FALLING IN LOVE IN KOREA L.A.

Misbah Zaidi

Copyright © 2022 Misbah Zaidi

All rights reserved

The characters and events portrayed in this book are fictitious. Any similarity to real persons, living or dead, is coincidental and not intended by the author.

No part of this book may be reproduced, or stored in a retrieval system, or transmitted in any form or by any means, electronic, mechanical, photocopying, recording, or otherwise, without express written permission of the publisher.

Edited by: Sarah Lamb
Cover design by: Emily's World of Design

Contact the author at: fallinginloveinkorea@gmail.com

Printed in the United States of America

You.

CONTENTS

Title Page
Copyright
Dedication
Falling In   1
Chapter 1:   2
Chapter 2:   39
Chapter 3:   76
Chapter 4:   108
Chapter 5 :   145
Chapter 6:   196
Chapter 7:   256
Chapter 8:   292
Chapter 9:   328
Chapter 10:   345
Books In This Series   359

FALLING IN ~~Love In~~ ~~Korea~~ L.A.

By: Misbah Zaidi

CHAPTER 1:

AJ-Zara

"**S**hit!" Of course I'd trip over a small rock in the most ungraceful way as soon as I step out of my car. It came out of nowhere! A couple walking into the restaurant scan to locate the idiot who just blurted out a bad word in front of a kid...who just happens to be theirs. They pass judgment with a short, sweet glare...putting my clumsy ass to shame.

"Sorry!" I apologize, covering my mouth to hide the sheer embarrassment in my shaky voice. I should've just worn flats instead of these five-inch heels! But no. Jace had the brilliant idea to channel my inner Beyonce for my date. Though, I must say...I look pretty good for a person who happens to look like the Grim Reaper's wife more than half the time. As I get closer to the door of the restaurant, I smooth down the fitted black midi dress Jace picked out for me. It's emanating a very 90s Chanel vibe—classy and elegant, the two qualities I do not possess. I unlatch my clutch with my manicured hands in an attempt to take out my phone, but it slips from the sweat of my hands, plopping onto the asphalt.

Why am I still nervous?! It's been around five months since we started dating. Yet, I still get butterflies when I'm about to see him. I wipe my hand across my dress and lift my phone off the ground. Yes! Right on the dot—seven o'clock. I was worried I might not arrive on time thanks to the infamous Los Angeles traffic. Oh, and parallel parking in Wilshire...it's my worst nightmare. Thankfully, for my ungraceful ass, there were two spots close to the restaurant so I only had to walk a few steps. I latch onto the doorknob, struggling to swing the door open. Jesus, did they steal it from the set of Game of Thrones or something?! Why the hell is it as heavy as a black hole?!

"Hi! Welcome! Do you have reservations?" The hostess greets me with the perkiest smile.

"Yes! It's under Felix." I match her energy.

"Oh, the rest of your party has already arrived. Right this way!" She scampers towards the left side of the restaurant as I follow. This side seems to be substantially less crowded with the lights dimmed lower, compared to the other, surrounded by russet walls.

"You will be dining in our private room tonight. It's right behind this door. Enjoy!" I thank her before she hurries back to the host stand. Before opening the door, I pat down the flyaways sticking out from my newly layered long, black straightened hair, trying to distract myself from my rip-roaring heart. I inhale and exhale all of the air particles surrounding me one last time and proceed to push open the door. Just a few seconds and the love of my life will be in my arms.

"Hi, baby girl!"

My heart pounds against my chest even faster, uncaging the butterflies as soon as I hear the sound of his sweet Australian accent. I don't think I'll ever get over it.

"AJ!"

I leap into his arms, clinging onto his broad shoulders, showing my transparent excitement. He lifts me off my feet and spins me around.

"I missed you so much...you can't even imagine." He snuggles his face—which is as smooth as a baby's bottom—into the nape of my neck. His side burns brush against my skin. "I missed the smell of your skin." His heart-shaped, plump cherry lips trail along it, leaving soft kisses.

"I missed yours more." I pull back to look at his face, which glistens from the dim yellow lights of the room. He flashes his million-dollar smile. Ah, those cheeks—sprinkled with pale gray freckles. They're deliciously kissed, with his deep dimples positioned by the corners of his lips on each side. In the twenty-five years I've had the pleasure of being alive, never have I seen such captivating dimples in my life before. Oh, and they get even deeper when he laughs, displaying his straight, leveled pearly whites. Oh, Allah! And his eyes! His chocolate-colored eyes are covered by a very light touch of brown eyeshadow, accentuating his beautiful, double eyelids and oval shape. If I weren't in grad school, I'd take the liberty of staring into them all day long.

I run my fingers through his soft, semi-slicked back hair, while a strand falls right above his forehead. Normally, it's fluffy and curly like a cute little puppy when he doesn't style it.

"Wow, I love the new hair. Purple—it suits you."

"Really? I don't look like a muppet?" He flicks his cascading strand of hair.

"A little...but certainly a hot one." I giggle like a little girl.

"As long as you think I look decent, I'm fine with it." He kisses the tip of my nose. "And also, thanks for driving closer to me. I know it was a bit of a drive from Downtown."

"It was only twenty-five minutes. Don't worry about it, silly. I'd drive hours just to see you."

"No, really. I feel really bad."

"Oh my gosh, don't! This works out even better, considering you only have two hours to spare for me tonight. We would've lost an hour with you going back and forth if you came by the apartment."

"Yes, that IS true. And I guess us dressing up and going on a date like normal people is actually...quite nice."

"I mean...I still love our small secret dates in disguise and stargazing...but it's a nice change, isn't it?"

"It certainly is." He tightens his arms around my waist even more.

I trail a finger along his chiseled jawline to the crescent moon necklace I gave him as a present, which matches his silver dainty hoop earrings. As I do, I can't help but notice something else different other than his hair.

"You look thinner, have you been eating properly?" My brows crease in worry on their own.

He smiles, placing one soft hand on my flushed cheek as his semi-calloused thumb strokes against my skin.

"Yes, my love, I am. I'm just on a diet for the K-Pop Fusion award show." Then he rests the other hand against the opposite side, pulling me closer until I feel his breath on my lips. "I love it when you worry about me, but I'm fine. Okay?" I glide my hands over his white button-down dress shirt, feeling the curves of his hard abs as his lips press against my forehead.

My gosh. It's like his lips were made just

to be grazed along my skin. It's an irreplaceable feeling...one that I long for when he's not around. He pulls back and taps his nose to mine. Ah, this man makes the forest of butterflies in my stomach flutter like no other. I remember how I tried to kill them when I first met him. Funny how things change.

"You give me premature ventricular contractions." I giggle as he plays with one of my

black 'jhumka' earrings like a baby playing with a jiggle toy.

He crinkles his brows but remains smiling. "I'm hoping that's a good thing?"

I place my hands on the sides of his face, "It means..." I pull him closer so that his lips are barely touching mine and whisper, "you make my heart skip a beat."

I press my lips to his and take my time, feeling his pillow-like lips melt into mine...until I hear a soft moan echoing in the room.

"That makes two of us, baby...especially in that dress you're wearing." The soft, minty kisses intensify as his insatiable need for my lips grows by the second. His hands clench around my waist, pulling me closer to him. I feel a rush of heat throughout my body, and I'm unable to breathe as he grinds his body against mine slowly...but I push him away like a priest exorcizing a demon.

"Slow down there, superstar." I compose myself. "We still have dinner to eat."

"Why?" He groans his question. "Aren't you having fun like I am?"

Oh...you have no idea.

"No...not at all." I lie, masking my heavy breathing by biting my tongue.

"No?" He whispers with a shaky breath. "Not at all?" His eyes pierce through mine, while he massages his tongue along his bottom lip.

I'm. Going. To. Pass. Out.

"Please...stop." I beg for his mercy.

His unforgiving eyes glow seeing me whimper.

"Fine." He strips me off of him with one hand gripped on my hip. "But...I won't be so forgiving next time." He tosses me a nonchalant wink and I internally fall on my knees.

"You're the worst." I gulp, trying to act as cool as I can, but it's evident that I'm failing miserably.

His fans probably can't even fathom this Christian Grey side to him, although they do witness it ONLY on stage. Besides that, he's practically Bashful from *Snow White*, except much taller and WAY hotter. He had me fooled in the beginning with this innocent boy act and 'oh, I'm so pretty and my ears turn red when I'm shy'. But damn...his duality surprised me, that's for sure. It's almost as if I'm dating two people all in one. I'm not complaining though, he just becomes more intriguing day by day.

Holding my hand, he guides me to my designated chair and pulls it out.

"M'lady." He bows, placing an arm behind him. "Also, did you see the moon tonight?"

"Thank you, my dear." I peck his cheek, curtsying my way over. "And yes, I did. It was shining as bright as you, my little superstar. There's also a full moon in a few days."

"Bright as ME?! No. Not at all. That's all you, my love." He lays a kiss on top of my head after scooting my chair in. "What are you in the mood for?"

"Um...the thing that I'm in the mood for, isn't on the menu..." I act coy, just to get a reaction out of him.

He clears his throat as he takes his seat. "You better stop talking." While turning a page of the menu, a mischievous grin appears on that scrumptious mouth of his.

"Or what?" I set my menu down, leveling my gaze to his eyes.

He lowers his as well, rises off his chair, and leans over the table to whisper, "Or I'll..."

But a knock interrupts him from finishing his sentence. Perfect timing. He plops back on his chair, with the 'you got saved' smirk. Reaching over, he pulls out a black beanie from behind him and wiggles into it. The waitress walks in, stopping in her tracks. She probably senses the sexual tension between us.

"Sorry, am I interrupting?"

Yes, you are.

"No, not at all." He responds with his fake American accent, which he's quite good at. I guess the practice from our little secret dates over the past few months made it perfect.

"Are you guys ready?" she asks, tilting her head towards AJ's direction. "Uh, I'm sorry. I don't mean to stare at you…but has anyone told you that you look like the spitting image of that K-Pop star on the billboard across the street?"

Shit. Here we go.

"Oh, yeah…I get that A LOT." AJ laughs.

"Yeah, everyone ALWAYS says that." I add on. We both have to play along when someone brings that up. Surprisingly, no one has ever figured out that he IS actually AJ. The trick is to hide in plain sight, acting like everyone else. No bodyguards. No big sunglasses. No over the top trendy clothing that will attract attention. And, a beanie is a must to hide his hair, ALWAYS. Plus, it helps we always see each other late at night and at places not around a lot of other people. Today might be one of the few exceptions we've made to be somewhat in public.

"Ah, I'm sure you do. But…you're a lot cuter." She smiles at him but his eyes are on me. HA! This little buttface.

"Yeah. He is." I enunciate my words.

With a quick annoyed glance at me, she pulls out a notepad from her apron's pocket and asks, "Anyways…you two ready to order?"

I order their special lemon pasta and AJ

orders the steak he's been raving about for days. He proceeds to hand over his menu to her, but she prances to him first.

"Oh, I can take that from you."

She brushes her finger against the back of AJ's hand and smiles. Oh, this little...buttface! I know exactly what she's doing...and right in front of me?! Clearly, I don't look like I might be his sister. The nerve!

"Oh, you can take mine, too." I lift the menu and place it on the edge of the table while flashing my fakest smile. The sexual tension in the room is quickly replaced by jealousy. On the other hand, AJ's smirk gets even wider.

"I'll come back with your food." She takes one long look at AJ before she leaves.

"What was that about?" He leans back in his chair, taking off the beanie and smoothing out his hair.

"I saw the way she looked at you."

"And? Jealous?"

I shrug.

"I didn't like the way it made me feel." I pick at my napkin with my red polished finger, trying to avoid eye contact.

He pulls the napkin out from under my hand and places my palm in his. His smirk fades.

"Talk to me about it?" Making an effort to meet my eyes.

"Nothing, don't worry about it."

I brush it off with a smile, but he remains

silent, waiting for me to answer.

"Alright. Well, you know…I'm aware how girls see you and I'm fine with it. Well, not entirely, but that's something I cannot control. They're drawn to you, clearly even in disguise when you're looking like a creepy man." He shakes his head as a tiny giggle escapes his mouth. "And…let's just say, I've heard from the grapevine that some female K-Pop idols are trying to get your attention. I just wonder if you—"

"Zara…" his gaze lowers towards the edge of the table, "don't finish that sentence."

He remains quiet for a few seconds, slowly brushing his thumb along the side of my pinky.

"Do you trust me?"

"I…" a sigh slips from my mouth, "I do." I trail my index finger along the lines of his warm palm. He hasn't given me a reason not to. At least…not yet.

"Do you trust me when I say I love you?"

His gaze is no longer lowered—but on me.

"I do."

"Then never, not even for a second, think I'll have eyes for anyone else but you. I don't care who's trying to get my attention…I only want yours." He squeezes my hand. "I trust you and you trust me…that's what matters. Right?"

"Mhmm." I nod consciously. I do trust him, and since I do…can I trust that he'd be open to talking about something that's a little more…serious? Something that's been haunting my mind for a few weeks now.

"AJ...I do trust you. I know you wouldn't do anything to break my trust, and neither would I. " I pause to clear my throat, knowing I'll falter the next few words. "Speaking of...I was, um...wondering about something."

"Uh-huh, go on, my love."

I gulp before asking, "Where do you see us going?"

He freezes as if I just caught him with his hidden porn collection...which I'm PRETTY sure he doesn't have.

"You mean...in the future?"

What did he say? Sometimes I don't understand his accent.

"The what?" I ask.

"Um, the future?" It sounds like he's saying 'fewch-uh'. Oh, wait!

"You mean future!" I shake my head. How disappointing, I've been dating the guy for almost five months now, I should be used to his accent.

"Yes, the future." He mimics, shaking his head as well.

My eyes roll to the side and back at him.

"Um, yes? Do you see this relationship going further? I know we love each other, but do you think we're at the stage where we can talk a little about where we're headed? Especially considering both of our situations...especially yours."

Dead silence. The sound of the bustling crowd from the restaurant envelops the room. I didn't hear it earlier, probably because the only sound I was focused on was his damn Australian accent...which clearly I still cannot understand.

"Um, I don't know." He props himself upright. "It's only been five months, Zara. Should we maybe just go with the flow right now?"

Maybe I am overthinking. I mean, it really only has been five months since we started dating. Our relationship is barely in the second trimester as an unborn baby.

Pursing my lips, I let out a sigh under my breath.

"You're right. Ahk, sorry." I wipe the edge of my thumb against my forehead. "I'm trying not to freak out as much. It's not working, is it?"

A soft laugh draws out his dimples.

"No, you're failing terribly." He places a quick peck on the back of my hand.

I reach out and push back the hair strand that's effortlessly draped over his forehead.

"And, you have no reason to apologize, my love," his fingers tighten around mine. "Look...truth is, I can't guarantee what will happen in the near future. To be honest, I don't even know what I'll be doing the next few months besides working. Since I started K-Pop, it's JUST been work. Then...you came into my life and I started thinking about things I hadn't before. I never pictured myself making it this far with anyone...but here you are, sitting beautifully in front of me." He coddles my face. "We have to meet by sneaking around, lying, using fake names, accents and props...but it's worth it to me. Is it...for you?"

I hesitate for a second. Gosh, why did I hesitate?

"Yes, of course it's worth it." I push back my chair and rush to wrap my arms around him from behind. "I'm so lucky to have met you. You ARE worth it." I feel guilty that I hesitated, even if it was just for a second. Maybe a tiny part of me is questioning the viability of our relationship.

"I'm the one who's the luckiest." He twirls me around, grabbing me by the waist and positions me on his lap. "I'm sorry if I made you feel insecure. I would never do anything to make you doubt me. I only ever want to make you happy. Your happiness is what keeps me going and I would travel thousands of miles just to see you smile."

"Like you did five months ago?" I smirk.

AJ throws his head back laughing.

"Yes, my love. Like I did five months ago." He twirls a strand of my hair with his boney finger.

"I'm glad you did. I really thought our little love story ended back in Korea."

"It would have, but...I couldn't bear the thought of not having you in my life."

Same, AJ. Same.

"But I still don't understand one thing. Why did you risk it? Why risk something you put your whole life into just because of a few dates with me?"

He scoffs, leaning forward, brows raised.

"You're really asking me this question, again?"

"Mhmm. Maybe I like hearing your answer." I nod like a child begging its parent to tell a bedtime story.

"Ah," he lets out a tiny sigh, "do you remember our first date?"

"How can I forget?"

What a silly question, AJ.

"You said something that struck me and those words replayed in my head all night."

He's never mentioned this before.

"Which were?"

"You said, and I quote..." he pauses for a second, "I couldn't help but wonder what else might be out there."

Out of everything I said that night, why did that resonate with him?

"I guess it made me realize how I never allowed myself to desire anything else BUT being a part of K-Pop. I only saw the world through a small lens, because as stupid as it sounds...being ignorant is safe. I was afraid of making my desires any larger and seeing a clearer picture that had been blurry. I'd think to myself, what if it makes me long for something I couldn't have?

What if I want more than what I've been working for? Would I be able to bear getting the taste of it and then pretend it doesn't exist?"

I know exactly what he means.

"But then...what I feared the most, happened."

"Which is?"

A smile beams across his angelic face.

"I got the taste of you...literally."

My lips separate as my jaw drops. Maybe I spoke too soon. For a person who possesses such an ethereal face, he sure is naughty. He indulges in seeing me thrown off guard by his polar opposite sides.

"But, really. The moment we exchanged our first few words with each other, I wanted more. You sparked a desire I never imagined. I didn't think it could ever exist within me."

"And what desire would that be?"

His fingertips trickle along the side of my arm to my thigh, looking at me with siren eyes.

"To feel...and to be felt." He whispers with his soft semi-raspy voice.

My eyes are met by his keen gaze, forcing goosebumps to travel throughout my body.

"To see and to be seen."

He digs his fingertips into my flesh like a ravening wolf, forcing me to feel the pressure of his strong grip around me.

"To love and to BE loved."

Relaxing his fingers, he grinds me against

his lap, pulling me even closer to his warm body.

"Both emotionally...and physically. You make me...insatiable."

His words implant themselves in every neuron of mine. No one has ever seen me in this way. I never felt I was worthy of even being desired. I'd think to myself, what's special about me? Is it possible for anyone to think the world of me? But I guess I was wrong because there is someone who does—my AJ.

I allow myself to linger in his words, which have been echoing in my head for the past few seconds before I say, "Okay, but that didn't answer my question," knowing really well he's going to find it incredibly annoying. He brings out this playful child in me that never had the chance to emerge before.

On cue, he throws his hands up in defeat and replies, "You are the queen of ruining romantic moments." Giggling, he flicks the tip of my nose with his index finger and I do the same to him, mimicking Rahul and Anjali in *Kuch Kuch Hota Hai*—my favorite childhood movie and now his, ever since he watched it...granted it was by force on my end, but still!

"To answer your question in the simplest way," he lowers his voice, "I'll say this."

He leans back in his chair.

"When I write songs, it is almost always from the emotions I've experienced. I've written songs about sadness, betrayal, accomplishments, depression and the list goes on. But, I also wrote love songs and realized...what a con artist I have been. They were nothing but careless words about something I've only seen in movies or listened to in songs. How can I write about an emotion I've never felt before?"

His brows crease as his eyes shift to a corner of the room.

"I wrote about love as if it's always exciting. And, don't get me wrong, it is. The beginning of us dating WAS exciting, a little anxiety ridden, but I felt an adrenaline rush all the time. Still do. But...I never thought there could be this sense of calmness in love. I felt that with you that night we talked under the night sky at Dongdaemun. And I know I had only known you for a day, but there was this connection between us which felt exhilarating but also familiar. It felt as if I've known you all my life. I didn't want to let go of it because I thought, what are the chances that I'd feel that again? Especially being a K-Pop star. Time is my worst enemy and I didn't want to spend another couple years without experiencing it again. I mean, I AM in my mid-twenties."

Ah, shit. We're...getting older.

"So, after I left your hotel the night of the concert, I sat the members and manager down, told them what happened between us. I wasn't sure how exactly my manager would react, but he was so loving and supportive. They all were. Luckily, we were leaving three days later for our tour in America, the first stop being Los Angeles."

"Yeah, I don't understand why you never mentioned that."

"Well, I never thought I'd ever see you after you left Korea. And figured, what's the point? Especially since you made it clear you didn't want to see me that night at the hotel."

"I did want to see you."

"But...you thought it'd be painful to get our hopes up for something that might not happen, right?"

"Mhmm." I pout.

"Well, I still had my hopes up." He smiles, deepening his dimples. "Normally, this would never happen, but somehow my manager pulled some strings which allowed me to come earlier than everyone else. And, around the same time you were getting on a plane, so was I with others in the managing team. I texted Ari to sneakily get the address from Jace, and showed up at your doorstep."

This is some movie shit.

"Also, speaking of Jace...I'm a little surprised he didn't know about the tour in America. I thought he's a fan."

"Yeah, a fake one!" We both laugh in unison. "Didn't the delivery girl recognize you?"

"No, thankfully not. She asked if I lived there. I lied and said yes, then quickly paid her so she could leave. I didn't want her to witness you telling me to get lost." His childish smile widens, making the tiny creases around his eyes more transparent.

"I remember being so nervous standing there, knowing you were on the other side of the door. The few seconds felt like minutes. But... seeing your face was priceless." He scrunches his nose and taps it against mine. "It seemed like you saw a ghost."

"It felt like I did." I raise my brows as my eyes shift to the side, remembering that exact moment.

"When Jace called me over and I saw you... STANDING at MY doorstep...I swear my heart stopped and sunk into my stomach. I thought I was losing my mind"

"Well, you did lose your mind when you decided to date a K-Pop star." He winks while biting his bottom lip.

"Yeah...I'm SUCH an idiot, aren't I?" I scrunch my nose at him. "But, we pulled through."

"You more than me. I mean, I didn't have to lie and hide a trip to a whole different country from my parents."

"I mean, what can I say? I'm just such a brilliant mastermind." I flip my hair over my shoulder. "But anything is possible if you have a friend like Jace and a credit card not under your parents' name."

"I guess God is on our side!"

He laughs, which comes to an immediate halt. AJ tilts his head while pushing a few strands of my hair behind my ear.

"It all makes me feel like I'm in a movie...and I kind of like it." He stares into my eyes as if he's trying to capture the details of my irises.

My life does feel like a movie right now, which is exciting and thrilling. But...unlike a movie, I can't fast-forward to the ending to see what happens. Will we end up marrying each other? Will my parents accept him as a son-in-law? Will he leave me once he realizes how hard it's going to be to fit into my world? Would I be able to manage to be in his? What if I have to sneak around for the rest of my life, or at least until he's allowed to have romantic relationships openly, despite the dating ban ending at the end of the year? Will this ultimately be a waste of time? Jesus, I really have to work on my overthinking abilities. Why can't I just freaking relax?!

As my thoughts are swarming through my mind a million miles per minute, I jump from the knocking at the door. I slide off of his lap and hurry back to my chair. He pushes his hair back, yanking the beanie down to his earlobes. The buttface of a waitress walks in with our food and places it on the table. I catch a glimpse of AJ staring at me as she sets his plate in front of him. He definitely has a way of making me feel like I'm the only person in the room—literally and figuratively.

"Enjoy!" Again, she glances at him, flashing a flirtatious smile before she leaves. These girls and their wandering eyes on taken men, agh, can I just gouge them out?! I felt a wave of heat flush throughout my face. Damn, I need to drink some water before my blood pressure skyrockets. I've been losing my temper for the past few days, which is so unlike me because I'm genuinely a very calm and collected person. Well, for most of the time. I don't get angry easily, but I've noticed I've been snapping at the smallest inconveniences. I swear, I feel like I'm going to manifest my inner Hulk one of these days.

◆ ◆ ◆

"How was it?" AJ wipes the corner of his mouth with his napkin.

"The food was actually really good. I just wasn't too happy with the service." I roll my eyes.

"Wow, Zara." He laughs. "I don't think I've ever seen you this way before. I mean, jealousy aside, you're angry as well." He pushes his chair back and grabs his jacket off of the top rail. "It's a very different look on you."

"What do you mean?" I furrow my brows, pausing for just a moment before reaching for my clutch.

"I mean it's okay to be a little jealous. I

get jealous, too." He gets jealous? Of whom?! It's not like the whole world is picturing themselves sleeping with me like they are with him! "Is something else bothering you, is that why you've been a little angry lately?"

Lately? Jesus, how long have I been unaware of this?!

"I don't think I'm angry."

"Are you sure?" The raspiness in his voice becomes more transparent as he lowers his tone, eyes flirting with mine. He slinks to me, just enough to get a slight whiff of his cologne that drives me crazy.

"Yeah, I'm sure." I raise my chin.

He slides even closer, and this time his lips are a few inches away from mine.

"Are you positive?"

Intensely looking into my eyes, he licks the corner of his mouth. His thumb fondles along my bottom lip.

"Maybe I've been a little frustrated." I gulp, though trying my best to come across as composed as I can possibly be right now. He's the only man who can affect me in this way.

"Sexually?" His eyes scan my lips. He gulps a breath of air before biting his bottom lip. Jesus, they're so scrumptiously luscious.

But I don't want to give him the satisfaction of knowing how every single nerve of my lips crave for a taste of his.

"Nope. Just frustrated." I stride past him,

intentionally bumping my shoulder against his. "Alright, how should we do this?" I lean against the door of the room.

Still biting his bottom lip, he strolls towards me while plucking his beanie off the table. He's so nonchalant, some could say he emits Chuck Bass's energy from *Gossip Girl*.

"You'll go out first. Go straight to your car and drive away. Then after ten minutes, I'll walk out. The Uber will be here for 'Felix'." He chuckles. "Sounds good?"

I try to not display any sort of emotion on my face to make a point. Not going to show any anger, jealousy, or the fact that I just want to pull some 'Fifty Shades of Grey' on him right now.

"Sounds great. I'll see you tomorrow." I rush to open the door, but before I even reach for the knob, he grips my wrist with one swift motion and pulls me in.

"Oh and just to let you know..." he grazes his lips against my earlobe and whispers, "I'm...INCREDIBLY frustrated," sending shivers down my spine and into my soul. "Goodnight, my universe. I love you."

AJ loosens his grasp, brushing his thumb softly against my cheekbone and kisses my forehead. My legs beg me to move away from him, but I stand there like a deer in headlights.

"Goodnight." I reach for the door knob again and this time I get the hell out before something happens in there. I should get an award for leaving the room without ripping his clothes off. He is a Greek Siren, luring me in with his sweet, beautiful voice, but the male version, with a microphone and instead of the sea, it's a stage.

◆ ◆ ◆

"Hey, my little Pakistani princess. How'd your fancy date go?"

I open the door to the apartment, set my keys down and find Jace in the kitchen pouring a glass of wine.

"It was good. Please pour me one, too." I don't deserve this glass of wine, but as Drake once said, you only live once.

"Oh, shit. Did it not go well?" He hands me the glass with the red nectar of joy.

"No, it did. It was like any other secret rendezvous of ours...but just dressed up nicely. Except this time, I was about to murder the waitress and resisted jumping his bones at the restaurant."

I take a sip and not a small one. He points his finger to the couch in the living room.

"Okay, those are two things I didn't expect to hear in the same sentence. That's like, a lot of weird emotions for a date. Bitch, are you okay?! You've been a little on edge lately."

We both plop onto the couch, making sure our wine doesn't spill over.

"Why does everyone keep saying that?! I'm

fine!"

"Uh...okay, who else said that?"

"AJ did."

"Well, if more than one person is noticing, then there must be something going on there."

"I'm just...frustrated."

"Sexually?"

"Jesus, no! Well, okay maybe a little, but no, it's not just that."

"First, take another sip of your wine." I follow his orders and do so. "Nope, do it for about five seconds." I don't even try to fight back. Damn, I must be going through it to be listening to Jace's orders. "Alright, how do you feel?"

One. Two. Three. Ah...hello buzzed Zara. I'm such a lightweight.

"I'm feeling it a little."

"Start talking. What's bothering you?"

"So...we've been dating for five months, and it's been truly amazing. I mean, it's hard, of course. We've barely had the chance to spend time together, but we've both made the effort to try to see each other. It was easier when he was touring in America since sometimes I'd be able to fly out to where he's performing. And he'd come to L.A. to see me. Granted, it would be for a night and rare—"

"Okay, sorry, can I just say I'm so proud of how you pulled that off. Your parents didn't even suspect anything."

He lifts his hand for a high-five.

"Well, practice made me perfect."

I smack my hand to his.

"Hell yes! Okay, sorry, continue."

"As I was saying, despite him being SO busy, he always goes out of his way for me. I mean, you wouldn't do that for someone you don't see a future with, right?"

"Well, I mean...if you're dating someone, you'd WANT to go out of your way to be with them. Which AJ does, and so do you. It's a natural part of dating. Why are you asking?"

"I guess I've just been wondering if this is long term. If there's a future here. I tried talking to him about it today by asking if he sees this relationship going further, but he doesn't have an answer. I mean, I guess we still are in the honeymoon phase and it's too soon to talk about, but five months is a lot. I mean, if my mom knew that I was dating a guy for five months, that's good enough to start wedding planning. Well, if she knew I was dating AJ, I'd probably be disowned by now, but okay—one anxiety ridden issue at a time."

I slurp a sip of the wine.

"I just want to know if he's thinking a little more about us like I am. He says he loves me and I think that should merit a conversation about the future, no?"

"Yeah, I think so. You both SHOULD talk a little more about your future together, considering that both of you could be in serious trouble if this leaks out, ESPECIALLY him."

"Right?! I don't know, maybe I'm questioning our relationship a little. But, Jace...I love him so much. You know that, right?"

"Yes, I do."

"Like, if he needed a kidney transplant, I'd give him mine in a heartbeat."

"Weird, but okay." He creases his brows.

"But maybe I need some reassurance that he's thinking about this long term as well. He just said it's too soon and that I should enjoy the present."

"He's right about that, you should...but we aren't in Korea anymore, Zara. We're back in L.A., where YOUR life is. I told you to be in the moment and you did. You lived out your teenage dream and boned AJ like a little starved cub chowing down food. But you both aren't having a vacation fling anymore." I take another sip of my wine and remain quiet, listening attentively to Jace's reasoning. "Though, now that I think about it...it might be too soon. He's never done this before, so maybe it's taking him a while to get to that conversation."

"Well, neither have I but I'm willing to talk about it."

"Zara, do you forget that...he's just not SOME guy. He's a..."

"A K-Pop star, I know." I nod, rolling my eyes to the side with a sigh.

"Yeah. You knew what you were getting

yourself into when you decided to date him. He was very clear about what has to happen for you two to be together. Even with the dating ban ending this year, you'd still have to continue meeting in secret."

Agh, Jace is right. AJ was VERY honest about the severity of this whole situation. A bit too much. I guess sometimes I forget he's a K-Pop star. I forget that he has so many responsibilities and it's a risk to see me. When he's with me, it feels like he's just my boyfriend, AJ...not the international superstar. I don't get to see the flashing lights on him from hundreds of cameras, or him being surrounded by crying fans, being escorted to places by his bodyguards. It's weird seeing him perform on T.V., watching him be this perfect specimen, showing off his godlike skills. For some reason, I don't see that as my boyfriend. It's just like seeing any other famous person.

There are times he'll be on T.V.—whether it's an interview, a performance, or a music video—and Jace casually comments, "Hey, look! It's your boyfriend!" And then, it'll take me a second to realize that the angelic, ethereal man on T.V., IS MY BOYFRIEND. On screen, he's covered by makeup, his hair is perfectly styled, wearing high end trendy clothing—what we imagine perfection to look like. It doesn't feel real seeing him behind a screen unless he's with me where I can see his perfect imperfections, making him look and feel like an actual person. I think we often forget that celebrities are people, too. In a way, we dehumanize them only because we see them behind a screen, accessible to everyone worldwide. They're just shown as what we think 'perfect' is. I guess that's why they're called 'stars'. They're out of reach from everyone else, shining brightly, perfectly from a distance. But I'm a witness that they eat, poop, sleep and have emotions, just like the rest of us. They're more than just the world's entertainment. Oh my gosh, I need to chill my thoughts. My mind literally goes from a teenage girl, complaining about her secret romance to Socrates Zara within a few seconds.

"I know...I'm really grateful for him being sent to me. I thank Allah everyday. I just wish it was just a little easier. The sneaking around, lying, the anxiety of getting caught...is a little too much. I mean it was really hot in the beginning, but agh, I just wanna hold his hand in public and stroll around under the moonlight, showing the world and girls that he's mine. Only mine! Why couldn't he just be a Pakistani Muslim K-Pop star instead, who can openly date?!" I groan.

"Do you even know what K-Pop stands for?" He chuckles as he sips his wine.

"Agh, and I feel so guilty. He asked if all of this was worth it and I hesitated like an ungrateful swine."

"I could slap you right now for calling yourself an ungrateful swine. I mean, are you ungrateful? No. He should also be grateful to have you. A swine? Maybe a little." I laugh under my breath, nudging his arm with my elbow. "But it must be tough being a K-Pop star's dirty little secret."

"I just want to punch something." I devour the last few sips of my wine like a person gulping down water after being rescued from a stranded desert. From my peripheral vision, I pick up the judgment coming from his gaping eyes. "I can literally feel the judgmental energy coming from your ass."

He surrenders his hands in the air.

"I'm not judging. Actually, quite the opposite."

"Oh yeah?" I snort.

"I can't offer you much solution to your frustration, but I know one thing that releases some steam."

"What?"

"SEX! You idiot, you have a hot ass boyfriend now. Are you forgetting he's a K-Pop star?! Use that as some sort of foreplay, I don't know! Play some of the RnB songs NOWus recently released to set the mood! Doing IT to his songs…are you kidding me? Who gets to do that?! When was the last time you got laid?"

"Uhh…" I count in my head, not that there's a big number to begin with. "Like, the day he surprised me in L.A. when we came back from Korea."

He doesn't move. His eyes are locked to mine as if it's the most absurd thing he's ever heard, but easily breaks that stare by slapping my wrist.

"IT'S BEEN FIVE MONTHS?! ARE YOU KIDDING ME?! No wonder you're a cranky little bitch."

"Hey! It's not like we have a whole lot of time when we do see each other AND I'd rather spend that time talking to him."

"Okay, fine. But now the tour is over AND he's here in L.A. for about a week. Take advantage of this sweet time Allah has literally presented to you with a bow on top…so get on top of that and unwrap your present!"

"Jace! You're so freaking gross."

I backhand slap his arm while he laughs with his whole body.

"Plus…it's not just because we've had limited time together. I feel a little…guilty."

"Why?"

"Because…my mom told me that good girls don't have sex before marriage. Whenever my little friend down there starts to…'act up', my mom's voice just appears in my head saying something along the lines of the devil has won me over by giving into temptation AND I will burn in hell for engaging in pre-marital sex."

"Then burn in hell! You're already going to! Might as well soak up the pleasure here because you ain't gonna get it there."

"Jace! It's not funny! If my parents ever found out, I don't know what I'd do. My mom would probably go into depression. She'd internalize it and make it about herself, thinking she messed up in my upbringing. And, of course, my pleasure will bring shame to the family. I don't know who the hell placed my whole family's honor in my vagina!" I plant my face in my hands. "As much as I tell myself I shouldn't listen to these outdated beliefs, there's this guilt I can't get rid of. Then, I freak out thinking about what will happen when they learn the person I love is not Muslim. I don't think I'll be able to handle seeing the disappointment in their faces. Like...I've failed them."

"I understand, Zara. And, I know how hard it is to just think about yourself. You're going to want your parents' blessing in everything you do, I understand completely. Especially since both of our cultures teach the value of always putting yourself after your family. But just try to remind yourself day by day that at the end, you have to make yourself happy as well. You're the one living your life, not them."

He rubs my back with slow strokes. "And plus, it's not like there was a post-it with instructions attached to your ass about who you can and can't fall in love with when you were coming out of your mother's womb!"

"I know all of that. It's honestly insane when parents expect their children to marry someone with the same ethnicity or religion as them. And you're right, it's not like I can choose who I can and can't fall in love with. That shit just happens without a warning! They act as if we've committed a murder! I think that will probably be seen as less of a sin in their eyes than this."

Jace pours more wine into my glass until the bottle finishes with faltering drops.

"I wonder if our immigrant parents realize when raising their kids in a country far from their own, that we're surrounded by people from different walks of life. They think we're genetically designed to fall in love with a person who fits the image that they brought back from their homeland. My mom thinks there are Pakistani guys at every corner of Los Angeles just waiting to serenade me like in Bollywood movies! It's hard to find them, man! I haven't met any eligible guys here, let alone Pakistani ones."

Jace chokes on his wine after taking a sip.

"I'm—" his violent coughs keeps him from finishing his sentence but he manages to prop a thumbs up.

"I refuse to settle down for a guy just for the sake of him being Pakistani and Muslim. I mean, would I love to? Sure. But...I want LOVE. I've gotten the taste of it and I don't want anything else. I wasn't brought up seeing healthy and loving relationships, especially my parents. They've never even hugged each other in front of me because it's considered 'shameful' to show affection...but somehow fighting and arguing in front of me is not traumatizing. I don't think they're even in love. They're just living together like...roommates. I don't wanna live like that! That sounds depressing as hell."

"You go off, girl!" He heads to the kitchen, still lightly coughing, and pulls another bottle of wine from the cabinet.

"Jace, isn't it crazy to know how infinitely huge our universe is? Filled with billions and billions of galaxies, planets, stars, and hello...parallel universes! We have no idea what the hell is out there! Earth is just a minor planet revolving around an average star. Yet, we act SO superior and think so small. People can't be with the person they love? Why?! Because we're bound by crap that us humans created! I'm SO incredibly lucky to have experienced real, genuine, passionate love. AJ and I happen to be born in this lifetime, on the same planet, sharing the same reality and having a common language. What are the odds? Yet...my hands are tied up in shackles made by others. Doesn't that boil your blood?!"

That heat I felt throughout my body back at the restaurant resurfaces.

"You both are living in some *Veer-Zaara* shit, man." He pours more wine into my glass.

"Yeah, but I just hope that unlike in that movie, I don't have to wait till I have gray hair and an ass that's hanging to the floor to see AJ again if we break up."

"You won't! I believe in you, Zara. It might be hard and nerve wracking, but you WILL convince your parents and they'll come around."

"Yeah, they'll come around...when I'm old and wrinkly! Maybe then, at that point, they'll BEG me to marry anyone with a pulse. Gah! I wish I were white at times. Things would be so much easier, at least that's what I've seen in movies. Might not be the actual case in real life, but in the movies, they don't have to hide things from their parents. If they do and the parents find out, they'll laugh it off saying, 'Oh! They're just living their youth!' They encourage their kids to live their best life and not worry about what others have to say, while mine ask to not let anyone know I even have a heartbeat. If my mom found out I went to Korea, fell in love with a Korean boy, SLEPT WITH HIM, and then came running to her, crying about a heartbreak...she wouldn't see how broken I am. She'd be fixated on the fact I had sex and probably imprison me in my room for the rest of my life for being a fornicator!"

"You make uncle and auntie sound like the devil. They're not!" He slaps my back.

"Ouch!"

"Get yourself together! Listen to me. You WILL bring them around to the idea of marrying AJ. Okay?!"

I sigh. "But...what if I'm the only one in

this relationship who's even thinking about it this far. I mean, I think I'm willing to fight for him, but he's not even open to the idea of talking about a future. What if we never talk about it and…continue living this teenage dream?"

"Zara, I wish I could tell you what you want to hear, but I think what you need is to be reassured by him. Just give it time, that's all I can say."

I wrap my arms around the couch pillow as a form of comfort.

"Is love enough to hold on to a relationship that may or may not have a future? Is it self-destructive knowing there's a huge chance that at the end…he won't end up being mine? I love him, so all this trouble…it's worth it, right?"

It is, isn't it?

CHAPTER 2:

Damon Salvatore

Ding dong!

I'm awoken by the one sound I didn't expect to hear on a Saturday morning. Confused, I roll over to check the time on my phone. It's nine o'clock. Who the hell is ringing my doorbell this early in the morning?! It rings again. Jesus, whoever is at the door is one impatient specimen. It better not be someone trying to convince me that I can still be saved by the grace of God and Jesus Christ...because it's a little too late for that.

I scout the living room. Jace isn't here. Normally, he'd be the one who gets the door since he's convinced that one day I'll get kidnapped. In a rush, I force my feet into my slippers and sprint to the door before I hear another bell.

I twist the knob and pull the door open to see a tall, well-built man standing in front of me. He has an olive skin tone, with short, jet-black hair that's styled back like James Dean's signature hairstyle, accentuating a chiseled jawline touched by a neatly trimmed beard. His features are very South Asian-like. He's wearing gray joggers and a fitted white crew neck shirt, which hugs his six pack...or is it an eight pack?! Let's just say...his outfit leaves little to the imagination. From the looks of it, he's way too put together to be straight...and definitely seems like Jace's type.

"Oh, sorry. I think I got to the wrong place. I was looking for Jace." His voice is deeper than his dark brown eyes, covered by thick black eyelashes. He definitely seems like Jace's past lover...but I would have known if he was, so who the hell is this guy?!

"He lives here, I'm his roommate and his best friend...Jace isn't here, but you're more than welcome to come in and wait for him."

"Don't mind if I do." He steps inside with his confident shoulders swaying side to side, flashing a...flirtatious smile? Huh?! Clearly, my gaydar was totally off...unless he plays for both teams.

"Would you like some water?"

"Sure, that would be great. Thank you." Okay...so he's polite.

"I'm Zara, by the way." I tiptoe to reach the glasses at the top of the cabinet but he extends his hand around me to grab one. He smells amazing. I recognize the scent since it's the same as the one AJ uses—Armani. "Uh, thanks." I accept the glass from his hand with an embarrassed laugh.

"No worries, I saw you struggling. It was a tad bit cute, not gonna lie." He grins from ear to ear, revealing shiny, bright teeth. Okay, he's for sure flirting. But damn...his smile resembles my favorite Pakistani actor—Fawad Khan.

"I'm Arsalan. Arsalan Haider Khan."

Khan, ha! What are the odds?

"Wow, powerful name. Are you Indian?"

"No, actually. I'm Pakistani. Well, I was born and raised here, but my parents are from Pakistan."

"No way, so am I!" My face lights up. The only other Pakistani's I know—other than family—are from my mosque but I haven't personally talked to any of the guys my age. He might actually be the first. "Uh, so how do you know Jace? He's never mentioned you."

"Ouch." He mutters under his breath.

Shit, maybe I shouldn't have said that...but it's the truth!

"I mean..." I laugh, trying to salvage the damage, "I've just never heard him talking about you and I'm his best friend. You're not his past lover...are you?" I joke, hoping he doesn't take it offensively. Unless he is an old flame, then I may have opened a can of past wounds.

His head jolts backwards as he laughs.

"Jeez, no! Do I give off that vibe?!"

"A little. You're way too handsome and put together."

My eyes widen, realizing the shit that just spurted from my mouth. That was totally unintentional, but I don't want him to think I'm flirting back! What the hell is wrong with me?!

"I mean, I'm totally supportive, but I don't play for the other team. I'm straight and single, if you were wondering." His eyes twinkle, accompanied by a slimy, cocky smirk.

Oh, gosh, NO! I wasn't wondering one bit.

"Well, I was just wondering about one of those things." I raise a brow. He's quiet, but remains smirking. "Coffee?" I ask.

"I could definitely use some caffeine, thank you."

"Black or with cream?"

"Just black."

"Ah, you take your coffee like me. Jace thinks I'm a sociopath for liking it this way."

"Well, are you?"

"Let's hope you never have to find out." I try to crack a joke, but lowkey sound like I might be a serial killer.

"Actually...now I do."

Uh...what?!

"So, how do you know Jace?" I change the topic, disregarding the flirty shit he's trying to pull.

"We are classmates at USC."

"Oh, nice. I go there, too. But I'm a PA student."

"Wow. Surprised I've never run into you. I would've remembered a pretty face like yours."

Yeah, a pretty face that normally looks like it got run over by a lawnmower, which is probably why he wouldn't remember me even if he did see me.

"Ah, you're such a flirt." I hand him a cup of coffee.

"That's what I've been told." With a slight tilt of his head, he raises both eyebrows. He reminds me of Kim Soo-hyun's character named Jang Tae-Young in the movie *Real*–bold and bad. "But no one usually calls me out on it when meeting for the first time."

"First time for everything, right?" I wink. I wink?! I've never acted 'badass' and witty before, what the heck is happening?! Who do I think I am, the main character? Gosh, I really need to chill out.

Thankfully, I hear the key entering the lock. Finally, Jace is back! Another flirty remark from this Damon Salvatore character from *Vampire Diaries,* would have made me throat punch the player out of him.

"Oh, hey!" Jace sets his keys on the entrance table. He has takeout in his hands from a local breakfast place he and I go to. "I went out to get all of us some breakfast." He looks at the both of us. "I'm guessing no introductions are necessary here?"

"Nope, we introduced ourselves. I thought he was your past lover." With long strides, I walk past Arsalan and out of the kitchen, totally embracing my newly found bitchiness...granted it's only been a few seconds.

Jace reacts the same way as Arsalan. "You're joking! He's probably the straightest guy I know. Trust me, I tried to test it." Jace winks at Arsalan.

"And failed horribly." Arsalan grabs a takeout bag from Jace's hands and sets it on the table. If he was a few seconds late, it would've slipped through Jace's hand. "But I was kind of flattered that I attracted both men and women."

I roll my eyes, away from his sight. He's getting cockier by the second and I've just met him ten minutes ago.

"What plans do you have today, Zara?" Jace unties the tightly wrapped knot of the plastic bag, placing the containers on the table.

"I was just going to work out and then see AJ later." Jace freezes, shifting his eyes to catch a glimpse of Arsalan's reaction, then at me. Ah, shit. I hope Arsalan doesn't know who AJ is. Although...I do want him to know I have a boyfriend. I walk over to the fridge, pulling out a bottle of freshly squeezed orange juice.

"Is AJ a girl?" Arsalan asks in a condescending tone.

"No, he's my boyfriend."

Silence fills the room. Jace has his gaping

eyes glued to the both of us.

"Oh, I thought it was a girl since AJ is usually a girl's name."

"Since when?"

"Aly and AJ? The sisters from that Disney movie, *Cow Belles*? Does that ring a bell?"

I loved that movie back in 2006, but still...I have a feeling he said it in a very mocking way and I hated that. "Yeah, I remember." I pour the orange juice in three glasses and carry them on a tray to the dining table.

We all take a seat around the dining table, and I lift the container with pancakes, carefully placing stacks on each of their plates.

"Whoa, this is too much." Arsalan gestures to stop.

"Too bad, you gotta eat it." I click my tongue.

"Don't argue with her, Arsalan. It's her desi mother instincts kicking in. She force feeds people even when they're full."

It's true. It's a nurturing yet annoying habit of mine that I inherited from my mom.

His cocky smile fades.

"Ah...I wouldn't know about the desi mother instincts."

"Oh, I'm sure your mom's like that." Jace responds.

"Well, she wasn't around growing up, so..." he trails the point of the fork along the edges of his plate. "Anyways..." he changes the subject, "tell me more about this boyfriend of yours."

I side eye Jace in hopes for an answer. He nods. Does that mean I can trust this cocky desi Damon with my secret?

"Um, well...what do you want to know?"

"What does he do?"

Ha, if only you knew.

"He's a singer."

"Is he any good?"

"Yeah, he is. He travels the world to perform." Maybe I should shut my mouth before he Googles him, but he's so irritating!

"Oh, wow." He chews on a piece of his pancakes as he replies with a dull tone. "How'd you two meet?"

I laugh in my mind. If only he knew how romantic it all was, he would wish something like that could happen to him. Gosh, I sound so mean. Stop, Zara!

"We met in Korea."

"Oh, yeah. Jace went to Korea a few months ago...did you go with him?"

How has Jace not mentioned me at all?!

"Yeah, we both went together because ONE of us got incredibly drunk and bought plane tickets."

"YOU got incredibly drunk...and yeah, I secretly bought the tickets, making it seem as if she did."

"Turned out to be the best trip of my life. I

wouldn't have met AJ otherwise." My face lights up by saying AJ's name. And he sees it.

"Are you two doing long distance?" Arsalan raises a groomed, thick brow.

"Yeah. But, he visits when he can."

"That sounds tough. Long-distance relationships never last." He says with a smug look on his face.

I change my mind. I may be mean to him but he totally deserves it. Who the hell does he think he is giving his two cents on MY relationship!

"They're tough, yeah." The muscles of my furrowed brows form slight lines above them. "But if you try hard enough to make it work, it can last."

"I don't think so." He leans back on the chair, propping an arm back on the top rail. "Let me ask you this...is he Muslim?"

How...DARE he. What's with the interrogation?! And by whom?! This Damon Salvatore wannabe?!

"No, he's not. So?" I hiss with a defensive tone.

"How would your parents feel?"

Jace scoots to the edge of his chair.

"Why do you care about how my parents feel?"

"Do they even know?" His fork and knife plop on the table as he sets them down.

"No, they don't."

"Well, will they even accept him?"

Wow, he's such an ass.

"Yeah, maybe. They're not like most desi parents."

"Ha! They never are, until it's one of their own trying to marry outside of the religion."

I officially dislike this guy.

"When the time comes, I'll handle it. Thanks for your concern, though."

"Just trying to look out for you."

Yeah, I'm sure you are...he has no concept of boundaries. I JUST met him.

"Don't worry about me, I'm a big girl."

"Yeah, I don't doubt that...but keep your options open."

I want to punch the smirk off his stupid face.

"Nah, I think I'm good. I haven't found real men around here who are worth my time."

"Maybe you just haven't met the right one."

"I highly doubt that." I puncture his ego, giving him my own smirk. "Well, I think I'm finished here. I'm going to go work out. Do you two need anything?"

Jace's anxious face made me want to laugh a little, but a part of me also felt really bad; it looks as if he's a child between divorced parents...which isn't funny at all now that I think about it.

"No, you go. I'll clean up." Jace clears his throat.

"Are you sure?"

"Yes, I'm sure." He's trying to get rid of me. I understand why. His friend is a total ass.

"I'll be here studying with Jace for our last final, so I'll see you in a bit." Arsalan interjects, taking a bite of his pancakes.

"Good luck." I mumble before dragging my feet to my room. I officially do NOT like him. Not one bit.

◆ ◆ ◆

Jesus, I'm sweating like a pig through my black workout leggings and sports bra. I lay on my yoga mat, trying to catch my breath after an intensive leg and ab workout. I've been working out a lot since I came back from Korea, mostly because I don't want to look like a sickly little boy or have people advise me I need to eat more. When people make comments about my weight or how skinny I am, it just adds to my low self-esteem. That's why I never took pride in my looks up until now. I steered away from wearing fitted clothing. I chose outfits that were a bit loose or oversized so people couldn't notice my skinniness, which made me feel most comfortable. As much as Jace would try to get me to embrace my body or be comfortable in my own skin, regardless of what others had to say, I didn't have the courage to listen to him until now.

The only demographic that glamorizes

my skinniness are desi aunties. They're obsessed with girls being incredibly thin and fair-skinned...and I DESPISE that. Especially when complimenting me for qualities I have no control over. What I hate even more is when they say it in front of a girl who doesn't fit this unhealthy beauty standard. These poor girls have been victims of their traumatizing words, leading them to having self-esteem issues, body dysmorphia, and eating disorders. Just because I'm skinny doesn't mean I'm necessarily healthy or even happy with the way I look.

It's astounding what a huge issue it is in our South Asian community. Many girls get rejected right off the bat for marriage proposals if they don't possess these unrealistic beauty standards. Like, sorry...didn't realize we still see women as objects that should be easy on the eyes, neglecting to see them as a real person with a personality and feelings! It's funny, I don't think there's a beauty standard set for men. They could be looking like they've been living in a trash can for a million years, but want someone who looks like Aishwarya Rai. In their parents' eyes, they deserve the best because they have an anatomical body part—an organ that if damaged, is completely useless—that women don't possess.

I don't think people realize what a traumatizing experience it is for a girl. I hear the whispers amongst aunties and sometimes uncles at my mosque who claim to be God loving but put girls down for their appearance, an aspect they have no control over. If they truly believe in Allah and follow the teachings of the Prophet and his family...how do they have it in their hearts to hurt someone's feelings in such a shallow way? Isn't it the cardinal rule in Islam NOT to hurt someone? If we believe that every human being is God's creation, then how have we as a society considered something that God designed with such detail a flaw? 'Ugly'? Those who hold such beliefs are ugly in my opinion, and should have leeches placed all over their skin before they comment on someone else's. Would love to hear God's thoughts about this. I wish I had the courage to question them and put them into their place, but then I'll be considered ill-mannered and disrespectful for spitting basic logic.

Anyways, I totally went off topic, but I guess my endorphins haven't kicked in yet. But, yeah, I'm trying to incorporate some healthy habits in my lifestyle to not only feel better but also to look better for myself...and AJ. I know that sounds so superficial, but it's normal to want to look attractive for your partner, right? If I feel better about myself, that should make me more confident, which I desperately need to work on. The truth is, there will always be someone out there who will be smarter and hotter, especially in the K-Pop industry where he's surrounded by model-like goddesses all the time. I've seen some fan sites and those who rave about him online. Some are gorgeous celebrities—I'm sure he's noticed, even though he denies it—and others are fans.

It makes me a little uncomfortable reading some comments where he's sexualized left to right. He's mentioned how some made him more self-conscious, like every move of his is under a microscope...I know that feeling, but of course not to that extent. There aren't a million cameras locked in on me. He did a performance a few days ago and his shirt raised up a little, showing a hint of his abs. It went viral all over the internet. Some fans were wilding out over it, fantasizing what they'd do to him, while others made the effort to educate them on the sexualized K-Pop culture. There's a difference between admiring someone and sexualizing them.

If I were in his shoes and read what some of the fans were fantasizing about me, I'd feel like my body has been invaded. Not only K-Pop stars, but those around the world who are a part of this industry are already sexualized as it is to be more appealing to the masses. Here's the inevitable and blunt truth—there's nothing more important than quenching the desires of the consumers for the sake of profits.

Nonetheless, there are millions around who see him the way I do. And, if the world sees him in that way, I'm sure that some of the rumors I read online about other female K-Pop idols crushing on him have to be somewhat true. Maybe dating another K-Pop star would be easier for him, and if the thought tempts him...that's something I cannot change. But I can change myself to feel confident enough that if he does, I'd have the courage to walk away.

Although AJ has never made me feel insecure, I want to keep becoming the best version myself. This way I can keep his eyes on me and only me. It might be a little psychotic and possessive, but I guess I am when it comes to him. I never pictured myself being this way. I guess it makes me realize how much I actually love him.

And as much as I would hate to admit this to Jace, I HAVE to work out more because to be completely honest... I AM FRUSTRATED, whether it's sexually or emotionally, I'm frustrated nonetheless. As Elle Woods once said in the movie *Legally Blonde*, "*Exercise gives you endorphins. Endorphins make you happy. Happy people just don't shoot their husbands.*" I'm relying on my neurotransmitters to keep me from shooting someone. In my mind...of course. I would NEVER resort to violence but I have had the urge to just go off on someone, like the waitress at the restaurant or Arsalan, ugh! Even though it's never happened in the past, I might just surprise myself one of these days.

Speaking of neurotransmitters, I should probably give them some fuel with a protein shake. I gather the strength to pluck myself off the yoga mat and force my sweaty arms through the armholes of my black NASA oversized shirt. I roll up my mat and set it against my bed frame before heading to the kitchen. As soon as I open my door, Arsalan's eyes land on me. They were fixated on my door before I even opened it. It's like he knew I was about to walk out. Does he have X-ray vision or something?!

His eyes trail me from head to toe, looks away and smiles thinly. Ew! I don't want him to look at me in that way. Only AJ has the right to do so. I drag my feet to the kitchen, only to see from the corner of my eye that his gaze hasn't moved from me!

"I'm gonna go use the bathroom, I've been holding it in since the last chapter we studied." Jace springs from his chair and quickly tiptoes to his room. Arsalan rotates his chair towards the kitchen. I can sense his lurking eyes directly on me.

"How was your workout?" he asks in a casual tone, as if he didn't infuriate me just a few hours ago with his stupid interrogation.

"It was great." With the stiff reply, my eyes pretend to search for something on the kitchen counter in an effort to avoid eye contact with him.

"Look...I'm sorry for drilling you with all those questions earlier. Normally, I wouldn't apologize."

Jesus, he's just digging more of a hole for

himself. "It's okay, don't worry about it." I try to sound as if it's genuine forgiveness, but if he normally isn't apologetic, it doesn't seem like he's a good person.

As I'm gathering my fruits, milk, and protein powder, he pops into the kitchen. He's so sneaky, like a cat. I didn't even hear him get out of his chair.

"I really am sorry." I turn around and crash into his abs as he's towering over me. "Maybe I judged you. You just didn't seem like the type who would date someone who isn't what Ami and Abu want."

"What type of girl do you take me for?" Annoyed, I dash around him, grabbing my blender.

"You seemed like the goody two-shoes, one who doesn't really do anything that Ami and Abu will disapprove of."

What? I didn't realize I radiated that 'holier than thou' persona, but I can't tell if he means it as a compliment or an insult.

"Well, first off..." I drop the fruits, protein powder and a bit of milk in the blender, "stop saying Ami and Abu. It sounds weird to hear you say Mom and Dad in Urdu...and you're not even pronouncing it properly."

I position myself in front of him with conviction.

"Secondly, I am NOTHING like the girl you think I am." I secure the lid on the blender and press the power button. The blaring noise from the blender vibrates throughout the apartment. We're both staring at each other as if it's a competition. He's smirking, as expected, and myself, glowering in hopes of turning him into stone. Ugh, he's so pretentious! No one has ever gotten under my skin like this. Before the minute ends, I switch the blender off.

"I want to know what kind of girl you actually are."

God, is he still on this? Where the hell is Jace? How long does it take to pee?! Did he fall into the toilet and get sucked into a black hole?!

"Arsalan, I'll be blunt with you." I pour my shake into a glass. "I don't think you and I will become friends. You don't strike me as the type that I'd associate myself with."

Wow, maybe those workouts aren't releasing any endorphins at all because that is probably the bitchiest thing I have ever said in my life. But, it doesn't even affect him! His slanted smirk is still on his stupid, unbothered face!

"Oh…I'll change your mind. Just give it time."

"Oh my god! You know I have a boyfriend, right?"

"Yeah…your point?"

"You're being really flirtatious and I think it's a little disrespectful."

"I'm not being flirtatious. This is just the way I talk." He cackles, fueling my anger.

"So, you talk to everyone like this?" I raise a

brow.

"Yeah, pretty much. Most of the time, people don't take it up the—" Right then, Jace swings open his door and steps out in the living room. He stops mid stride as both of us shift our heads towards him.

"Uh, sorry. That took a while. Everything okay out here?" He assesses my facial expression.

I squint my eyes in disgust at Arsalan before stomping into my room without saying a word. I fling my door shut, flopping onto my bed and chugging the protein shake as if it's a shot. I feel like hurling the glass at the wall. How and why am I letting this desi Damon get to me?!

They continue to study, while I head to the bathroom to take a shower, hoping the cold water brings my hypertensive ass down. I take deep breaths and glance in the mirror as I take my clothes off. The definition of my abs are getting more prominent and my muscles are getting bigger. That brings a smile to my face. Putting effort into something and seeing results you hope for is such a rewarding feeling. Speaking of rewarding feelings...I'll see my AJ soon. It's the only thing I'm looking forward to after having my blood boiled all morning.

◆ ◆ ◆

Before heading out to meet AJ, I glance

one last time in the mirror, flipping my freshly straightened hair over my shoulder. Damn, Zara. You can dress yourself up now without any fashion advice from Jace. Oh, wow. Am I...growing up? Ha! Nope. Not yet.

Lately, I've been experimenting with different clothing styles, trying to see which one I like most. Figured it's time for me to retire from my former style, or as Jace calls it...hobo chic. I just choose comfort over style, there's no harm in that.

I went with a black, fitted bodysuit with half sleeves and a scooped neck, pairing it with dark washed skinny jeans. I top it all off with some dainty gold 'jhumka' earrings and gold 'churiyan' my mother bought for me from Pakistan. Oh, and can't forget my black doc martens. Feminine but edgy, kind of how I've been feeling lately.

I step into the living room and grab my keys out of the glass bowl placed at the entrance table before turning around towards the dining table.

"Hey, Jace, I'm heading—" I stop mid-sentence as I glance up to see both of their jaws hanging, especially Arsalans.

"Wow." Arsalan, yet again, has his gaze on me, scanning head to toe. "You clean up nicely."

"Thanks." I roll my eyes without making the effort to hide it from him.

"Just take the damn compliment. Like I

said before, you'll come around to liking me."

"I wouldn't hold my breath." A devilish grin hijacks my face. "On second thought, I would love to see you pass out from low oxygen levels, so be my guest."

"Alright, you two, calm down...no one's dying here today." Jace acts like a parent. "Are you heading out to see AJ?"

"Yup, don't wait up." I wink at Jace and then glance at Arsalan. The smug look is wiped off his face. Now THAT releases endorphins.

◆ ◆ ◆

"Hey, gorgeous." Ah, his Australian accent is music to my ears. There he is, leaning against the wall of my apartment building effortlessly. He makes an 'o' with his mouth while eyeing me up and down. "Wow, you look stunning as always, my Pakistani princess."

"Thank you, my dear!" I wrap my arms around his neck, and he around my waist. "I missed you."

I inhale the smell of his skin ricocheting off of his black hoodie. I love it when he wears one of his MANY black hoodies—his off duty street style—and I love it even more when he lets me borrow them.

"I saw you yesterday. Miss me that much?" He rests his forehead on mine and kisses the tip of my nose.

"I miss you all the time." I sigh.

There's a split second of silence from both ends, but it breaks quickly.

"I just wanted to get through this morning just so I can see you."

"Same." I groan. "I had such an irritating morning. Oh, I also reserved a room in the clubhouse. It's right over there." I point a few feet away from us. Holding his hand, we walk in the direction of the building.

"What happened?"

"I met Jace's annoying friend." I roll my eyes while placing the keycard against the door scanner to the room and punch in the reservation code. "Probably the worst human being I've come across." The door's loud unlocking echoes throughout the hallway as we walk in. There's a brown couch against the wall as soon as you enter, with an ebony coffee table in the middle and two rustic armchairs on either side.

AJ laughs. "Wow, what did he do? Claim aliens don't exist or something?" He waits for me to take a seat on the couch and then he follows.

"I would've been able to get past that if he did. But, no. He's just so arrogant and entitled, and says anything that comes to his mind. It's funny, I thought he might've been Jace's old flame because he looked too good to be straight."

AJ purses his lips and creases his brows. "So, straight people don't look good? You think I don't look good?" I can't tell if he's joking or is actually concerned. "I know I'm barefaced right now, so I might look hideous. But, am I still good looking?"

HOW CAN HE ASK SUCH A QUESTION?! What gives him the right to have low self-esteem?! This boy, I swear...doesn't realize his presence in this world.

"AJ, are you really asking me that question?" I caress his face. "You're the hottest guy I've ever laid my eyes on."

"Okay, okay. Good. Better stay that way." He playfully taps my nose with his index finger. "So, was he Jace's old flame?"

"No, he's Jace's friend from medical school and he made it quite clear that he's straight and single. Oh and get this...he's also Pakistani, which is crazy because I don't know any Pakistani boys besides the ones in my family."

"Well, in that case, shouldn't you like him?"

"Just because he's Pakistani doesn't mean I should like him as a person by default. So far, he seems like the son of the devil."

"Okay, but you just met this guy. What exactly did he do to make you dislike him this much?" I bite my tongue. Should I tell him how he interrogated me like a police officer about HIM?

"He just...hit a nerve."
"And...that nerve is?"
I bite my lip and mumble, "You."

He tilts his head, casting a squinting gaze towards me.

"ME? You told him about me?"

"No, not about you being a K-Pop star. Just that I have a boyfriend…and he just kept drilling me with these inappropriate questions that he has no right to ask."

"Like what?" he asks in an irritated tone. I think he's starting to dislike Arsalan as much as I do.

"Like…" I hesitate to say the next few words, "he asked if my parents knew about you not being Muslim. He was basically insinuating that you and I won't last."

AJ's jaw clenches. "Who the hell is he to make that sort of judgment, let alone ask these questions he has no business asking, unless…" he scoffs, "the mate's jealous."

"Why would he be jealous?"

"He probably likes you." He crosses his arms.

"No, he's just an ass. He's probably like this with everyone."

"Maybe, but I don't think he would care this much if he wasn't interested in you. He wouldn't be putting down our relationship if he wasn't."

"Okay, even if he is, I certainly am not."

"Why not? Things might be easier with him than they are with me." He clenches his jaw even harder, enhancing the appearance of his masseter. This boy needs to relax before he pulls a muscle!

"Can you stop? What's gotten into you?"

"Nothing, sorry." With a passive reply, he pierces straight ahead at the door.

"Are you mad?"

"No...I guess I'm just a little irritated with this guy commenting on our relationship."

"Yeah, I agree."

I mean...I don't like Arsalan by any means but he brought up some points that eventually I have to address to AJ.

"But AJ...I hate to admit it, but the questions he asked...are some I ask myself when it comes to us."

He uncrosses his arms and turns his whole body to face me.

"Okay, like what?"

I gulp. "Well, I mean if we plan to have a future together, we should talk about some things right now. Like, how I'd get my parents to come around. I'm kind of just waiting on you because for me to even do that, I have to get the green light on your end."

The room echoes from his exasperated sigh.

"Zara, I'm gonna be honest...I hate talking about this. I think it just causes more stress on us than anything."

"AJ, if we want to have a future together we need to think about this stuff."

"I know that, but why can't we just live in the moment for now and see what happens?"

What happens...with us? Does he have doubts?

"What do you mean?"

He clicks his tongue, followed with a loud sigh.

"I just don't feel like talking about this. I don't know, it makes me sad and anxious."

"Sad? Why?"

He props his bent elbow on the armrest and fiddles with his small, silver hoop earring.

"I'm not very good with my words, so...I don't know how to explain it."

"Are you kidding? You're a songwriter and a producer. It should be second nature."

"Not when it comes to you, Zara." He strokes my cheek with his thumb as his favorite silver bracelet rattles down his pale thin wrist. "I can't seem to find the proper words in any language to describe how I feel about anything when it comes to you."

Lines between his brows form into the number eleven. His eyes penetrate into mine, switching from looking into one eye to the other.

"So, until I know what to say, can we please not talk about it?"

"Alright." Before he can say another word, I ask, "So...how're rehearsals going?"

Right when he separates his lips to answer, his phone rings. He closes his eyes before forcing them open. "Just one second, love." With a deep breath, he inhales and exhales as he answers with, "Hello?" AJ nods while having his eyes centered at the coffee table before shifting them towards me. "Alright, I'll be there in ten minutes."

You know that feeling when you've been waiting all day to go back home and eat that gooey, cheesy, sizzling hot burger while indulging a documentary about space? Then you trudge back home after a tiring day and the one joy—which is every dairy lover's safe haven —that kept you from punching someone in the face...turns out spoiled? You know the disappointment that spreads throughout your tiring soul at that very moment? Yeah, I feel that shit right now. He has to leave...again.

"You want to talk to her?" He hands the phone over to me and mouths 'Lee'.

I grab the phone from him and place it against my ear, clearing the lump in my throat before speaking.

"Hey, Lee!"

"Hey!"

His beautiful deep voice always throws me off, especially with his Australian accent. That voice just doesn't match his intriguing soft, boy-like appearance. I thought he was in his late teens when I first met him, but he's actually twenty-four! After Sir David Attenborough, he should really consider being a narrator for those natural history series.

"How are you?" he asks.

"I'm good, my dear. How about you?"

"I'm great...I wanted to just make sure you are. I'm really sorry he has to come back that quickly. Our manager and I tried to hold off as much as we could, but the event planners for K-Pop Fusion need to speak to him right now."

"No! It's totally fine, please don't worry."

"I know you're hiding it with a smile, but I can only imagine how it must feel. I'm so

sorry, again, Zara. I really am."

"Oh my gosh, can you stop? It's okay! I completely understand."

"Hmm...good job trying to convince me. Don't worry, I'll make sure this doesn't happen

again. You know...I still don't get how you're handling all this and being so understanding. Hyung better marry you after putting you through this!" We both giggle at the same time, but mine was disingenuous.

"No, it really is okay." I glance at AJ. "He's worth it. Again, don't worry about me!

Take care of yourself."

"I will and you, too. Okay? I better see you at the event! Bye, Zara!"

"Bye, Lee. I'll see you then!" I tap the red button and hand back his phone. The corners

of my mouth are met with a frown. "You should leave right now."

He grips my fingers in his palm and kisses

my knuckles.

"Yeah…" he sighs, "I know, my love…I'm so sorry. I don't want to though." Closing his eyes, AJ presses the surface of my bent fingers against his lips. "I never want to leave you…I always hate it when I do."

"Me, too." I nestle my face into his chest. It's heaven here. "But, I understand."

He plays with a strand of my hair and pushes it behind my ear.

"You know, Zara…I really do appreciate everything you're doing. I'm so thankful you decided to still be in my life considering everything. I don't think I could be as patient as you have been." I remain quiet. "Also…I'm going to New York next Saturday, but I'll be back a week later…and then…" I know what his next few words will be and I don't think I have the heart to endure them, "I'll be going back to Korea."

Yup, I did NOT want to hear it; those words felt like a burning knife that ripped through my gut.

"I know. I don't want to remember." I squeeze him in my arms a little tighter and for a bit longer…because pretty soon, I'll be longing for these moments.

◆ ◆ ◆

"Oh…you're home already? What happened to 'don't wait up'?" Jace is in the kitchen, washing dishes as I enter the apartment.

"Clearly things didn't go as planned." I kick my shoes off.

"You know for a performer, I would think he'd have a little more stamina in him." I proceed to chuck my keys at him but he dodges them. "Whoa there, if I knew I was getting assaulted today, I would've kept Arsalan around so he could be your target instead."

"Ugh, don't even mention that asshole's name. And, BY THE WAY, why haven't I heard of him up until now? I didn't know you had another Pakistani friend."

"Yeah...sorry, I decided I'm replacing you with another Pakistani since I can only have one at a time."

I roll my eyes and take a seat on the bar stool, crossing my arms on the kitchen counter as Jace continues to wash the remaining few dishes.

"I'm joking, of course. Well, it's just I didn't want you guys to meet because while he may be a really good friend...I have seen the way he is with women and I didn't want him to pursue you. He's definitely a player and I don't trust him with someone I care about, especially you."

"Well, regardless...I still ended up meeting him, despite your efforts."

"I figured now that you have a serious relationship, it shouldn't be a problem."

"Are you kidding? He was still trying to hit

on me."

"I could tell by the sexual tension when I walked in."

"There was no sexual tension! Maybe some tension, but it wasn't sexual!" I protest.

"Um, I don't know...there was just something weird between the two of you. You both banter like an old married couple."

I don't agree with him one bit.

"Speaking of couples...why are you back so quickly? It's hardly been an hour. Is everything okay?" He asks as he lifts a washed plate to dry with a dish towel.

"He...had to go back to work. They called him in."

He sets the plate on the drying rack before leaning over on the counter.

"Are you okay?"

"Yeah, I am." I lie but he doesn't buy it.

"I don't know why you continue to try to lie to me when you know that I know you better than you know yourself."

"Um..." I try to comprehend his babbling words, "that sentence had way too many pronouns to keep up with."

"Stop lying to me. I think at times you forget, I am YOU."

"I can't believe I'm saying this, but I have a feeling...that Arsalan might have been right about my relationship with AJ."

"YOU think Arsalan is right? Someone call

an ambulance because there's definitely something wrong with you!"

"Don't ever mention that I said that about him or I will kill you."

"I won't, but don't listen to him. He's never been in a committed relationship before...or knows the struggles of banging a K-Pop star." He saves me with a laugh.

"Man...I REALLY don't like him."

"Yeah, another reason why I never introduced you to him. You two are polar opposites. You have a kind, gentle soul while he's just a hot piece of ass that breaks hearts left and right."

I laugh under my breath. "Yeah, a hot piece of ass that would instantly get my parents' approval without even lifting a finger." I wonder how Jace's parents are with him dating someone who isn't Hispanic. I'm surprised we haven't talked about this. "What about your parents? Do they approve of Ari?"

"Yeah, well, as you already know, I told them about her the minute we landed back in Los Angeles. They've even spoken to her through FaceTime and REALLY like her...and I think her parents like me, too." He shrugs as he grabs another plate.

"Really? Are they okay with the whole cultural differences?"

"My parents were a little thrown off when I told them, but they said it doesn't matter as long as I'm happy. I don't know exactly how her parents feel, but they seem to like me from what she's said. Yeah, there might be a language barrier and she might not understand some things in my culture, just like me with hers, but I think we both are willing to learn. I'm fine with it because she and I know that our babies will be the cutest as long as they inherit all of her features. She's so...beautiful." His eyes gleam into the distance as a shy smile brightens his face.

"She really IS gorgeous." I nod. "I'm kind of jealous of you, actually."

"Why?" Jace arches his brow.

"Because your parents care about your happiness."

"Yours do too, dumbass."

"Yeah, I know they tell me to do what makes me happy...but ultimately, I don't think they'll be fine with what ACTUALLY brings me happiness. Maybe parents say that because they don't think we'd want anything other than what they've imagined for us. They believe we wouldn't dare to go against their wishes. Until we do and then..." I project the pain of millions of desi kids like me. "It's just a betrayal in their eyes. They'll guilt us with, 'After all the sacrifices we made for you, how could you do that to us?', thinking they have ownership over our happiness. Do they not realize that we put aside our interests, wants, and love for their sake as well? And for what?! To please and impress the uncles and aunties I barely speak to? I'm pretty sure they care less about our well-being and more about the latest gossip to fill their lonely evenings with, while sipping on a cup of chai."

He hurries to my side and pulls me in for the hug I need at this very moment.

"You're a great daughter, Zara. You need to stop thinking this way."

"I feel selfish for being happy. It feels like I'm doing something wrong."

"How could you be doing something wrong if it makes you happy?"

"Honestly, I ask myself the same question, but can't seem to find the answer to it."

"Zara, you really have to stop. Okay? This is your life. You need to keep reminding yourself of that. You're the one living it."

"Easier said than done." As he continues to hug my pessimistic, tortured ass, a thought surfaces in my head. "Jace...you and Ari talk about having babies together?"

"Oh...yeah, that kind of slipped, huh?"

"Mhm."

"Yeah, we do."

"So, you both talk about your future together?"

"Yeah, all the time, actually."

"That makes me happy." It really does.

"Thanks, bubs. I don't know, she put a spell on me or something!" He pulls away, and his laughter rings throughout the apartment. "But because of her, I questioned a couple things about myself."

He takes a seat beside me, resting his wrist on the counter.

"I started wondering why I avoided emotions in relationships. I liked keeping things sweet and fun. No complications whatsoever. But, as soon as the other person became clingy in my eyes, I'd run away faster than Usain Bolt in the Olympics."

We both chuckle. Even in the most serious conversations, he still manages to add a bit of laughter.

"Now that I look back at what I considered 'clingy', that was just them expressing their emotions and needs. And I found that INCREDIBLY annoying. In my head, I thought they're complaining, not having a clue that other people have it worse. But now, I realize I was projecting my parents' words. As a child, whenever I told them I didn't like something or felt scared, they'd always tell me to suck it up, others have it worse. Or they'd throw in the classic line—'Stop complaining, be thankful we've given you food, water, and a roof over your head.' Maybe it's the immigrant parent mentality, I'm not sure, but they thought that was enough for a person's needs, rejecting any of my emotional ones. They expected a child to be more mature than it can possibly be. I guess that's why I felt like I grew up so quickly. I became overly independent, suppressing my emotions and needs, struggling to ask for help. But then...I met you."

He places his hand over mine, giving it a gentle squeeze.

"I found someone who understands where I'm coming from because you are a lot like me. Minus the gross jokes and killer clothing style."

I nod as he taps two fingers on the back of my hand.

"For the first time, I felt like I didn't have to comfort myself alone...you made me feel safe enough to lean on you and I felt very protective of you. I wanted to make sure your needs were met. You brought this side out of me that I didn't think was possible. But I was afraid to be as vulnerable with anyone else as I am with you. I didn't want to hand anyone the power to have a hold over my emotions. It's scary to do that, but I guess sometimes you just have to take that risk in order to gain something beautiful...and I'm glad I did with Ari. I'm not scared anymore and I cannot tell you WHAT a relief that is."

Seeing his huge smile makes me happy. There is nothing more that I love than to see Jace this way. It prompts a smile to my face as well.

"She doesn't invalidate my feelings even if I try to do it myself. When I look at her, I see the parent I wish I had growing up and that's why I want her to be the mother of my children."

My eyes tear up hearing Jace's heartfelt words. I wish parents could see the effects childhood trauma has on us as adults. Whether it's big or small, it manifests itself in a way that leaves us confused about why we are the way we are. Parents are supposed to protect their children from any harm...but maybe they weren't protected as well. I often wonder if perhaps our parents' needs and emotions were neglected by their parents, continuing this cycle of intergenerational trauma. Maybe they're also victims of trauma just as much as we are.

"I hope she's the mother of my future nieces and nephews. I'm really rooting for you two."

"Well, I'm rooting for you and him as well."
"Me, too."
But now I question...is AJ?

CHAPTER 3:

A Hidden Rose

"Come closer, baby." Tugging on his tie, I pull AJ towards me. "I love you so much, AJ."

I breathe in the air of romance set with the dim lights of candles scattered around. Rain trickles down the window pane, filling my room with the faint sound of raindrops.

"I bet I love you more." The light touch of his hand trailing along my spine and halting at my waist sends goosebumps throughout my body. Gosh, I'll never get over how his Australian accent—emitting Hugh Jackman vibes—just makes everything sound ten times sexier.

Eyes closed, I smile and ask, "Is that so?" I indulge in his hands moving around my waist, and down to my own. Lifting my arms with one hand, he locks his fingers around my wrists. I try to tussle myself out from his grasp, but that only makes him tighten his grip. He works his other hand up my thigh, shooting me a wink that goes straight to my toes.

"Would you like me to show you?" he whispers, sending chills down my spine. I feel AJ's lips brush the back of my neck, tilting my head a little to the right and placing a lingering kiss. My heart beats faster and faster against the sternum as his provocative breathing on my skin gets heavier.

Unable to move, I moan under my breath, "Yes."

"Good girl." He lays a ravaging kiss on my neck. "Now, you have to listen to what I say."

I nod obediently, unable to move.

"I'm going to turn you back around, but you can't open your eyes."

I remain quiet, as words have escaped my mind.

"Do you understand, princess?"

Oh my gosh, he's driving me crazy.

"Yes," I mumble into a moan.

He tightens his grip around my wrist even more and I revel in the soft strokes of his lips against my skin.

"You can't just say 'yes'."

Confused, I ask, "What am I supposed to say?"

His lips retreat from my neck and gravitate to my ear. Oh...dear god. I inhale deeply as it feels like I'm running out of oxygen.

"You have to say…" his lips glide over my

earlobe, and with a shaky breath whispers, "yes, sir."

Uh, what?! My eyes open wide and break free from his grip. I turn around towards him but he clamps his soft hand forcefully over my eyes.

"I told you, you have to keep your eyes closed." He whispers, but with an undertone of threat behind each word.

"I'm not calling you 'sir'." I scoff in disbelief. Did he really just say that?

"That wasn't a suggestion, baby girl." He grunts, pushing himself off of my body, his hand still over my eyes. "It was an order."

God damn, AJ. That was smooth, real smooth, even if I wanted to burst out laughing.

"If you move your hand off my eyes, then I'll say it."

"Not. A. Chance." He says each word slowly with an intimidating low voice, making the raspiness of his voice more apparent.

"Then, I won't. We can stay like this forever."

"I'll just kiss you."

"Do it." That's exactly what I want you to do, honey.

Silence fills the room. There's not even a hint of sound. A few seconds go by. I contemplate whether I should say something and before words slip out of my mouth, something else slips in. I feel his plump lips press against mine. He teases me by brushing the tip of his tongue against my lips. I melt into it, soaking it all in. He lifts his hand off of my eyes.

"You can open your eyes, meri jaan."

Meri jaan? I never taught him how to say 'my love' in Urdu.

I open my eyes fleetly, only to see...

"Arsalan?!"

The horror that burns through my body feels as if my veins are caught on fire. I take a step back and he takes one forward. My heart crashes against my rib cage. What the hell is happening?! AJ was just here!

My window flings open, shattering the glass into pieces all over my floor. The gust of wind blows out every flame of the candles, making my room pitch black. The only source of light strikes every few seconds as the sky roars with thunder.

"What—what are you doing here?!" I trip over a sneaker as I continue to stagger backwards.

"Meri jaan."

He leaps towards me before my room fills itself with a faint flickering red light. Where is it coming from? Why has my room become an episode of Black Mirror?

"Stop!" I yell as I plop onto my bed. My heart feels like it's an atom bomb, about to explode! "How did you get in here? Where's AJ?!"

Answer me, damn it!

He smiles, towering over me. Arsalan

lowers himself down on his knees. He levels his eyes to mine and says, "Wake up, meri jaan."

"What?" I stare into his eyes in confusion.

He braces his hand on the back of my head, pulls me closer to his face, and whispers, "Wake up."

"WAKE UP!"

My eyes swing open as my body flings off the couch from Jace's screaming and the blaring ruckus of the vacuum.

"Jesus, Jace!" I press my hands over my heart that's beating as if I've overdosed on drugs.

"Damn, my bad." He turns the vacuum off. "Sorry, I didn't mean to wake you up like that. I was vacuuming and thought you'd sleep better in your room." He offers his hand to help me up, but I smack it away. "Are you okay? You were moaning and stuff...were you having a sex dream?!"

If I tell him what I dreamt of, I wouldn't hear the last of it.

"Uh, no. I don't remember my dream." I touch my face as I feel it's starting to get warm.

"Bitch, your face is more red than Donald Trump's tie...literally. Don't lie to me."

"Oh my god, I don't remember!"

"Geez, okay, damn. Whatever it was, put you in a grouchy mood."

"I'm not, just tired." I play it off.

"I bet. It can be tiring from all the sex you're having in your dreams!" He laughs.

"Again, I wasn't!" I head to the kitchen to drink some water. I feel dehydrated from the nightmare I just endured unwillingly.

"Okay, okay. Damn, I'll drop it. Also, why are you still in your scrubs? You know you're supposed to take them off as soon as you get home. But, I'm sure you were tired...from all the sex—"

"Oh my god, you said you'd drop it! It's not even funny anymore!"

"Okay, NOW I'll drop it. Anyways, how was volunteering at the homeless shelter this morning?"

"It was good. Dr. Johnson came in today to supervise."

"I love her! I think she's one of the best doctors at the medical center."

"I know! I think out of all the doctors I've met, she seems to be the one who cares the most about the students and patients. She has a genuine, pure heart. We both shared some of the stories we've heard at the shelter and they're just...gut wrenching. Some of them get treated so poorly, like they're not even a person. Would it kill for people to be a decent human being and help those who need a little love and support?"

If there was a genie and granted me one wish, I'd choose to end homelessness all over the world, but I don't think it's possible unless we all collectively try to do something about it.

"Human beings are the WORST. No wonder aliens don't want to contact us. They're probably disgusted by our kind."

"I would be, too. Unless somehow they're worse than us, which I highly doubt." I pour some water into my glass. "Also, why are you vacuuming? We just cleaned the house a few days ago."

"Zara, don't you remember?! Ari is coming today! I want everything to be spotless! There should be no traces of any human beings living here!"

Shit, that actually slipped my mind. Crazy to think that just a few months ago, both me and Jace were single. And now, both taken by a pair of Korean-Australian siblings.

"Oh my god, that's right!" I place my glass down on the counter. "Are you excited?!"

Widening his eyes, Jace knocks over the vacuum.

"No, I'm not excited at all. I'm just cleaning our whole apartment for my own enjoyment. What do you think?!"

I guess I'm not the grouchy one anymore.

"Okay, stupid question. I deserve that."

He picks it up while shaking his head and laughing.

"But do you think you can do me a favor?"

"Sure. What's up?"

"If you're free for the day, do you think you can take Ari out and just show her around for a few hours? I have to go study for my last final tomorrow and by the time you guys get back, it'll be dinner time. I'll cook something up for you both. Is that okay?"

"Yup, I'm free. It would be my honor."

"Thanks. I figured you had nothing to do since you're not doing AJ...clearly. It's probably why you're having all these sex dreams."

"You ass!" I throw the kitchen towel at him. I mean, he's not wrong, but still he doesn't have to rub salt in the wounds that I essentially made myself.

"Where's Arsalan when you need him?!"

My face heats up when I hear his name.

"You're so...dumb." Scoffing, I turn away from him and chug some more water down my dry throat.

"Why is your face turning red again? Oh...my...god." He throws his hands up and onto his face. "Don't tell me...you had a sex dream about...Arsalan!" His infamous mischievous smile fills his face.

"No, I didn't!" I hurl the other kitchen towel at him.

"You totally did! Wow, you dirty little harlot!" He bursts into a spate of laughter, with one hand on his stomach and the other on the handle of the vacuum.

"Oh my god, please stop." I plant my hand on my forehead.

"Wow, I didn't think you had it in you...or should I say, him instead of 'it'." Jace checks his watch mid laugh. "Oh, shit. I have to go in like five minutes, but she'll be here in about an hour."

"Sounds good to me." Anything to make this conversation stop.

"Oh, and...I'm studying with Arsalan. I'll make sure to tell him you've been thinking about him. I'm sure that's something he's been dying to hear." He winks.

"I swear, if you say a word, I will end you first and then myself."

"Okay, tiny killer. Go get ready. You look like a hot mess."

"I'm going! Geez."

"Maybe a cold shower would help with those dirty thoughts you're not having about your boyfriend!"

Oh my god, did I just cheat on AJ in my dream?! No, right?! I said no to Arsalan. But, why is my subconscious...thinking about him?!

◆ ◆ ◆

"Let's stop to get some coffee, Zara. I'm exhausted!" Ari glances down. "My feet are killing me. Why did I think walking around Rodeo Drive in new heels was a good idea? Oh, that's right. Because I'm an idiot."

"Girl, look at me. I'm wearing an oversized T-shirt with sneakers. At least you're an idiot who looks like she just stepped out from a photoshoot." We laugh while assessing our outfits. "Oh! We can go to Laudree! You'll love it."

We walk over to the next street, while Ari stumbles as she holds onto me. Before we walk in, she stops to take a picture outside of Laudree —one of the cutest cafes I've been to.

"Oh my gosh, Zara! This place is so cute!"

"Just like you." I tap her nose. Ahk, I really love her. I don't have any siblings and I always wished to have a sister. In a weird way, she's kind of like that sister I never had.

We place our orders, and as always, we fight over the bill. But I knock over her wallet and win. I learned that one from the best—my parents.

"Zara, you cannot do that again, okay?!" She yells as we make our way to a table towards the back of the cafe.

"Yeah, I can't promise you that." I tap her nose again.

"You and AJ are the same. He never lets me pay for anything. Speaking of...how are you two?"

Should I tell her how we really are or just pull something out of my ass? I mean, it's still weird talking about her own brother to her.

"We're good." I nod and smile.

"Hmm, promise? You know...I can kick his ass if you ever need me to."

"I don't think that would be necessary. Your brother treats me well." Which isn't a lie. I change the subject. "How are you and Jace?"

Instantly, her face lights up. "Zara, I am so

in love with your best friend."

"Yeah, I can see it all over your cute little face." Hearing her say that brought out a similar smile on my face. Jace has never been in a serious relationship, so hearing someone else talk about him in this way is new, but it brings me so much comfort and joy knowing he has someone like her as a partner. They're perfect for each other.

"I've never felt like this before. In Australia, I never really met any guy who made me laugh until my stomach hurts or could keep up with me because I can be a handful at times! He makes me feel so loved and safe, which is something I have never experienced."

What kind of shitty guys has this poor girl dealt with?! Well, to be fair, it's not like I've had the pleasure of knowing any quality men out here in California besides Jace. Granted, Jace was kind of a player, but still, not a shitty person.

"I don't think he's ever met anyone who matches his energy. I remember when he first laid his eyes on you back in Korea. It was DEFINITELY love at first sight for him." I wink.

"It was for me, too." Her eyes crinkle from smiling.

Our order arrives, with a cheerful, "Here's a cappuccino and a tea, along with some croissants. Enjoy, ladies!"

Without waiting for the scorching coffee to cool down, I take a desperate sip. I don't even know why I'm so tired. My body is probably catching up to me from being sleep deprived from finals week.

"Zara..."

"Hmm?" I set my coffee down on the table.

"I really want to marry him." She pushes a strand of hair behind her ear, joining the rest of her layered black long locks. Ha, what do ya know. Her hair actually looks very similar to mine.

"Yeah?" A smile sweeps my face.

"Mhm....Jace and I even talked about it." She cuffs her hand over her smile. I know I shouldn't be surprised at hearing that since Jace also mentioned how serious they are about each other, but I still am. They've only been dating for as long as AJ and I have but they're both so sure about each other.

"About getting married?"

"And where we would get married. Pretty much have all the details planned. Jace is the one who seems more excited about a wedding than me." She chuckles.

"Tell me the details!" I'm excited to hear this.

"Okay! Well, we planned to have the wedding in Australia. He thought it'd be nice to get married where I grew up. A while back, apparently I said that I wanted a wedding in Australia and he remembered, even though I completely forgot! Plus, he said it'd be nice to have a destination wedding. Oh my god, how cute would it be?! You and Jace, in our hometown! AJ and I would show you both places we loved growing up!" She brings her hands together in tiny soft claps, something AJ does as well when he's excited.

"That actually does sound like a lot of fun." I slurp my coffee, allowing her to shine through this moment of excitement.

"I've never been so excited about anything before, not even when I got promoted to be a fashion creative director." She laughs. "Just waiting for him to propose. I'm not even pushing it because I know he still has to finish medical school, so I'm kind of just letting him take the reins on this."

"Yeah, but you guys can always get married while he's in medical school. A lot of people do that."

"Really?" Her eyes light up, widening as much as her smile. "But I would understand if he wouldn't be willing to. I mean, if I were in his shoes, I don't know if I would." She finally takes a sip of her tea.

I wonder how her parents would feel about this. I really want to ask what they think about the cultural differences between her and Jace. Maybe that would give me insight about how his family views interracial and interfaith marriages. That way I can be prepared for when they find out about me and I finally meet them. For now, I'll remain hidden like a dirty little secret.

"Ari, what do your parents REALLY think about Jace?"

"Ah, yeah...I was worried they wouldn't be accepting." Guess she's not the only one. "But to my surprise, they're more receptive than I thought. Though, I won't lie...I did have to convince them A LOT. I haven't told Jace that, actually. They were more worried about how we'd navigate through the cultural differences. And, I know it will be a little hard but I told them that's an issue for him and I to work through it. I think we love each other enough to make that effort, you know? That's about it so far. They ask about him a lot, so that's a REALLY good sign. I don't know if they'll a hundred percent accept our relationship, but I guess living in Australia opened their eyes quite a bit. They were super conservative when they moved there before AJ and I were born. I'm sure if they still lived in Korea, maybe their conservative views wouldn't have changed as much. Thankfully, they did a little...for mine and AJ's sake!"

I feel a little better hearing that. I just wish that if the time comes when I talk to my parents about AJ, they would have at least half of the same reaction.

"Zara, if you're worried about my parents accepting you...don't be. They'll love you as much as I do." Damn, was I thinking out loud?

"Thank you. That means a lot to me." I reach out to hold her hand.

"Damn, if people didn't know we're like sisters, they'd think we're lovers instead!" She whispers and we laugh under our breaths.

"Also, Zara…if they have any issue—which they won't—they'll feel my wrath!" She squints while making a fist and pressing it against her other hand.

Wow…I'm so lucky to have her in my life, not only as a potential sister-in-law or my best friend's potential future wife, but as a friend. I'm glad AJ has her as a sister. In a way, she's AJ's 'Jace'.

"Zara, have you and AJ talked about your future together at all?"

Ha, if only she knew that I've been trying to do that.

"We just haven't had the chance, really. He was so busy touring and then after that ended, he had to get ready for the K-Pop Fusion event."

"Ah, I see. I'm sure he's going to talk about it, eventually."

I wish I could tell her he hates talking about it, but I also don't want her thinking of her brother any differently.

"Yeah, maybe." I click on the home screen of my phone for the time as a way to end this conversation about AJ and me. Shit, Jace should be getting home soon. "We should head out in a few minutes. Jace should be getting home and he's making dinner."

"Perfect! I'm almost done with my tea."

I chug down the last few sips of my coffee, leaving me all jittery. Now, the only thing on my mind besides the jitteriness is AJ. To be honest, as much as I am over the moon hearing about her and Jace talking about their future, it makes me wonder why AJ and I aren't there. Are we not as close to each other as Jace and Ari are? I mean, I think I am. I'm willing to talk about it but he isn't. I know I shouldn't have these thoughts, but I can't help but wonder if he even sees me in his future. What if he doesn't? Maybe that's why he avoids the subject. Or maybe he really is just stressed out right now. Ah, I'm overthinking, AGAIN! He loves me so much! Zara, get it together! I have to keep reminding myself that he's not living a normal life like Jace, Ari, or me. He's a damn K-Pop star.

◆ ◆ ◆

"Honey, I'm home!" Ari peeks her head into the apartment—which is filled with a mouthwatering aroma—and leaps into Jace's arms.

"Hi, mi amor!" He picks her up and spins her around. "I missed you, babe! Oh, I never want to let go of you."

"Well, you have to because you're suffocating me." She struggles to even mumble her words.

"Oh, I'm sorry, my baby!" He slowly lowers her down till her feet hit the floor. "Did you two have a fun time?"

"We had an amazing time, except for my feet. I think there's no blood circulating to them anymore."

"Well, I can take a look at them later tonight if you like." He winks and kisses her lips.

"Geez, you guys! Get a room!" I deliberately cover my eyes with my hand to get a laugh out of the two. "What's on God's menu today?" I lift the lid off the pot.

"Ah, well, I'm attempting to make bulgogi and rice. So far, I can't tell if it'll be good, but it's safe to say the kimchi will be since it's store bought."

"Aww, you're making Korean food?! My heart!" Ari kisses Jace on the cheek, and he returns one on her forehead.

"It might not be edible, babe."

"I don't care." She holds his hands so tightly. "The fact that you tried to make a Korean dish means the world to me, baby." They embrace by the simple act of staring into each other's eyes in such awe, it almost made me tear up. Seeing the love and appreciation they have for each other's cultures really gives me hope for a future with AJ.

In the past few months, I've been asking AJ things about his culture, like his favorite dishes, learning some Korean phrases, and even watching some Korean dramas and movies during my free time. Boy, I get the hype now. They're SO good and speak to the soul. I realized some of their cultural beliefs are as conversative as the ones I was raised with. Even though my parents didn't believe in those values as much, the brown aunties and uncles around me never failed to mention them constantly. AJ asks about different things in my culture as well, especially when it comes to music. He absolutely loves most of the Bollywood songs that I like, but the one artist he fell in love with is Pakistan's legend, Nusrat Fateh Ali Khan. It makes me happy knowing he likes the one artist I grew up listening to because my parents played his songs from morning till night. Hopefully, that would earn him some 'mithai' points. 'Mithai' points, ha! I crack myself up sometimes, although it's clever, I must say. I should use that often, even though I don't eat that many Pakistani sweets because it's practically diabetes central but so delicious. Jesus, I just go off topic in my own head! I bet they're probably wondering why I've been staring at them for a while.

"Zara, I have a surprise for you in your room." Jace breaks me out of my mind banter.

"What surprise?" I squint. "Don't tell me you filled my room with phallic objects or some crap."

"Why do you think I would do such a thing?" Jace places his hand over his chest as if he's offended.

"Because you DID such a thing two years

ago on my birthday."

"Oh…" he bursts out laughing, "yeah, I did do that. That was hilarious. But, no. Nothing like that…but you might find the real deal in there."

What the hell is he talking about? With him, I just never know.

"Jace! What—"

"Just go!" He thrusts his arm, pointing to my room.

"Okay, okay. I'm going."

I twist the doorknob and push open the door and…nothing. Nothing is there. What in the world was Jace even—

"Boo!"

I scream every air particle out from my lungs! I turn around and behind the door is…

"AJ!" I jump into his arms and kiss the nape of his neck, which gratefully was within the reach of my lips.

"Sorry, love. I didn't mean to scare you." He nuzzles his nose in my hair. "Just kidding."

"Well, you aren't the only one who scared the crap out of me today."

I laugh and loosen my arms around him to see that gorgeous bareface. His soft purple hair is all natural today, curly and fluffy—just the way I like it. He's dressed in black joggers and a loose black workout tank top with cut open sides exposing his latissimus dorsi and serratus anterior. Allah took time to make him. He's…a work of art. Even when he's dressed down, he looks like a king.

"How are you even here?! I thought you had to be at practice all day."

"I was, but I sneaked out for a bit. I felt bad I had to leave early the other day and...I really missed you." He pauses, pressing his lips ever-so slightly against my forehead. "I just needed to see your face." I don't think I'll ever get tired of hearing that. It's not that the words on their own hold such depth...but they become a whole lot more meaningful coming from someone who's filled every crevice of your soul.

"You made my day, AJ." I intertwine my fingers with his. He smiles, but it's not his usual energetic one. "Are you okay? Gosh, AJ...you look so thin." I brush my hand against the side of his face. "Are you eating properly? Please tell me you're not staying up late working. You promised me you'd try to get enough sleep. Do you know you're supposed to get about eight hours of sleep, not four?" I sound like my mom.

"Yeah, I'm fine, my love. I told you, just dieting. Nothing else, don't worry so much." He purses lips and diverts his eyes from mine as if he were hiding something in them.

That's not reassuring at all. I arch a brow.

"You know, you can put on a strong face in front of your members and everyone else...but you don't have to with me. Plus, I can't be fooled. It's my superpower, remember?" I place the side of my index finger under his chin and lift his face.

Avoiding eye contact, he gives a thin smile.

"No, it's nothing, I'm just…" grabbing my finger, he drags his feet and positions himself at the edge of my bed, "I'm disappointed in myself."

Um, what?

"What are you talking about?" I hover over him as he's holding onto my finger before I take a seat beside him.

"Ah…" he releases a long sigh as if he were exhaling all his tiredness from the day, "we did a performance a few days ago with other K-Pop groups. I normally don't watch the fancams afterwards because I cringe at my mistakes and it kinda makes me self-conscious. But today, I did and oh my gosh…I made so many mistakes! Ah!" He groans into his hands. "And the whole world is going to see it!"

He jerks his head back as he runs his hand through his hair.

"So what?! It's ONE performance, AJ. AND I bet no one can even notice them."

"But I know for a fact it's just not one performance. I always know when I've made a mistake…I wish it was just once."

He lowers his gaze towards the ground.

"You know, my whole team…the stylists, the dance team, my managers, the stage crew…they work so hard day and night for us. Me making even the tiniest mistake is just letting them down. They deserve way more credit and recognition than I do. I'm the leader, damn it!" He smashes his fist against the bed.

"AJ, my dear, it's okay. Breathe." I pat and rub his back, trying to calm him down.

"Zara, you don't get it. I should have everything perfected. Sometimes I feel like I shouldn't have gotten this privileged role as a leader. Maybe I'm not as talented as most people think. The members are far more talented than me. And, they're SO loving. They would move mountains for my happiness...which happens to be you."

My heart is in awe. His members truly are gems.

"I'm their protector, a big brother, someone they should look up to, but if I make mistakes...am I really a leader? I don't know. They deserve better, especially the fans—our loving WON's. I do everything for them. They're the only reason why we've been able to climb a step further to our goal."

He nestles his face into his hands.

"Without their love and support, I'm nothing...no one at all. "

God, I hate seeing him act so harshly to himself. I bet WON's would also hate hearing him say these words.

"Any mistake, whether it's slipping during a dance move or not hitting a note high enough, makes me so upset because I KNOW I could've done better. I lost that one shot, that one moment, to a mistake that I practiced so hard not to do. So many people have invested their time, energy, and money in me, so when it's not the perfection I envisioned...I feel as if I've let them down. Being a K-Pop star is such an honor and a huge responsibility to BE these idols who deliver only the best and...I don't feel that way."

"AJ, I'm going to punch you in the face...out of love, of course."

I yank his hands off his face and force him towards me. There's that half smile, again.

"Why are you beating yourself up over tiny mistakes? You're entitled to make mistakes, even as a leader. Do you think the leaders around the world were born perfect?" I wait for a response, but he doesn't answer. "No, they weren't. No one can be perfect. I get that you're a K-Pop star, but last time I checked, you're also still human. It's natural to make mistakes. I honestly don't know how you can think of yourself this way, especially with all the talent oozing through your veiny veins."

He shrugs the joke off with a fake smile.

"You do know that you're incredibly talented, right?" I pull him closer to me, placing one hand on his bicep, and the other stroking the back of his neck.

"You compose your own music and create your lyrics within a few minutes like magic... PLEASE tell me you know that a lot of people cannot do that. I've seen you and the members perform and I've NEVER witnessed anything like it. I mean, the themes you come up with, the detailed stages, the deep hidden messages behind every song, dance performances, the music videos...it's beyond anyone's creativity. You put your soul and emotions into it and I promise you...it shows. The world sees it, so why don't you?"

I run my fingers through his curly, fluffy, purple hair, massaging that brilliant worldhead of his that is desperate for a break.

"AJ...let me put something into perspective. Your music...it brings happiness to people. And I mean LITERALLY. Music can change brain chemistry by releasing chemicals that instantly alter mood or ease pain by lowering some stress hormones. A person could be having the crappiest day, and then listens to your music and just like that...it brings a smile to their face. A complete sense of comfort. I think that's the greatest gift you can give your fans and those you work with who get to be a part of your beautiful, creative mind. I guess that's why they say some artists are incredibly gifted because you offer the greatest gift to the world through your music... complete euphoria. AND a glimpse of that beautiful mind of yours." I tap his forehead with my finger and smile, hoping I'd get to see those pearly whites of his, but I'm left disappointed. The sadness in his eyes has also hijacked that gorgeous mouth of his.

"People from all over the world form connections and beautiful friendships with one another, even if they're thousands of miles away and don't speak the same language just because they have one thing in common—your music. So how can you say you're not enough? Some people pay money to get therapy, and for some...your music is their therapy. Life can take some unpleasant turns, but your art makes it a bit bearable. Do you get what I'm saying?"

He nods, hesitantly.

"No, say it out loud."

Rolling his eyes, he smiles and says, "Yes, madam."

"I know that wasn't genuine, but good enough for me. So, please. I never want to hear these words out of your mouth. Okay?"

"Okay."

"You're more than enough, AJ. You're beyond what this world expects. You're...sensational."

He props my chin between his thumb and forefinger.

"Thank you. I really needed that."

I weave my fingers in his, laying a gentle peck on his cheek.

"I wish you could see yourself through my eyes, then maybe you'd love yourself the way I love you."

He smiles. The tiny creases surrounding his eyes become visible as well as his dimple.

"You hypocrite. I can say the same thing to you because you never believe me when I tell you how beautiful you are." Ah, he got me there. "Maybe one day...I can see myself the way you do." He sighs and puts his arms around me in a tight hug. "But until then, I'll smile, nod, and pretend I know exactly what you mean."

"Well, I'll be waiting for that day."

We take the moment to admire the sanctity of our love for each other by simply locking our hands. I can't believe a man like him exists. Despite how I'm feeling about him and our future, it's true when I say I've never met someone like him before. He's so selfless, always wanting to be better and useful for others, but so harsh to himself.

"Zara...thanks for never seeing me as weak when I'm at my most vulnerable. I don't like showing much emotion to others, but I never hide mine from you."

"Being vulnerable doesn't make you weak." I wiggle an arm out of his grip, and ruffle his hair. "It makes you human. Something I think you forget that you are."

He rests his forehead against mine, closing his eyes for a brief moment, and placing gentle strokes along the side of my jawline.

"Saranghae...Zara." I feel his warm breath as those words escape his mouth. What a K-drama moment.

We stare at each other for a few seconds before he slides down from the edge of the bed and onto the floor. He places his head on my lap and wraps his arm from under my legs, pulling me in tightly.

"You're my...safe place." He pauses, nestling his face against my leg. "I don't know if I ever told you this but...when I'm having a hard day at practice and feeling a little anxious before a performance, or even getting overwhelmed by the million things I have to do...I close my eyes, and picture you smiling in my arms. And just like that...I'm whole again."

He squeezes my legs with his arms as if he's afraid to let them go.

"The peace I feel in my heart when I think of you, I promise, I've...never felt that before. You say that I'm gifted, but really I think it's you and your beautiful soul, my love."

I take a deep breath. Hearing these words...leaves me not only emotional, but again, speechless. He claims he doesn't have the right words to describe how he feels, but I think he does it beautifully without even noticing. Knowing I provide that sort of comfort to someone—especially him—I don't know, I guess it makes me feel important. Like...my presence matters in someone's life.

"I love you more, AJ." I gently stroke his hair, smoothing it back. "I love you more than life itself." I try to hold back my tears. I know I think about the future a lot, but for once I'm here...in the moment.

He kisses the top of one leg, looks up and

whispers, "I love you with every fiber of my being." A few seconds pass by and he breaks the comfortable silence with, "Anyways, Oprah, let's go outside and eat with them. I don't want them thinking we're in here doing some...funny business." He winks and he pushes himself off the floor, offering his hand to me.

I place mine in his as I get up and then... come close to his face. Without blinking, I look him in the eyes and say, "Let them."

His jaw drops, morphing into a seductive smile. "Damn, baby girl. You've become a little cheeky since the first time I met you."

The way he calls me baby girl in that accent...ah, smooth as soft butter.

"It's about time." I lock my hand to his. "Let's go eat."

"Wait, before we go, I wanted to ask you something."

"Yeah?"

"How do you say...my love in Urdu?" Immediately, my face heats up. My terrifying dream plays before my eyes.

"Uh, why do you ask?"

"Well, I always call you by 'my love'...and I want to learn how to say it in Urdu." I remain quiet. "Do you...not want me to say it?"

Shit. Well, I want HIM to say it, but now I associate the Urdu version with that stupid, desi Damon.

"No, of course I do." I clear my throat. "It's

easy. Say it with me."

"Okay." He squints his eyes in concentration, bringing his ear slightly closer to my mouth.

"Meri...it sounds like 'merry'." I wait for him to follow.

"Okay, meri." Wow. Nicely done.

"You pronounced it correctly, good job!" I high-five him. "Next word, say jaan. It's pronounced juh-an." I enunciate, extending the sound of 'a', "Now say it together."

"Jaan. Meri...jaan. Ah, did I say it right?" He hides face behind his hands.

"Yes, you said it perfectly! Meri means 'my', and jaan is a term of endearment for love." I peel his hands off of his gorgeous face.

"How beautiful...meri jaan." Hearing him say it in his Australian accent made me forget about my dream. The Bollywood heroes got nothin' on him.

We make our way outside and see the reunited lovebirds setting up the table with plates and utensils.

"Glad you guys are joining us. We figured y'all were...going to get busy or something." Ari says smirking and Jace follows with a laugh.

"Yeah, we were busy. I was playing Oprah." AJ and I look at each other sideways, while trying to stifle our giggling.

"Damn, okay. I didn't take AJ to have that sort of kink but if that works for you guys..."

We all burst into laughter.

"Alright, alright, everyone sit down and eat," Ari mothers us.

We take a seat around the dining table. Both Jace and AJ serve Ari and I first before themselves. Ah, what chivalrous men.

"Okay, guys. Tomorrow, I'm throwing a party in celebration of finishing our first year. You all have to be here!" Jace announces.

Jesus, when did Jace plan this without telling me?!

"I guess I'll be here!" I shrug and turn to AJ. "Would you be able to make it?"

"Yeah, I'm sure I'll be able to. We start practice earlier in the day so I should be able to sneak out by evening. I've gotten better at hiding my tracks and dodging the cameras." He chuckles. "Plus, I wouldn't miss celebrating you two." AJ runs his hand on top of my head and then feeds me a piece of his bulgogi. He's so nurturing. I guess being the leader of his group made him quite fatherly. I wonder if I'll get to see his father-like skills one day with children of our own. I'd love to pass down his values and beliefs—which are similar to mine—to tiny gremlins.

"Well, you already know my answer, babe. I'm in!" Ari bounces in excitement.

"It's going to be so much fun! Speaking of fun...AJ, are you excited about performing at the K-Pop Fusion event?" Jace asks.

"Oh my gosh, so excited! A bit nervous, but

we practiced a lot, so hopefully it all goes well. You all are still coming...right?" He scans around the table.

"Yes, we will ALL be there, don't worry." Ari reaches out to pat AJ on the shoulder. "Zara and I saw your poster for K-Pop Fusion on our way here along Sunset Boulevard."

"Oh, yeah! I totally forgot about that. It was phenomenal. A very regal theme with the crowns and sashes you guys wore. YOU looked like a true king." I smile at him and he taps the tip of my nose with his finger.

"I don't know if he looked like a king... sorry to break it to you." Ari sticks her tongue out at him and he does the same. "But, jokes aside, I'm sure my brother is going to look like one at the event. And, I'm sure others will agree, screaming and chanting your name!"

"Yeah, we'll join in with the other teeny-boppers." I subtly wink at AJ.

"BUT we will scream the loudest. All of Staples Center will only hear our voices! Especially mine. People in Canada could hear it. An arena? No problem." Jace's confidence never ceases to make me laugh.

"I'm sure they won't just scream his name but also Rose Lin's! I'm so jealous that you're performing with her!" Ari chimes in.

Who's Rose Lin? I've never heard of her. I glance at AJ as he drops his chopsticks on his plate before he takes a bite of his bulgogi. Weird.

"Yeah, uh, it should be fun." AJ clears his throat. He's acting strange...am I overanalyzing?

"Fun? How are you not ecstatic?! She has an incredible voice! Oh my god and her group, Bliss8, is absolutely talented and breathtaking."

"She's so beautiful. Ari and I literally love her so much. I'd say she's our bias. Please tell me she's as beautiful in person as she is on screen!"

AJ stays quiet, giving a hesitant nod. Jace and Ari continue to obsess over Rose Lin. He's acting the same way he did before he told me he's a K-Pop star. He wouldn't hide anything from me so...why hasn't he told me about her before?

CHAPTER 4:

Paranoia

"**W**OOO! WE'RE DONE WITH FIRST YEAR!" Jace runs into my room as I'm applying my eyeliner carefully...or at least I was, until he scared the shit out of me. Now, I just look like a hooker after a long night of work.

"Jace! Look what you made me do!" I grab a q-tip to salvage what's left of the wing.

"Okay, T-Swift, calm the hell down and hurry your ass up." Jace turns around to leave but stops, circles around, and trails me with his eyes from head to toe. "Also, damn girl. You're filling that tank top and skirt out really well."

I praise my inner confidence with a cocky smile reflecting in the mirror.

"I guess those workouts have been paying off."

"Yes, they have. AJ won't be able to keep

his hands off of you when he sees you tonight." He wiggles his phone out of his pocket. "Oh, also, Gigi and Alyssa are on their way here. Wow, I don't think we've seen them since before we left for Korea. You know what that means?!" he screams in my ear.

"What does that mean?" I ask while pushing him away before he ruptures my eardrum even more.

"We're gonna get WASTED, and I mean even more wasted than we did before the Korea trip!"

I gag as I remember the revolting taste in my mouth from the morning after.

"Never. Again." I shudder as I tug on my earlobe, wiggling in my small, silver 'jhumka' earrings with turquoise embellishments. They match perfectly with my white flowy skirt and turquoise tank top.

"Yeah...okay, maybe not to that extent, but still to a good amount. I don't care, we are young, dumb, and full of…"

My phone rings before he can finish that sentence.

"Hello?"

"Hey, girl!" Gigi and Alyssa scream through the phone. "We're outside! Open it up!"

I hear Gigi knocking on the door, both on the phone and outside.

I throw my phone on my bed, running towards the door but Jace beats me to it and has already let them in.

"OH MY GOD!" I greet them with high jumps and screaming, like the sorority girls I knew back in college. "I missed you guys!"

"Yeah, I missed you, too. But you both left us back in Irvine while y'all moved to L.A. for bigger and better things!" Alyssa hugs me and doesn't let go till she finishes her sentence. Her dark brown hair is still as long and luscious as I remember. Her Afro-Latino ancestors blessed her well with her gorgeous, prominent dark features and green eyes. A rare gem, if I may say so myself.

"Well, the men here are bigger and the women are better, if you know what I mean!" Jace winks while licking his lips.

"Still as deranged as I remember. I MISSED IT." Gigi leaps into his arms. "Que empieze la fiesta! Let's get the party started!" She flips her short, wavy black hair, while running her hands down her curves. Then, whips out a bottle of tequila from her bag and holds it up like Rafiki showcasing Simba to the kingdom in *Lion King*.

"So, Zara...Jace told me and Gigi everything. Are you really banging a K-Pop star?! A FREAKING K-POP STAR?! Who are you and what have you done with our friend!"

"Yeah, didn't know you have some nasty tricks up your sleeve!" Gigi and Alyssa tackle me to the floor and tickle until I can't breathe.

"Oh my god, you guys, stop!" I squirm, trying to catch my breath from laughing.

"Girl, we're so happy for you! And, don't worry...we won't tell a soul about it. Finally, you let someone pop that..."

Ding dong!

Gigi jumps from the sound of the bell in the middle of her finishing the sentence...thank God.

"Is that Ari?" I ask.

He shrugs before opening the door.

"My man!"

No...please tell me that's not who I think it is.

"Arsalan, you dirty dog! You made it!" They bump chests as if they're prepping for battle. Gosh, no! Why is he here?! I feel my face flush just like it did when I dreamt that nightmare about him.

"Hey, Zara." He shoots his sleazy smile from the doorway as soon as we lock eyes.

"Hey." I reply cordially as Alyssa, Gigi, and I get off the floor.

"Oh my god...who is that tall sexy cup of agua?!" Gigi eyes him up and down.

"Oh, I don't know, girl...but I'm trying to climb that like a tree!" Alyssa joins in.

"No, you don't want anything to do with THAT. Trust me, he's a total player." I turn my back to Arsalan and Jace who are in the kitchen, talking about God knows what.

"Girl, does it look like I care? I've been

drier than the Sahara desert the past couple of months. He can play with me in any way he wants." Gigi giggles.

"Yeah, I'm right there with you, Gigi!" Aylssa high-fives her.

"No, you guys, he's so disgusting. He's like...a desi Damon Salvatore."

"You think Damon Salvatore from *Vampire Diaries* is...disgusting?" Alyssa's jaw drops as if I've said something blasphemous. "And what the heck is a desi Damon Salvatore?!"

"Oh hell no, girl. Damon Salvatore was the essence of that show. I would have my arm chopped off if it meant that I could have one night with him." Gigi sighs.

"Okay, the actor isn't. But the character is just so selfish and…"

"Complicated? Protective? Mysterious? Hot? Everything your heart desires?" Arsalan cuts me off.

"Excuse me?" I turn around, not hiding how annoyed I am. Jesus, Alyssa or Gigi could have warned me that he was right behind. He really is like a sneaky cat.

"I'm assuming you girls were talking about me." He shines his stupid, seductive smile at both of the girls, which lowers their jaws and apparently their standards as well.

"Hi, I'm Gigi!" She extends her hand.

"Pleasure to meet you. You have a beautiful smile." Gigi blushes as she shakes his hand, then fans herself once he looks away to greet Alyssa. "And who do we have here?"

"I'm Alyssa!" She goes in for a hug instead.

"Wow, I haven't had a hug in a while. Thank you!" Arsalan laughs and lies at the same time. I highly doubt he can survive a night without having a girl in his arms.

"Arsalan! I need your help in the kitchen." Jace hollers at him.

"Coming! Ladies, we have to take a shot after this. Promise?"

Both Alyssa and Gigi nod and giggle like little schoolgirls. Am I the only one who is immune to his coquetry?!

I slap both of their arms. "You guys are too smart to be fooled by him."

"Zara, are you kidding? Okay, whatever, he's a player. So what? We don't care. Do we, Alyssa?"

"Not. At. All." Alyssa has her eyes on him like a hunter on a prey. "Also, I don't think he's even interested in either of us, Gigi."

"Yeah...you noticed that, too?!" Gigi whispers, looking straight at Alyssa.

"Noticed what?" I ask as I'm clearly not catching on to anything they're saying.

"Dude, he totally has his eyes for you, Zara!" Alyssa jerks my arm.

"Okay, I thought I was the only one who noticed!" Gigi does the same to the other arm.

"Ouch! Oh my god, no. That's definitely not

true. Trust me, he's a womanizer. He's like that with everyone."

They both glare at me as if I've said something completely mindless.

"Okay, you may have a hot K-Pop boyfriend now, but you're STILL the same oblivious Zara. How do you NOT see it?!" Alyssa yells, yet manages to do it under her breath so eloquently.

"Girl, he's tryin' to get on that...or should I say IN that!" Gigi chimes in.

"I don't think so. Even if he is, he's an asshole for even trying since he knows I have a boyfriend."

"Welcome to the life of a player, girl. They don't care if you have a boyfriend. As long as you have a pulse, it's a greenlight on their end." Alyssa wraps her arm around my neck.

"When's your man coming, anyways?" Gigi asks.

"Oh shit, I have no clue." I actually haven't heard from him all day. Poor guy is probably busy with practice. "He should be here soon with Ari."

"Should we ask AJ to serenade us with his beautiful voice?" Gigi elbows Alyssa. Hearing his name made me giddy with excitement.

"Yes, please! He really does have an incredible voice. It's smooth yet slightly raspy, which is more relaxing than the sound of the ocean's waves gently crashing on the shore." I stare out at a distance thinking of him. Once I snap out of it, I see Alyssa and Gigi looking at me with the corners of their mouths extended across their cheeks.

"Awe, sweetie. You're so in love!" Gigi leaps towards me for a hug.

"We've never seen you like this before!" Alyssa joins in. "We can't wait to meet the man who stole your heart."

"And some other things, if you know what I mean." Gigi winks at Alyssa, totally channeling Jace's energy.

"Jesus, you guys are too much! But, I can't wait for you guys to meet him."

Jace's phone vibrates against the kitchen counter.

"She's here!" He rushes to open the door.

"BABY!" Ari springs into his arms as he lifts her up and spins her around.

"I missed you SO much, little mami!" Jace showers her with boundless kisses. I can never see myself being that affectionate in front of others with AJ, probably because I never saw that in my own household. My parents act as if they've never kissed each other before.

Jace cradles her from behind as he begins to introduce her, unable to contain his excitement.

"Guys, this is the woman I've been dying to introduce to you. The love of my life!" He pecks her on the cheek.

"Hi!" She giggles, "I'm Ari!"

"Wow, she's even prettier in person." Arsalan walks towards her with swaying shoulders. "It's nice to finally meet you. I can't get this guy to stop talking about you!" He welcomes her with a hug.

"You must be Arsalan! I've heard...MANY interesting things about you."

Even SHE knew about him?!

"Oh, yeah...I get that a lot." He grins like the Grinch.

Ari turns her attention towards the girls.

"I feel like I already know you two!" She skips over to both of them, wrapping one arm around Gigi and the other around Alyssa, all in a jumbled hug.

"Wow, you're absolutely stunning! And your accent—ah! Can you just keep talking?!" Gigi cries in awe.

"Damn, you're nice AND pretty?! Jace is one lucky man!" Alyssa eyes her head to toe. "You better watch out, Jace. I might just steal her!"

Jace walks over and snatches her away from Alyssa like a toddler would do with a precious toy, "No, no. I don't think so. She's all mine, now and forever." He leans in to kiss her on the cheek. I admire the two lovebirds, but can't help noticing that my lovebug didn't come.

"Also, I convinced Ari to stay till her birthday and you all better be there at her birthday dinner next week!" He waves his arm around in a circle as he points at each one of us.

"We won't miss out, scouts honor." Arsalan sticks out three fingers, with his thumb over the nail of his pinky.

"Count me in!" Gigi follows.

"Me, too! It would be an honor." Alyssa places her hand over her heart as she glances at Ari, whose smile is wider than a valley.

We all take a seat in the living room besides Arsalan, who's in the kitchen, sipping out of his red cup. My eyes are glued to the door.

"Oh, Zara...don't worry. He's on his way up!"

"Oh, no I wasn't even..." I shake my head out of embarrassment and forget how to talk. I didn't think she'd call me out on it!

"You don't have to hide it! I know you're dying to see him as much as I was to see Jace." She flutters her eyes at Jace.

"I'm actually looking forward to meeting this boyfriend of hers." Arsalan interjects as usual with his disdainful commentary.

"Well, you'll be meeting him very soon!" Ari walks over to the kitchen and gathers shot glasses. "As soon as my brother walks in, we are all taking shots and getting this party started!"

"Wait...Zara's boyfriend is YOUR brother? So, he's also Australian?"

What a dumb, stupid question, Arsalan.

"Last time I checked, he was!" The room joins Ari as she laughs. Everyone except Arsalan.

I could care less about his stupid questions. My eyes just yearn for my little star. The anticipation is killing me! I guess Allah was listening because right then...there's a knock on the door. Like Jace, I bolt to the door before anyone else does, especially since I saw that desi Damon take a step towards the door.

My eyes beam with joy like a kid in a candy store as soon as I see his deep dimples. The energy of his smile matches mine. Gosh, I can definitely see this smile for the rest of my life.

"Hi!" I grab his arm to pull him in for a hug, but notice he's carrying baggage.

"My love, just one second." He struggles his way through, but still manages to lay a kiss on my cheek which makes the butterflies in my stomach come to life.

He sets the bags down by the entrance table, and pulls me in by my waist for the hug I've been craving all day long.

"Took you long enough!" Ari chuckles as she pours vodka in each shot glass.

"Well, if only a little someone helped me with her bags, it wouldn't have taken me so long." AJ raises his eyebrows.

"I'm glad you decided to stay a few days with us, Ari! Me and Jace practically had to beg you to check out of the hotel."

"You guys were very convincing. Love you, Zara!" She blows a kiss to me and I pretend to catch it. "Well, now that my brother is here, who's ready for some shots?!" Ari raises a shot glass and everyone piles up in the kitchen.

"I think introductions are in order." God, of course Arsalan was going to open his mouth. A second hasn't gone by and I already feel sick to my stomach. The butterflies are replaced with a strong gut feeling that this won't be good. "Hey, I'm Arsalan. You must be the boyfriend I've been hearing so much about." He slightly steps forward and extends his hand.

AJ's jaw clenches faintly, but enough to see that he's definitely not happy about Arsalan being there.

"Hey, I'm AJ...the boyfriend you've been hearing about." AJ clasps his hand to Arsalan's for a handshake.

The veins in their hands bulge out. If they keep this up, I swear one of them is going to pass out from poor blood circulation. The two glare at each other as if they're rivals. The room becomes so eerily quiet, one could hear the sound of my heart pounding. Each of us have our eyes glued to the two men raging with testosterone. My eyes switch from AJ to Arsalan. I gulp so loudly, everyone in the room reacts with a small giggle under their breaths...besides those two. Jace eyes me and I back at him. I read somewhere that if you stare at a person for more than twenty seconds, you either want to kiss them...or kill them. I swear it feels like it's been more than that, so for my sake, I hope they just kiss and lower their masculine outburst.

"Okay, now that introductions are over,

can we start drinking?!" Jace swiftly breaks the staring contest between the boys. I take a step towards AJ to hold his hand. That was a side of AJ I didn't think he possessed. He's so fatherly, soft and gentle like a teddy bear.

"Say less, I already poured out the shots!" Ari passes a shot glass to each one of us. She raises hers to make a toast. "Here's to a night that will become a part of our maze of memories!" We clink our glasses with one another, except I made an effort not to with Arsalan.

"You know, Zara, it's bad luck to not look into someone's eyes while toasting?" I jump and turn around to see Arsalan behind me and AJ. When did he get there?!

"Uh, I'm not that superstitious." I roll my eyes.

"It's bad sex for seven years." He rests the corner of his elbow on my shoulder and turns his head towards AJ. With a lopsided smile he says, "Just looking out for your boyfriend."

"I think that's impossible for us, but thanks for your concern." AJ reciprocates the same smile as Arsalan. I look down, biting my bottom lip so I don't burst out laughing. That was a proud girlfriend moment.

◆ ◆ ◆

Ari and Jace took the role of being the bartenders for the night, which led to all of us being slightly more tipsy than expected, especially AJ. His pale complexion has been introduced to a flush of red. The last time he had a drink was back in Korea when us four went to the bar and I was met with my first medical crisis.

So far the night is going better than I expected. The girls LOVE AJ. I knew AJ would get along with them. He just becomes in sync with whoever he meets. Everyone instantly falls in love with him because he really is THAT charismatic. They kept asking him to sing their favorite songs and he agreed, if everyone sang along with him. He always makes an effort to include everyone so that they have way more fun than him. Ahk...I love this man.

We all sway to the 90s songs Arsalan's playing as he's become the unofficial designated DJ. He might be an ass, but has great music taste. We pour our hearts out, singing along to Backstreet Boys. As we're jamming to the music, AJ gets a little touchy...with his hands all around me. Feeling a little puzzled with his public display of affection, I face him...only to see his eyes fixated on my lips. He wraps his arm around my waist and moves me close to him, laying a lingering kiss on the corner of my lips. I don't know why, but my eyes gravitate towards Arsalan for his reaction. My eyes meet his for a brief moment. He's stoic, not breaking a sweat of emotion. Granted half his face is covered by his red cup.

AJ whispers in my ear, "Come with me," clutching my wrist and hurries towards my room. To my surprise, AJ pushes me against the door after closing it. This feels incredibly familiar, but thankfully, unlike in the dream, Arsalan won't switch places with AJ.

"Turn on the light, silly." I drag my hands on the wall, searching for the switch.

With a swift motion, he grips his hand over mine, seizing my searching fingers. He presses my hand against the wall hard enough for my knuckles to feel it's glazed, cool surface.

"No," he whispers, moaning as he brushes his lips along the crevice of my collar bone. "Leave them off, baby. Just…feel me."

As "Loveeeeeee Song" by Rihanna and Future plays in the living room, seeping through the walls of my room, he studies me closely, paying attention to my eyes. With a gentle stroke against the sides of my cheek, he places my face between his palms before moaning into a kiss… massaging my lips with his. It's like he couldn't wait to kiss me. He traces his fingers up against my thigh, making his way up my skirt while simultaneously laying soft, gentle kisses on the nape of my neck. The simmering touch of his lips gliding over my skin leaves every quivering nerve satisfied.

"God…I missed you so much. I miss you…every…second." He moans with a wispy breath as he sweeps his lips along the side of my cheek, lingering just below my earlobe.

"Are you okay?" I giggle, trying to catch my breath and stay as composed as I possibly can. But, my god. He makes my toes curl unwillingly.

"Oh, I'm more than okay, baby girl." He swallows his groan, murmuring in my ear. "But, in a few seconds...you won't be." He tugs on my hair...pulling back to see my reaction.

"What do you me—"

Without waiting for me to finish my sentence, he lifts me up. With a firm hold of one of his hands under my thigh and the other on my back, he lays me down on the bed as if I were made of fragile diamonds. My breathing becomes heavier by the second from his insatiable stare while standing against the edge of the bed. The city lights and the moon's rays beam through the window, forming a scattering pattern from the shadow of the window rails on his face. He looks heavenly, kissed by the lights of MY city.

He lowers his wrists just below his chest, rolling his sleeves up to his elbow with his bulging, veiny hands...keeping his eyes fixed on me. My heart plunges against my sternum before he reaches out for the first button of his black button-down shirt.

My 'churiyan' rattle as I run my hand over his shirt to feel his abs. He closes his eyes before opening them to say, "Gosh...I love it when you wear those. You look like a queen, my love," with a low tone as his breathing gets heavier, making his distended vein that sits above his right brow more visible.

He unbuttons the first button with his calloused thumb and forefinger without breaking eye contact. It feels like deja vu. His breathing gradually gets heavier, syncing beautifully with mine.

Separating his lips, he unbuttons the second. Ah...that mischievous smile appears right before he undoes the third.

Then the fourth, exposing a small part of his chest which is as flushed as his face.

Then the fifth, showing the curves of his upper abs and the moon necklace I gave him, resting gracefully on his equally defined pecs.

The moment cannot get any better than it is. It seems as though time has slowed. Everything slips out of my mind, blurring out every worry of mine which rarely happens. The music, the city lights, and the moon all work their magic to make me fall more in love with this man. I didn't think that could be possible.

"I've been looking forward to this all day, princess," he mumbles with a raspy moan. And before he reaches for the sixth and final button...there's banging on the door.

"AJ and Zara, you guys can bang it out later, COME OUT AND PLAY!" Jace and Ari drunkenly fall against the door, sliding down laughing.

"Saved by the knock." AJ falls on top of me

as I lay there like a corpse. "Agh, I want to murder them." He growls.

"Me, too." I laugh, consoling him with a hug. "Don't worry, we have our whole lives together for this." Jesus, why did I say that?! AJ doesn't move an inch of muscle. "I mean...like, if we happen to get married." I should've just shut my mouth.

He pushes himself off of me and stands up stumbling.

"Let's go outside," he says stiffly, buttoning his shirt without looking at me. If he's upset because of what I said, he can fall off the stage for all I care. Well, I wouldn't want him hurt. Just a little, enough for him to quit being so passive. I'm not even going to apologize. Annoyed, I slide off the bed and rush towards the door. He looks up, eyebrows raised high and pauses buttoning his shirt as I walk past him with fast-paced steps.

As soon as I open the door, the first person my eyes lay on is Arsalan. He's in the kitchen making a drink. His eyes wander, only to lock with mine. He arches his dark brows and squints as he looks over my shoulder. I fidget with my skirt, making my way to the kitchen. I could really use a shot...or two.

"Is everything okay?" Arsalan whispers in my ear as I reach for one of the shot glasses.

"Uh, yeah. Everything's fine." I pour some Amsterdam, trying to keep the shot glass still from my shaky hand but end up spilling a little on the counter.

"Doesn't look like it." He arches a brow while grabbing a napkin to clean the spilled vodka beside my glass.

"What makes you say that?"

"The way you two seem right now is polar opposite from how you both were before going into your room."

Well, he's definitely not wrong about that, but there's no way I'm letting him get the pleasure of knowing.

"No, we're fine. We just wanted to hang out with everyone outside."

"Okay, you won't tell me and that's fine. Chalo, take a shot with me?" Chalo? I didn't think I'd ever witness him spitting Urdu.

I know I shouldn't because it will most likely feed his ego, but I'm kind of in the 'I don't really care' mood. Plus, I think right now I need my own ego fed. I can't believe I'm even saying this.

"Fine, but don't think for a second that we're friends." I raise my shot glass and he follows.

"Look me in the eyes this time, or else whatever happened in your room might become your reality." He poses his signature smirk which instantly makes me regret the decision I've made. But I do as told because as Michael Scott from the show *The Office* once said, *"I'm not superstitious, but I am a little stitious."*

"Cheers." We clink our shot glasses. His eyes haven't moved from mine and mine from his. Both of us proceed to chug what tastes like rubbing alcohol. There's something about his leering eyes. It's unsettling...like he's undressing every hidden thought of mine. If this were a movie, his entrance song that would perfectly describe him would be, "Do I Wanna Know?" by Arctic Monkeys. I always pictured the devil strutting to it.

His eyes are no longer glued to mine but to something behind me. I set my shot glass on the counter and catch a blurry reflection on the toaster of what he's staring at...or should I say whom.

Arslan's eyes shift to the vodka bottle I poured from and twists the cap open.

"You missed taking a shot with your beautiful girlfriend, so...I took the liberty to take one with her instead. You don't mind, do you?"

In a panic, I turn around only to witness AJ's face more flushed than before. His eyes dark with anger. He flares his nostrils as he clenches his jaw, making his distended vein seem as if it's about to pop. His chest rises more and more as every breath passes. Arslan managed to do the one thing within a few seconds that other fandoms have been trying to do—piss AJ off.

"Oh, by all means go for it. She probably took pity that you were drinking alone. She's nice like that." My head jerks in AJ's direction. Is that...coming out of my boyfriend's mouth?! He wouldn't hurt an ant, let alone talk back to someone...granted that someone is a complete jerk.

"Nah, I don't think that's it. I think she wanted to. Right, Zara?" He asks without moving his eyes from AJ.

My jaw is left slightly open, unable to organize my thoughts and words. Is that a rhetorical question or does he actually want me to answer it?

"You know, I don't want MY girlfriend to get sick by drinking so much. So, I'll take the shots on her behalf." AJ takes a step forward.

"I don't think you'll be able to handle it." Arsalan snorts.

"You'd be surprised." AJ is expressionless, which is lowkey...a frightening image of him.

"I was in a frat back in college, so I think I know what I'm talking about," Arsalan boasts with a conceited smile on that devilish face of his.

"Well, as a performer, I've been trained to be resilient...something I think a former frat guy wouldn't know anything about." AJ glowers at his undeclared rival. Is this really happening?!

"What does resilience have to do with sitting down on a stool and singing?"

Why is Arsalan deliberately trying to rile him up?! He's enjoying every second of it, but I'm at a point where I want to murder both of them—Arsalan more than AJ because unlike Arsalan, AJ would never act in such an ill manner intentionally.

"You think I JUST sing?" AJ takes another step with a slight manic laugh. I extend my foot towards AJ just in case he decides to surprise all of us by throwing a punch. To be fair, Arsalan deserves it wholeheartedly, but I REALLY prefer not to patch anyone up with stitches.

"Uh, yeah. I'm assuming that's what singers do. They sit on a chair in front of a bunch of people and sing. That barely breaks a sweat." Arsalan jeers with an arrogant smile.

AJ isn't any less cocky than Arsalan right now...which shouldn't in any way make me more attracted to him but it is...just a tad bit. I do not condone this behavior in any shape, but there's something alluring about AJ being so confrontational to someone who may pass as a Bollywood movie villain.

"Do you listen to any K-Pop?" Smirking, AJ cocks his head, waiting for Arslan to reply.

"Yeah, I've heard a few songs. I don't live under a rock."

AJ takes his third step towards him.

"Have you heard of a K-Pop group called NOWus?"

No, no, AJ! What are you doing?! Is he just going to OUT himself? And to whom?! This idiot?! I should chime in and stop this toxic masculinity debacle but it feels as if someone's sucked the air out of my vocal cords.

"Uh, yeah I've heard of 'em." Crossing his arms, Arsalan replies quietly, but loud enough so only AJ and I can hear him. Is he...getting nervous? Arsalan's getting intimidated by...AJ?! But, to be fair...AJ is pretty scary right now. I'm even feeling the secondhand intimidation.

AJ takes a fourth step and stops right in front of him.

"Do you know who the leader of that group is?"

Arsalan remains stationary, squinting at AJ for a few seconds before his eyes widen and jaw opens to mutter, "AJ."

His sneer is wiped off his face.

"Yeah...me." AJ clicks his tongue as he takes one final step towards him. "Next time, know who you're dealing with before you say something you cannot live up to."

The main chorus of "Humble" by Kendrick Lamar plays as an awkward silence fills the kitchen. It couldn't be any more appropriate for AJ's badass moment. There's a lot I want to say right now, but I simply cannot fathom where to begin. Normally, I would encourage AJ to take the high road and remain true to who he is. But that was handled with such impeccable grace by none other than my soft K-Pop star. I mean, he IS only human. A person can stay patient for only so long before someone as devilish as Arslan tries to get under your skin. Though I never thought I'd ever get to witness it.

A while back, Lee told me in confidence that AJ rarely ever gets mad...but when he does, you DON'T want to be on the other end of it. I had a hard time imagining that...up until now. I always see him laughing or being silly on T.V., and I guess others may see that and think there's absolutely no way he could have a vice. People get stunned, SHOCKED when a celebrity exhibits such a natural human emotion. Him being angry made me see him as more of a human being.

I snap out of my AJ analysis after a few seconds when Arslan leaps towards AJ. Ah, shit! This can't be good!

Panicking, I search the room for Jace, hoping to telepathically communicate with him before all hell breaks loose. I don't even know what to expect from AJ at this point. I've never seen him angry. Nothing really makes him upset unless the members or the people he loves are in an uncomfortable situation. But this time...it's personal.

Thankfully, Jace already had his attention towards the kitchen and witnessed the soon-to-be bloodshed. I gesture with my eyes at the boys and mouth 'help'. He nods and a sense of relief cascades throughout my body.

"Alright guys, let's play a game!" He raises his voice over the blaring music. The boys remain staring each other down, but I nudge AJ's hand, pulling him to the side.

"AJ, what the hell was that?! I thought you

wanted to keep the whole K-Pop thing a secret, and you told that idiot?!"

He flares his nostrils and clenches his jaw even harder.

"I did, but I hate being provoked by assholes like him."

"Aren't you afraid that he might tell someone?"

"Ha!" He scoffs. "He won't, I know that."

"How could you be so sure?"

He looks straight into my eyes.

"Because...he's into you."

Am I blind?! Does everyone see it?!

"And, I'm sure he wouldn't do anything that would make you hate him even more."

I don't hate him, but I do dislike him...A LOT.

"Guys, over here!" Ari signals. AJ holds onto my hand, walking in front of me.

"So, any suggestions?" Jace asks as we all gather around in a circle. Arsalan took his sweet time to join and plops between Gigi and Alyssa.

"Truth or dare?" Ari suggests first.

"Mafia?" Alyssa chimes in.

"Okay, I'm making an executive decision and saying no to both of those." Gigi takes a sip of her drink and pauses. "Wait, you guys...remember playing Paranoia?!"

No, not this game...not right now. Let's just say this game has led to some heavy consequences and heartbreak back in college.

"Yeah, I don't think we should play this game." I shake my head in disapproval.

"Is this a game where we tell scary stories?" AJ questions.

"No...but it can essentially become a scary story." I answer.

"Well, in that case...I think we should play." Arslan voices his opinion.

"What are the rules of this game?" Ari's eyes light up.

"So, you whisper a question to the person sitting next to you and they answer out loud. It could be anything. Normally, people would ask a question relating to people in the circle. This way, they would want to know why their name is brought up...hence the name Paranoia. Once you answer out loud, you play rock, paper, scissors. If the person who asks the question wins, the other person has to say the question out loud." Jace explains as thoroughly as he can.

"Well, what if the person who asks the question loses?" Ari asks.

"Then we don't get to hear the question." Jace brushes his thumb against her chin.

"Oo, I'm gonna have fun with this one." Arsalan moves his eyes around the circle and zeros in on AJ. I already have a feeling this is NOT going to end well.

"Since I recommended the game, I'll start it off." Gigi turns her head to cuff her hand to Arsalans ear and whispers her question.

He grins and without hesitation replies, "Zara."

His eyes pierce into mine, knowing damn well AJ's eyes are on him. AJ's hand tenses into mine. Gigi's gaping eye's leaves me curious but I have a feeling I don't want to hear the question...especially AJ. They stick out their hands to play rock, paper, scissors. Jesus, please...please let Gigi lose. I'm surprised I haven't had a heart attack so far from all of the physiological effects my heart has been going through today.

"Rock, paper, scissors!" Arsalan leads. My hand, interlocked with AJ's, sweats profusely against his.

Gigi shoots scissors and Arslan...paper. Allah, take the wheel, PLEASE. Arsalan smirks with sheer happiness. He wanted to lose.

"The question was...." Arslan pauses, "who in the circle would I like to kiss?"

Ari, Gigi, Alyssa and Jace's eyes land on me. I'm afraid to even look at AJ. From the tight grip that my poor hand is experiencing, it's probably best if I don't or else my anxiety is going to skyrocket to the moon.

"Ah, who wouldn't?! Even I would!" Ari attempts to defuse the transparent tension in the air. "Next person!"

◆ ◆ ◆

We went in a circle asking questions—

none too controversial considering what had just happened—and now it's Ari's turn to ask me.

"Alright, let's do this!" She comes closer to my ear and whispers, "Kiss, marry, kill. Say the names in that order."

Oh, now I'm going to have fun with this one. Without thinking, I reply, "Ari, AJ, and Arsalan." I bet this one is going to kill Arsalan...and not just in the game. It makes me want to actually lose so that I can enjoy the pleasure of seeing the disappointment in his face.

"Ooo, I see you." Ari nods and winks. "Rock, paper, scissors." Ari shoots paper. I purposely wait a split second so that I can act accordingly—I need to lose. I shoot rock.

"Oh, man!" I act as if I totally didn't plan that.

"You gotta say the question out loud!" Ari shouts.

"The question was..." I mimic Arsalan's energy from earlier, "kiss, marry, kill. In that order."

I cast my eyes over at Arsalan, hoping to see the smugness off his face. But, to my surprise...it's still there! How is it that he can get under my skin, but I can't with him? What is he...a sociopath?!

We continue to finish this round and both Ari and Jace stumble into the kitchen to refill our drinks. They come back with them in hand and an added shot for everyone as well. Much needed after that last round. We rearrange the circle to begin the new round. I sit between Gigi and Alyssa, following Ari, Jace, Arsalan…and AJ. How did Arsalan and AJ end up sitting next to each other?! I swear Arsalan's evil mind did that on purpose. All of us besides those two men exchange nervous glances.

"I volunteer to go first." Arsalan raises his arm. Oh, no. I try to conceal my nerves by placing my hands under my thighs. AJ rolls his eyes.

Arsalan moves his lips close to AJ's ears and whispers. Three seconds hadn't passed before AJ's eyes widened and the color drained from his face back to his pale complexion. AJ's eyes shift to mine with a stern look.

"I'm not answering this question." AJ stands his ground.

"Why not? Are you scared?" Arsalan challenges. "Not so bad and boujee afterall, popstar."

Oh my god, what did he ask?! I swear the anticipation is going to make me have a brain hemorrhage as well.

"No, it's a stupid question and I don't think it deserves an answer."

"It's just a game. I didn't think K-Pop stars could get stage fright."

AJ's jaw clenches hearing his snide comment. His hands turn into fists. Please, AJ. Don't punch him.

"Come on…don't be a little…bitch." Arsalan riles him up. Everyone exchanges nervous glances at one another.

AJ's chest rises, his ears turn red, then... without blinking, blurts, "Rose Lin."

After a few seconds, his eyes widen in surprise.

Arsalan's reaction is the same as Gigi's when she asked him a question. Rose Lin...where have I heard that name?

Ari leans into Gigi and Alyssa and says, "I love her voice. I can't believe AJ gets to tour with her!" She probably hopes saying this would defuse the tension that's invaded the room.

The light bulb in my head turns on. That's the K-Pop girl Ari mentioned yesterday at the dinner table.

"Rock, paper, scissors shoot...big boy." Arsalan forms a fist and places his other hand under, waiting for AJ to do the same. But AJ holds back. The anger in his eyes dissipates and is replaced with regret. He glances at me, barely able to meet his eyes with mine. Like Arsalan, he forms a fist.

"Rock, paper, scissors." Arsalan motions each word in sync with his hand.

Arsalan chooses rock and AJ...scissors.

"Time to confess, buddy. Say it."

"I think we're done with this game." AJ raises his voice.

"Yeah, you'd like that right now, wouldn't you?" Arsalan narrows his eyes on him. "Very well, if he won't, I will."

My curiosity is killing me inside, but do I really want to know the question?

And before I can answer that for myself, Arslan looks directly into my eyes and says, "I asked if he could hook up with one person, who would it be? And the answer cannot be anyone in this circle."

Gigi gasps under her breath, but she just projects what everyone is feeling. Me, on the other hand, my curiosity has turned into mere anger. My jaw tenses, my fingers dig into my palms, my eyes well up...and not from sadness.

Ironically, one of AJ's songs is playing in the background called "Tell Me The Truth, Won't You?".

I lock eyes with Jace. In a panic, he says clearing his throat, "Uh, alright. I think we're done for the night. It's getting pretty late and we have an early morning, don't we, Ari?"

Ari's eyes are glued to her brother, squinting from disbelief. "Uh, yeah. I totally...forgot about that." She muffles her words. "Let's clean up. Gigi, Alyssa, AJ?"

I remain frozen as everyone gets up, trying to piece everything that just took place. What the HELL just happened?! I'm so angry, but I can't pinpoint who I'm most angry with...Arsalan or AJ?

"You okay?" Jace stands over me, offering his hand. I reach out and pick myself up.

"All I know is that there is a conversation I

do not want to have."

"Hey, it's just a game. Don't think too much of it."

"Well, I'm trying not to, but he could have said a million other names. Not someone he's with most of the time."

"Don't get too into your head. He loves you and you know that."

Does he though? I mean, people say they love someone, but only they know their own true intentions. I need to shake off these thoughts but I can't help it. This was sort of like a slap to my ego, which has been pretty non-existent up until now.

"Hey, I think I'm going to head out now. Thanks for a great night." Arsalan hugs Jace, but Jace isn't as receptive. Arsalan turns to me and leans in for what I thought would be a hug but instead, he whispers, "I know why you killed me off in the game."

Confused as to what he's thinking, I ask, "Why?"

"Because..." He leans in closer, "with me out of the picture, you wouldn't have any temptations."

He pulls back, lays his eyes on my lips as they gradually move to my eyes. I stare icily back at him. Does he really think I want HIM?! Regardless of what my subconscious thinks, I wouldn't dare to ever hook up with his slimy ass. I know most girls would be falling for this bad boy swagger, but honestly it's SUCH a turn off. He's so full of himself! As more time passes knowing Arsalan, the more I realize he's not any different from some politicians—he thrives on creating chaos.

He makes his way around the kitchen, saying his goodbyes and both Gigi and Alyssa follow him out. The one good thing that came out of this night was for the girls to like AJ as much as I do. Well, my bar of liking him has lowered as of right now.

"Alright, sweetie. Me and Jace are off to bed. Get some rest, okay?" Ari hugs me, pressing her cheek against mine.

"Goodnight, Ari." I slant my smile. I really hope they aren't worried about me. They should be more worried about AJ who's probably shitting himself right now. I also have no clue where he is either. He's probably hiding out in my room, practicing his aegyo...which won't work out in his favor this time. I pop open the door to my room and peek my head in to see him positioned at the corner on my bed, watching one of Kevin Hart's stand-up comedy shows. He's trying to distract himself with humor, considering this whole night has been anything but that.

He pauses the video and sets his phone down on the bed. I act as if he's not in the room and race to my dresser, pulling out a pair of pjs.

"Hey, Zara, we should talk." His tone is soft and low. I continue to get ready for bed without replying to him. My mom once told me that if you're angry to a point where you might say something hurtful you don't mean, don't say anything at all. I plan to do just that.

"Zara." He calls out my name, but I choose to ignore it. I walk into my bathroom, strip the clothes off of me and force myself into my black pj pants and black NASA shirt. I twist the bathroom knob and step outside to see him standing before me. "Can we please talk?" The desperation in his voice melts my heart.

"What?" I leave no hint of submission.

"Look, I'm really, REALLY sorry I said her name. I wasn't thinking."

Hearing that made me more mad. He had the option to say anyone's name. Like, I don't know...maybe Betty White for giggles!

"AJ, I think it's best if we don't have this conversation right now." I remain calm.

"No, we're talking about this right now. I can't leave knowing you're mad at me."

"AJ, please. Just go. We can talk about this later." He grabs my arm and draws me closer to him.

"Please, just talk to me. Tell me how you feel."

"AJ, just...drop it." I push him away and march towards my bed.

"Zara, I want to talk about it right now, please!"

Sorry, Mom. I tried.

"Fine, you want to talk about it?" I walk right back and fix my eyes directly to his. "I'm SO pissed at you!"

"I deserve it," He says with an apologetic nod.

"What was going through your head, AJ?! You could have said any other name. But, no! You said hers, someone you're with all the time. Was this some sort of Freudian slip?"

Is he subconsciously thinking about Rose Lin?

"No, of course not!" He steps forward, attempting to get a hold of my arm but I push his hand away.

"How would you feel if someone asked me that same question in front of your friends and I said...Arsalans name?!"

"I..." he inhales deeply before answering, "I would feel like punching him." His furrowed brows relax and jaw clenches.

"Well, that's not far from how I feel about you right now." I cross my arms. "You saying her name instinctively just raises some thoughts that...I never thought I'd have about you."

AJ diverts his eyes from mine. He reaches to grip his hand around my wrist, gently pulling me closer to his body. Then, places his forehead against mine as he seals his eyes shut.

"Please...don't break up with me over this. I won't be able to handle it."

I was fuming but hearing the crack in his

voice as he said those words felt as if someone poured a bucket of cold water over my burning body. To know he's so afraid of losing me gave me a little comfort in that very moment. Maybe I was overreacting. I mean...my subconscious has betrayed me, too.

I let out a defeated sigh.

"AJ...I'm not breaking up with you. It just felt like a slap to my face. I've worked so hard on my self-esteem and I don't want that stripped down again, which is so hard not to do considering you're surrounded by those who literally look like goddesses."

"Meri jaan...no, don't think that way." He cradles my face with his warm hands. "Look at me." He forces me to meet his eyes. "You're the most beautiful woman I have EVER laid my eyes on. I could never, ever think of anyone else. I'm sorry if I made you feel that, even for a second."

Damn YOU, your hypnotizing deep brown eyes and your Australian accent, AJ. Damn you.

As reassuring as that was, I have to ask.

"AJ, I believe you. You haven't given me a reason not to but...do I have to worry about Rose Lin? Is there something you want to share?"

Please, AJ. Say no.

Without hesitation, he says, "Absolutely not, Zara. You never have to worry about any other girl catching my attention. I'm all yours."

Funny, he says that now but couldn't an hour ago. But, I'm not in the mood to fight with him anymore. He realizes what he did and honestly, that's good enough for me. Plus, he's already had a day of being Arsalan's victim so I'll cut him some slack. He has a tendency of getting under people's skin.

"I forgive you, AJ. I love you. I think Arsalan got to both of us."

"I love you more, my universe." He kisses my forehead. "And, please don't mention that snake's name during this beautiful moment." We both laugh in unison. "The universe waited too long to bring you to me and I wouldn't do anything to hurt you...ever. I don't know what will happen in the future, but I promise you one thing...no one, and I mean NOTHING can ever come between us, whether it's my career, our parents or anyone else at all. I'll fight head on against anything that blocks our paths together."

He places his hand over the back of my head and brings me against his chest.

I hope you stay true to your words, AJ. I really, really hope you do.

CHAPTER 5 :

Tick-Tock

"Hey, sleepyhead. I made you coffee." Jace's voice echoes in my head. Is it in my dream or is he actually in my room? Reluctantly, I turn my head and open my eyes, only to see him standing beside my bed with the Grey's Anatomy mug that says 'you're my person'.

"Agh, no. Let me go back to sleep." I groan, pulling the sheets over my head.

"Zara, are you kidding? It's one in the afternoon. I let you sleep in ALL morning!"

He sets the coffee mug on my nightstand and rips the sheets off of me.

"Jace!"

"Get up! Why are you even in bed?!"

"Because! I'm...tired." I pull the sheets back over me.

"Bitch, we all are! But we still got our asses

out of bed! Come on, we're on break!"

"I want to enjoy it by sleeping."

"We can sleep when we're dead!" He yanks the sheets off of me, again! I lay there like a vegetable, refusing to move.

"Can that BE any sooner?"

"What's the matter with you today?!" He taps my elbow to scoot over and lays down beside me once I make room.

"I don't even know. I just feel...off."

"Are you on your period?" he asks while patting his tummy.

"Yeah...I just started this morning. Wait. How the hell do you know?!" I furrow my brows. Does he have a sixth sense of when I'm menstruating?

"I just know."

"Okay, Cole Sear, calm down with your sixth sense. But I don't think how I'm feeling is because of my period, although it has intensified what I've been feeling since last night."

"Is it because of what happened yesterday?"

"Maybe. I mean, AJ and I talked it out and we're fine. I just...miss him."

I sigh as I drop my hands over my chest.

"You saw him yesterday, idiot."

"I know but...I miss him all the time. And a part of me hates that. He has such a huge hold on me. I thought I became strong enough that even if we do break up, I'd pull through. But, hearing him say her name last night, I don't know...the thought of him being with someone else or losing him...I don't think I'll be able to handle it."

"I understand that, bubs."

"I'm trying to hold on to EVERY second I spend with him. I can't even imagine how I'll be once he leaves back home...with that K-Pop buttface."

"Buttface...really?" Jace makes no effort to hide the judgment in his voice.

"Okay, maybe I shouldn't call her a buttface. She might be a nice buttface, but still!"

"You can say bitch. What are you, five?" He slams a pillow on my face. "Well, as much as I like her, she might be a 'buttface'." He wiggles two-finger peace signs into air quotes. "Who knows! Don't think about it. AJ's yours and it's going to stay that way if I have anything to do with it...even if I have to cut a bitch."

"I'm trying not to think about it. Ugh, I just want AJ right now! I wanted him to stay longer, possibly stay the night, but he promised WON's he'll do his weekly v-lives a day earlier. It's like the SWEETEST thing in the world. There should be a temple named after him because that's some 'big saint energy'."

AJ never misses any v-lives because for some fans, it's the one thing they look forward to every week. If he ever does miss one, he promises WON's that he'll do three the following week! If that doesn't radiate some 'hyung' spirit, I don't know what will

"So, like a total idiot, I downloaded the app that K-Pop stars use for their v-lives, and watched him as I sobbed. I even sent an 'I love you' in the chat like a sad little cat, thinking he'd see it." I smother myself with a pillow. "I just want one day with him without anything to do with K-Pop! Why have I become such a needy, idiotic bitch?!"

"You're not an idiot, idiot." He forces the pillow off my face. "It's natural to miss your partner, especially if you don't see them often. I miss Ari ALL the time. It's normal! But, unlike mine...your relationship is anything but normal. Maybe he's having a hard time balancing everything."

"Meaning?"

"Well, before you, he only knew K-Pop. That was his only world. Then your little sexy, Pakistani ass walked into his life and now he has something else to think about other than that. And I kind of understand the stress of the risk he's taking. So, maybe he's just trying to figure it out, pleasing both you and his own world."

"But see...that's the thing. I'm not part of his world."

"Okay, Ariel. Calm your fin. Stop getting emo here. I'm just saying, it might be hard for him as well as it is for you, right?"

"Yeah, I mean...he wouldn't fit into my world either, huh? I guess I've been so occupied with trying to fit into his, I forgot that I'm also battling the same issue."

"You both are on the same boat. Except...he has a fancy stage and microphone and yours has a stethoscope and a 'lengha'."

"I know, I know. I guess...last night just got to me."

"Yeah...last night got to A LOT of people."

"Yeah, what the HECK was up with Arsalan and AJ?! I thought I was literally going to have a panic attack right in the middle of the party. There was some weird toxic masculinity type of battle crap going on between them. AJ is the most humble person I've come across and he was being so cocky in front of Arsalan."

"Well, yeah, milady. These men were fighting for the honor to enter your secret chambers." He attempts to bow as well as he can laying down.

"Oh my gosh, STOP. But you know what... Gigi, Alyssa, and even AJ thought that Arslan might have his eye out for me. I don't know how accurate that is."

"Clearly, you need to grab your glasses because you're the only one who doesn't see it. Even Ari noticed how Arsalan acts around you. Anyone who has eyes can see that he likes you."

"Really? Like...with actual feelings? I thought he was just messing with me."

"Yeah...I mean he hasn't said anything to me but I was watching his body language like a hawk. He definitely felt jealous seeing you all lovey-dovey with AJ and that riled him up. Ari said she's never seen AJ get mad like that with anyone before."

"Oh, man. Am I...toxic?"

"Yes, Britney, you are." He laughs. "No, not at all. It's not your fault that you're so appealing to these men! You're a sexy, bad bitch. Own it!"

"Um...I don't want to if it means it'd cause any drama."

"Zara, you're dating a K-Pop star. Your life is literally a Korean drama."

I smack myself with a pillow, again.

"Agh, I just want to have a normal relationship, not starring in a K-drama series."

"No, you don't. If you had a normal relationship, the butterflies you feel in your stomach when you see AJ would have been covered in cobwebs by now. Kinda like that coochie since you haven't been getting any."

I pluck the pillow off of my face, and slam it right onto his.

"Ouch!"

"Stop mentioning it! I'm perfectly fine with that. Just, don't rub salt into my wounds."

"Well, then get something else rubbed!"

"Jace! You're so gross." I smack his wrist. "And...MAYBE I was about to last night before you and Ari banged on the door."

"Ah, shit! Had I known, I would have left y'all doing the nasty."

"No, I'm glad you did or else the guilt would have crept up eventually."

"You should be letting something else creep up...if ya know what I mean." He winks.

"You're LITERALLY disgusting."

"Yeah, you should be, too! Maybe then you wouldn't be so freaking emo. Look at me, I'm glowing like JLo."

"Oh my gosh, I'm not having this conversation right now."

I spring off my bed to end this misery.

"I just want to forget about the drama from last night, ESPECIALLY from Arsalan."

"Uh...well."

Ding-dong!

No. No. NO!

"Jace?" I close my eyes and bring my fingertips to my temples. "Please...tell me that's not who I think it is."

"Okay, I won't."

I glare at him.

"Okay, he just wants to apologize. He feels bad about what happened last night."

"Oh my gosh, is that why you woke me up?! Because he was coming over?!"

"Partially...but I also wanted to make sure you were alive."

"Well, I feel like I'm alive, but dead. I'd rather be that than to talk to him right now."

"Stop being dramatic. Go brush your hair and teeth and come outside."

"No!"

"Zara, stop! Just hear him out! You have a heart of gold, use it right now and just see what he has to say."

I inhale deeply and try to relax every agitated muscle fiber of my body.

"Fine."

I drag my feet to the bathroom and change my pj bottoms to some gray sweatpants. Staring at my reflection in the mirror, I tie my hair up in a ponytail while unkind words for Arsalan escape my mouth without a sound. I aggressively brush my teeth, taking out my anger on my poor gums.

I shut my eyes and inhale deeply before I open the door. I swear, he's going to hear it from me today. As the door squeaks open, I immediately regret it. Arsalan is sitting on the couch with Jace, while Ari is in the kitchen. She pretends to crack her neck when she sees me, rolling her eyes to land on Arsalan, then back on me. Ah, you and me both, girl. I'm not too happy about him here, either.

"Hey, Zara." Arsalan stands up, wiggling his hands in the pockets of his dark wash denim. His black v-neck shirt matches the gloominess in his voice.

"Hey."

An awkward silence fills the room, allowing the buzzing sounds of the streets of Los Angeles to creep in. Arsalan brings his palms together, glancing at Jace, Noticing, Jace nods at

Ari.

"Uh, well. I gotta get going. I have a meeting with some of my colleagues, but I'll see you guys later!" Ari mouths 'good luck', away from Arsalan's sight, and grabs her purse from the entrance table.

"I'll walk you down, babe." Jace follows her out the door. I know his sneaky ass is trying to leave me and Arsalan alone. I don't get why Jace is okay with this, knowing damn well that he likes me and I have a boyfriend! But, at the same time, if Jace thinks it's a good idea to hear him out, I'll trust him...one last time.

I make my way to the couch as his eyes follow me. I sit as far as possible from him...even though our couch is way too small for that to happen.

"How are you?" Arsalan maintains his soft voice as he sits back down. His eyes pierce through mine, resembling those of an injured puppy.

"I'm good." My eyes wander around the room to avoid making contact with him. I'm still extremely annoyed.

He clears his throat.

"Listen, Zara. I'm...really sorry about yesterday." He rubs his thumb against the index finger of the other hand. "I...shouldn't have been such a dick to AJ, or in the game. That was unnecessary."

"Mhm." I nod in agreement.

"I'm trying to apologize, Zara." He scoots closer to me.

"I hear you." My tone isn't as soft as his.

"Well, it seems like you're not accepting it." He scoffs.

"Do you think anyone would after what you did last night? Do you even realize how much anxiety I felt?" I voice my frustration.

"Oh…" his eyes widen, "I…I didn't know. I'm so sorry, Zara."

"Yeah, you wouldn't because you don't think! You just seem to do whatever you want without thinking about the consequences." I raise my voice. I should really just accept his apology and move on.

"I-uh," he stutters.

"Why do you feel so entitled? Huh? Did Ami and Abu feed your ego, like all brown parents do to their little boys?"

"No, I-uh—"

"Oh, let me guess. Your parents just let you get away with everything without even a slap on the wrist. So, now you just do whatever your tiny heart desires!"

"Zara, let me—"

"No! I don't want to hear it. I don't like people who purposely cause problems in other people's lives." My voice keeps getting louder and louder by the second.

"I'm not who you think I am." His remorseful eyes match his words, but I can't seem to find any empathy for it.

"You're exactly who I think you are!" I look him dead in the eyes. "You're nothing BUT trouble and I don't like you!" I catch myself off guard with the words that echo throughout my apartment.

"Ouch." His mouth hangs slightly open, averting his eyes from me.

Shit, I...maybe I said too much. I didn't mean to hurt him but it might be too late. I guess that's why you never speak when you're angry. You might say something hurtful you really don't mean.

I sigh.

"Arsalan...I—"

"No, it's okay." Still avoiding eye contact. "I deserve all that."

"I...didn't mean to say the last part." I tuck a strand of hair behind my ear. I suck in my pride and gather the strength to say something I never thought I'd ever say to him. "I'm sorry."

"Please, Zara. Don't apologize." He pauses, locking his hands together tightly. "You're right...I have been able to get away with a lot of things."

I stay quiet and quite confused with his unexpected contrition. Is he...playing me or is he being genuine?

"It's just...no one's ever confronted me about my mistakes. I guess you just took me by surprise."

What do I say to that?! You're welcome or sorry...again?!

"Just try not to be a dick, okay?" I reach out and gently pat him on his back. This was the most awkward gesture I've done in a while.

"I'll try and I really am sorry about last night. I didn't mean to cause you any sort of pain. I just wasn't thinking." He slants his smile.

"It's okay, let's just try to move on. How does that sound?"

"Sounds like something I don't deserve."

"Well, you don't." I soften my expression. "But everyone deserves a second chance, no matter how much of an ass they can be. Plus, you're one of Jace's close friends and I think we'll be seeing each other a lot more, unfortunately."

He chuckles. "Yeah, we do owe him that much. For Jace."

"For Jace." I nod.

Speaking of the devil...the door slowly opens as Jace assesses the vibe in the room.

"Uh...may I come in or should I call 911 and report a homicide?"

"You may come in." I roll my eyes and minimize my smile.

"Okay, good. I didn't know what I might be walking into."

"She almost killed me." Arsalan laughs and shoots me a wink. "But I think we're good now."

"Oh, THANK GOD! I thought I'd have to treat Arsalan like a mistress!" He speeds over to the couch, sitting between Arsalan and me, forcing us into his arms. "I'm so happy right now."

"Uh, well can you loosen up a bit? All this affection is making me slightly uncomfortable." My face brushes against his textured shirt. I'm sure that's going to leave a mark.

"Deal with it." Jace pulls us in even closer, bringing mine and Arsalan's face just a few inches from each other. His eyes switch from one eye of mine to the other as a shy smile sweeps across his face. And my heart...flutters?! The HELL?! Without waiting another second, I wrestle myself out of the headlock Jace has us in.

"Uh, anyways." I gulp. "Um, does anyone want water or something?"

"No, I'm good. Thank you, Zara." He smiles with kind eyes. Ew, stop saying my name, Arsalan!

"Nah, my thirst went away." Jace chimes in.

I press the back of my hand against my forehead as I slowly make my way to the kitchen. Do I have a fever? Did I eat something bad last night that's causing reflux or something? Why the hell did my heart flutter, despite the fact that it was for a second...it's what I feel when I see AJ. Honestly, I think it was nothing for me to overthink about. I think it was just Jace holding onto me too tight which probably caused some sort of palpitation. Yeah, that must be it. That seems to be the most logical explanation.

I pour myself a glass of water. Arsalan and Jace watch me as I chug it all down at once. Noticing how loud I am, I defend myself by saying, "I'm thirsty."

"Yeah, I bet you are." Jace sneers at my defense. I roll my eyes and set the glass in the sink. As I do, I hear a muffled buzzing sound. My phone! Ah, it must be AJ calling me! I sprint to my room, study where the sound is coming from, but can't find my phone! I rip the sheets off my bed and my phone lunges on the wall and onto the floor. Ah, shit. Did I break it?! I lift it off the ground with both hands as if it were a baby. Thankfully, it's still okay but...it's not AJ calling. It's my mom FaceTiming me. I swipe across the screen to answer.

"Salamu-Alaykum, Mom."

"Wa-Alaikum-Salaam, beta. How are you?"

"I'm good, just cleaning my room," I lied. Why did I lie?! Honestly, I find myself lying over the littlest things when I talk to my parents. It's probably out of panic, which ultimately has become an instinctive habit. Like I said, my parents aren't as strict as other brown parents, but definitely do a great job conjuring fear. They have always told me not to lie, and I normally don't but then if I do start telling them the truth about the majority of things that I do, they'd probably disown me. Plus, I did tell the truth throughout college and I always just heard lectures regardless of what I did. It only caused a lot more stress on my end. For example, I used to study at the library because there were less distractions there—and no, it wasn't as an excuse to hangout with a boyfriend or to go out partying—and they'd get mad at me for not being home! Like, I'm in the library...studying! I heard somewhere that strict parents make the best liars. Mine made me a semi-liar. Not proud of it, but it just keeps peace between my parents and I.

"Oh, acha. Well, I was calling to see if you and Jace wanted to come over for dinner."

"Let me ask Jace if he's free for the evening."

"Oh! Let me talk to him," she insists.

"Uh, okay." I walk on out to the living room, hoping Arsalan keeps his trap quiet.

"Jace, my mom's on the phone. She wants to speak to you." I hand him the phone.

"Salam Sonia Auntie! How are you?" Jace greets her like he does with his own mom.

"I'm good, beta! I wanted to ask if you and Zara are free for dinner tonight. I'm making your favorite biryani and karahi gosht."

"Oh, Auntie! You know I can never say no to that. I've been missing your cooking so much. My mouth is drooling already."

"Good! I can't wait to see you, beta."

"Me, too, Auntie!"

"Uh, I'll be there, too." I feel a little left out.

"You know I'm the favorite child." Jace jolts his head to make his point, moving the camera away from his face and the next thing I hear is…

"Oh, who's that sitting next to you?"

Ah…shit. She saw him.

I snatch the phone from Jace's hand as quickly as I can say, "It's just—uh—Jace's friend Arsalan."

"Oh, is he Pakistani?" Oh, no. I know why she's asking.

"Ji, Auntie. I am." Arsalan responds. NO! He jumps off the couch and walks behind me. "Salam, Auntie. I'm Arsalan. It's nice to meet you." He shines his pearly whites, taking the phone out of my hand.

Her face lights up like the Eiffel Tower at night.

"Nice to meet you, too, beta!" She pauses. "If you're not busy tonight…you should come for dinner with the kids."

NO, what is she doing?!

"Uh, he might have plans. It's short notice, he probably—"

"I would love to." He cuts me off.

Ah! He's the worst.

"Perfect! I hope you like my cooking, beta. I cannot wait for you kids to come over!" Her smile is radiating through the phone and onto Arsalan.

"I'm sure I will love it, Auntie. See you soon. Khuda hafiz." He hangs up.

Jace and I are taken back from him saying goodbye in Urdu. I was under the impression that he doesn't speak our mother tongue, let alone pronounce it correctly. I'm sure he just got some 'mithai' points by saying something as simple as that. My mom probably thinks he's a child of Allah. Not going to lie, he spoke so politely to her, for a second I forgot what an ass he is.

"Uh, you...don't have to go, Arsalan." I say as he hands me back my phone.

"Do you...not want me to go?"

Jace and Arsalans eyes are fixated on me, waiting for an answer.

"Oh, no! Uh, you're more than welcome. I just...didn't want you to feel pressured."

Honestly, I don't want him to come. He's so unpredictable. Even though he's apologized and seems remorseful, I don't like being around him. AND I have a very strong feeling my mom will pressure me about him.

"I don't feel pressured. I...actually want to go. Your mom asked in such a loving way...it felt really nice. Plus, I haven't had homecooked Pakistani food in years. I forgot what it tasted like. But if you don't want me to—"

"No." I blurt out before he finishes his sentence. "You should come."

Ah, shit. I feel bad now.

"I'm just going to finish up a couple things in my room and then we'll head out in a few hours. Sounds good?"

"Right on, boss." Arsalan gives a little nod.

"Yeah, sounds good, little one." Jace follows with a pretend punch to my arm.

I grab a glass of water from the kitchen before heading into my room. I can't stop thinking about what Arsalan said. Hearing him say he hasn't had homecooked Pakistani food made me feel a bit sad for him. From what Jace told me, he's from Los Angeles...so, he could easily go home. It just makes me wonder...what's going on in his life?

◆ ◆ ◆

I take a deep breath in and ring the doorbell. I hear my mom's faint voice calling my dad's name behind the door.

"Ah, hello, beta!" She swings open the door. Wow. I didn't realize how much I missed her infectious smile. Why is she all dressed up though? Normally, when Jace and I come over, she's in her American clothes but today, she's wearing traditional Pakistani clothes. I wish I knew we were dressing up. I came in with skinny jeans and a white fitted T-shirt.

"Hi, Mom!" I leap towards her, giving a long tight hug.

Arslan clears his throat and steps forward.

"Salam, Auntie. I'm Arsalan." He leans in so she can pat his head. We do it out of respect for our elders when we greet them. I'm a bit surprised seeing him all cultured.

"Salam, beta!" She pats his head with the

biggest smile on her face and places her hand on one of his cheeks when he looks back up. "Come in! Come in! Don't stay out here."

"Sonia Auntie, you forgot me!" Jace crosses his arms and feigns a frown.

"Oh, beta!" She steps outside to hug him. "I could never forget you!"

"It's okay, I'll forgive you if you tell me you made biryani."

"Of course I made it, beta!"

"Then it's okay, Auntie." He hugs her back.

"Okay, kids. Please come inside now, we've been standing out here for so long!"

As the boys make their way in, my dad strolls down the stairs gracefully. Awe, he's wearing the button-down white dress shirt I gave him for Eid! Since I was a kid, I've always seen him dressed up, wearing button downs with cufflinks. Clearly, I didn't inherit his posh style.

"Hi, Uncle Adil!" Jace leans in again and Dad pats his head.

"Hello, beta. Did your exams go well?"

"Yes, thankfully they did, thank God."

"Well, I didn't doubt that you'd do well."

Dad spins around to greet Arsalan.

"And you must be Arsalan. Zara's mom has been talking about you all afternoon." Both shake hands. "Strong grip. Good. Very good."

"Thank you, Uncle. I hope she said good things." Arsalan is actually really good with parents. He didn't show a sign of nervousness or awkwardness that normally people have when meeting anyone's parents. Maybe he really is a lowkey sociopath.

"She was excited to meet you, I'll tell you that, beta." Dad gestures to the family room. "Come, sit down. I think Zara's mom is almost done with dinner."

Jace and Arsalan follow my dad to the family room but my mom yanks my hand, pulling me to the side.

"Zara." She whispers as if she were about to tell me a secret plan.

"Uh, yeah?"

"Change your clothes. I put a set of salwar and kameez in your room. Uncle Ahktar and Amna Auntie are coming for dinner."

Oh. My. GOD! Someone please pour a bucket of cold water over me right now because I'm about to set myself on fire.

"MOM!" I scream as quietly as I possibly can without alarming the boys. "Why are they coming?!"

"Well, they called before you guys came and said they wanted to stop by and say hello. I obviously couldn't say no."

"Yes, you could have! You should have said you had guests coming."

"You know I couldn't say that, Zara. They're family and our elders. That would be very disrespectful."

"So?! Who cares! It's called setting boundaries! It's not like they're good people to begin with or give a flying crap about you and Dad. They don't act like elders. All they do is gossip and spread their negativity, something elders who have grown and evolved don't do! And I hate Uncle Ahktar's voice, ugh! Especially when he fights with Dad over stupid things. I can't believe they're even brothers."

"Zara, just change your clothes. Don't make a fuss about this."

"What's wrong with my clothes?!" I examine my outfit.

"They are too tight. I can see the outline of your bra."

"No, you can't!" I protest. It's not like I have any boobs to begin with! "And so what if you can? God forbid if the world knows I have boobs, something that ALLAH gave me."

"Okay, but do you have to show it? Amna will think I didn't teach you how to dress in front of elders."

"Yeah, and somehow it's my responsibility to hide the existence of the one thing I had no control over." I chuckle in anger. "Nothing's wrong with what I'm wearing. The only thing that's legitimately wrong is their narrow-minded, repulsive thinking!" I cross my arms to emphasize my point.

"Beta, I agree with you. But do you feel comfortable wearing such a tight shirt in front of your uncle? It's just shameful, beta. You already know how they think."

"Shameful? Because it's a little tight? Really?! Listen to yourself! Look, I have no problem changing but please DON'T make me feel as if I've made a mistake because they choose to objectify my body. Maybe you shouldn't be inviting people like that over to our home! Why do you even care about what they say?"

"Amna has a big mouth and will go around spreading things about you in the community!"

"She can be my guest!"

"Calm down! What's gotten into you?" She creases her brows as I cross my arms again. "Listen, wear whatever you want in secret. But for now, please go change your clothes." She points to the stairs.

"Fine, but you should have canceled plans with us if you couldn't say no to them! You knew the boys were coming. You don't think she'll run her big mouth around the community with an elaborative story about them? She'll probably spread a rumor that both are my boyfriends and I'm slutting it up at USC."

My head's about to explode! First day being on my period isn't helping either! I'm probably going to die today from a vein popping. This is a thousand times worse than being angry at Arsalan or that buttface of a waitress.

"Zara! Watch your language."

"I'm twenty-five years old, Mom! I don't need to be disciplined anymore."

"Stop arguing with me and go change!" She glares at me as if I'm a whining little kid.

I bite my tongue, close my eyes, inhale in and out. I stomp my way up the stairs and into my room. I strip my clothes off and force myself into the clothes she laid out for me. Although I'm furious—and if one had supersonic vision, could see the hot air flowing out of my nose like a dragon—I missed wearing Pakistani clothes. I feel like a princess whenever I dress up my outfit with kundan jewelry and bangles. Agh, whatever. I'm not going to waste my energy on those people and ruin my evening. Instead, I'm going to channel that anger into dressing up and doing my makeup.

◆ ◆ ◆

"Zara! Come downstairs!" Mom hollers from the staircase.

"Coming!" I push down my nose ring, making sure it's secured. I haven't worn it in SO long, but I think I'm going to from now on—gotta embrace my Pakistani heritage. With one last glance at myself, I switch off the bathroom light, and run downstairs before Mom has to call me down again.

I stroll into the kitchen only to find her giggling like a schoolgirl. Arsalan is leaning against the kitchen island cracking jokes with the woman who gave birth to me.

"Uh, hey, Mom. Do you need any help?" I ask while she laughs hysterically.

Arsalan turns around at the sound of my voice and his lips separate as his eyes trail down and back up at me. He looks at me as if it were his first time seeing me.

"No, everything's done, beta. Just set the table with Arsalan." She elbows me as she struts past, her dupatta flowing after her. She hands me a set of plates that leave me unbalanced. I know EXACTLY what she's trying to do. It's funny how she's trying to play matchmaker. This is the same woman who told me in elementary school not to talk to boys…but now, she's all for it because I'm getting older and should be married soon. Well, to be fair, her mindset changed a lot when I started college and warmed up to the idea of having boys as friends. She never had the chance to have male friends so she didn't realize that girls and boys can have a platonic relationship. In our culture, when a boy and a girl are friends, it's automatically assumed that they're lusting over each other because God forbid there could be anything else going on besides just that.

"Here, I can get those. They seem heavy." The weight of the plates lifts off my hands as Arsalan takes them. As he does, the side of our hands brush against each other. Ah…shit. Both of our hands jerk away as if we'd touched a burning pan.

"Uh, you don't have to help. It's okay." I

have trouble looking him in the eyes.

"I want to help. And...it's okay, Zara. Don't worry, I'll try my best for your mom not to like me." He chuckles and stops with a bashful smile. Jesus, is this some sort of Bollywood movie?!

"Too late for that." I say as we make our way to the dining room.

"Your mom is really loving." He places plates down, one by one in front of each seat at the table.

"Yeah, she is." I grab the utensils from the drawer, placing a fork and spoon on each plate he sets down.

"You take after her." He glances at me and I at him but his gaze lingers on me with an adoring smile on his face. Jesus, what's gotten into him?

"What makes you say that?" I move my eyes from his and focus on placing the utensils on the plates.

"Because you have every right to hate me right now, but...you still forgave me. Only a person with a kind heart would do that."

What do I say to that?! That's actually-...sweet.

"I may have forgiven you, but that doesn't mean you're off my bad list."

He laughs while shaking his head.

"That's fine. I'm planning on getting off of it anyways." He places the last plate on the table and turns around, bumping into me, leaving my clumsy ass unbalanced. As I'm about to fall backwards from the impact, I feel his strong hands grip around my waist—one on my back, and the other on the side of my waist. My arms, having a mind of their own, wrap themselves around his neck like a monkey clinging to a tree branch. His eyes shift from my left eye to my right...coming to a halt on my lips. The reflux from earlier comes back. Jesus, could this BE any more of a Bollywood movie?!

His lips separate...trying to slow down his slight heavy breathing.

"Are you okay?" he asks in a low, concerned tone while licking his lips.

Why am I still in his arms?! GET UP, ZARA! I wiggle out of his grasp, making sure the remaining utensils in my hands don't poke him.

"Yeah, thanks." I gulp. The reflux won't go away!

"No problem." He clears his throat as he runs his hand down his shirt to smooth the wrinkles caused by our Bollywood moment. "By the way, Zara..." he slows his breathing as his eyes find their way to mine, "I don't mean to be disrespectful to AJ but...can I say how beautiful you look in Pakistani clothes? I love the nose ring on you. You should wear it more often. That desi girl look suits you."

I completely forgot I wore it. I'm not used to getting compliments from any other man besides AJ...what the heck do I say?

Before I even get the chance to say anything back, I'm saved by the bell. Agh, but...it's THEM. I'd much rather have an evening trapped with Arsalan than speaking to these devils. Allah, if I have done anything nice in my lifetime, PLEASE MAGICALLY PLACE SOME XANAX IN THE PALM OF MY HAND. I take a few steps away from Arsalan in preparation before the two devils walk in and fabricate some story in their narrow-minded heads.

Mom hurries to open the door.

"Salamu-Alaykum!" My mom perks up her voice. I know you don't like them either, so

why hide it in your voice, MOM!

Both devils greet her while my dad and Jace make their way to them.

"Salam, Amna Auntie, Uncle Ahktar." I bow my head and fake a smile. Uncle Ahktar nods without a smile as usual but Amna Auntie ALWAYS smiles. Anyone can mistake it for a friendly one, but it's never JUST a friendly smile. It's more of a smirk that never fails to turn my stomach upside down. But what makes me feel even more sick to my stomach till this day is...Uncle Ahktar's voice.

"Oh, Salam, beta. Nice to see you." Amna Auntie trails me head to toe with her nasty gaze as she tucks a strand of hair into her hijab. "You've gotten darker, but you look nice." Was that supposed to make me feel bad or something? I love my tan skin. It's called melanin, BITCH. Take your colorism mentality elsewhere!

I wish...I WISH I could say it to her stupid face right this second.

"Oh, thank you, Auntie! I've been working on my tan. I'm glad it's showing." I channel Blair Waldorf's energy. Jace and Arsalan jerk their heads towards me with a surprised smile on their faces. To be honest...I've been surprising myself as well.

She raises her eyebrows and a petty smile appears on her face that's shaped like a basketball. Arsalan and Jace say salam to both of them BUT they don't reply back and just nod. How. RUDE. She keeps glancing at them and then at me. I'm just waiting to hear the elaborative story her peanut brain comes up with.

◆ ◆ ◆

"The food was incredible, Auntie. Especially the samosas." Arsalan compliments my mom as he blows on his cup of hot chai.

"Yes, Auntie. It was delicious as always." Jace adds on.

"Thank you, beta. I put some in the oven for you guys to take home. It tastes best when it's fresh." She smiles at them. "Oh, Zara. Can you set the timer on your phone? They should be done in about six minutes."

"Ji." I slide my phone out from under my thigh and set the timer to exactly six minutes.

"It could've used a little more salt, but still

okay," Amna Auntie says in her Pakistani accent.

Agh. I am so sick and tired of Amna Aunties backhanded compliments. She did that throughout dinner and clearly...is still going. I just want to drink my chai in peace without her unbearable voice making me want to throw it at her and Uncle Ahktar! Jesus, I really need to relax right now but I can't stop shaking my restless leg. I keep glancing at the clock...as if that would make the time go by faster! The two sounds echoing throughout the dining room that are driving me insane are the voices of those devils...and this damn ticking of the clock.

"I thought it was absolutely perfect." Arsalan says as he takes a sip of his chai. Damn, Arsalan. Thanks for having my mom's back. "And... this chai is perfect, too. Thanks, Zara." He turns to me and smiles, knowing damn well Amna Auntie and Uncle Ahktar are watching both of us with their evil gazes.

I purse my lips, making sure I don't show any emotion. I don't want the devils of honor to assume there's something going on between us, but Arsalan isn't helping with his compliments...which he also made throughout dinner AND he sat right next to me. I even tried to have a chair empty between us, but no. He wanted to sit next to me and I couldn't even say no or else they would have become even more suspicious!

"Zara, how is your roommate?" she asks and I choke on the sip I was taking from my chai.

"She's good." I answer while coughing. I glance at Jace—who has his eyes on his cup of chai—and catch Arsalan's confused face.

"Oh, acha. It's good you have a nice Muslim girl living with you. Others can tempt you onto the path of hell with their secular ways."

Well, I guess I'm going to hell then.

"So, Sonia...have you looked into any marriage proposals for Zara?" Amna Auntie asks...AS IF I'M NOT SITTING THERE LIKE A DOLLED OUT STATUE.

"Oh...no. She's still in graduate school, so we told her she can decide when she's ready." Mom glances at Dad while he slurps on his chai.

Amna Auntie makes a face as if my mom said something blasphemous.

"Just get her married as soon as you can. She's not getting any younger. It's a sin for a girl to be unmarried when she's at the age of marriage."

UM, I'm literally...RIGHT HERE. I don't understand how and why adults feel entitled to state their opinions...right in front of you! Like, I'm a person! WITH FEELINGS! I'm not invisible! Agh! My blood churns hearing her insensitive words...and my mom just takes it! Jesus, this ticking of the clock! Why did my parents think it was a great idea to put a wall clock in the dining room?!

"Children these days just focus on getting ahead in their career and then get TOO old.

THEN, they just marry whoever they want...like the Sadiq's family daughter, Noor! Did you hear she's marrying some white guy?"

Ah, here we go! The train of gossip is about to leave the station...the station being Amna Aunties ass flaps she calls a mouth!

"No, I didn't." My mom takes a sip of her chai, avoiding eye contact to hint her disinterest. She hates talking about others behind their backs, but she doesn't have the courage to stop them from doing so.

"Haan ji, their daughter is marrying a white guy she met at her university. It's so shameful. Children nowadays don't even care about their parents' feelings and end up marrying outside of religion. Back in our time, we didn't have the courage to refuse anything our parents told us to do."

I glance at my parents to see if they'd agree. My dad's eyes are wandering around the dining table, and my mom has hers on her chai. At least they're not nodding their heads...or else my heart would break.

"I would never let my daughter marry someone who isn't Muslim. But, I know Myra would never do that to us."

HA! I hate to break it to ya, Amna Auntie. Ironically...SHE'S DATING A WHITE GUY. How do I know? She accidentally snapped me a picture of herself and her boyfriend in the park, and THEN had the audacity to convince me it's a friend of hers...WHO'S A GIRL. Like, does she think I'm blind? Would I NOT somehow know the difference between a guy and a girl? Second of all, I couldn't care less about who she's dating! I'm not like her and her family, going around spreading rumors and butting into people's business. She's EXACTLY like her parents—judgmental, pretentious, self-righteous, and thinks she's the only one going to heaven with her parents because she reads namaz five times a day and never misses a fast during Ramadan. Yet...does the one thing her parents are shaming another girl for.

"We raised her better than that," Uncle Ahktar chimes in.

I chuckle, but not quietly enough from the death stares I'm getting from both devils sitting across from me. I may have done that on purpose. Sorry...not sorry!

"Children these days are moving away from religion. I am SHOCKED." Auntie emphasizes her words.

Every word escaping her mouth is manifesting itself in me as a gallon of fuel for my anger! My parents are just silent. Not even a speck of sound is escaping from their mouths! I wish the same was happening with Amna Auntie and Uncle Ahktar...and this damn clock! It's just a TICK, then one of their insufferable voices, and then another TICK!

"What a disgraceful daughter. That marriage won't last, I tell you. What religion will she teach her children?!" She cackles like Ursala from *The Little Mermaid*. "Those who go against their religion ALWAYS suffer."

Amna Auntie glances at me RIGHT when she says 'suffer'. THE...HELL?! Who does she think she is looking at me as if I'm guilty?! Does she secretly know I have a non-Muslim boyfriend? Actually, she's probably assuming I have a secret non-Muslim boyfriend...because that could be the ONLY reason why I don't wish to get married right now. Even if it's true, why the hell did she look at me?! AGH. I can't take them anymore! My chest rises as each tick passes. My merocrine glands are more out of control than they were before I saw AJ at the bar in Korea. Ah, my God! This ticking...is driving me crazy! Can I just hurl this clock at them?!

"She strayed away from Islam and Allah, just like the other children these days. I blame all this social media! They only want fun but don't bother to pray to Allah and ask forgiveness! Some drink and go to parties and...do sinful things. Tauba, tauba! Haram things!" Uncle Ahktar adds on.

I feel so attacked right now.

"How will these children show their faces to Allah?! Good thing they have practice protesting since that's all they seem to be doing." She scoffs. "They probably will have to protest their way out of hell!"

YEAH, because we're trying to make this a better place for future generations and cleaning up the messes that people like YOU have made with your backward-mindedness! ALLAH, please. Can I JUST scream my lungs out to them?! Agh! Gosh, I feel like I can't breathe normally from this heat of anger spreading throughout my veins! Or maybe it's because of the shit ton of biryani I gorged down...agh, no! I AM angry! I should really try to mask it but I just can't! I don't even care if others even notice it at this point. And it seems as though someone has already caught it. From the corner of my eye, I see Arsalan glance at my leg...which is now in sync to the ticking of the clock.

"Forget Allah, how will her parents show their faces in the community knowing their daughter is marrying outside of the religion?! She lowered their heads in shame." Uncle Ahktar places his cup on the table while having his eyebrows raised.

Shame? She lowered their heads...in SHAME?! For what?! Loving another human being?! A human being that god they believe in created?! His words hit too close to home. The fuel that was adding to my anger throughout dinner has reached its maximum capacity. My chest rises more and more, breathing heavier. It's become uncontrollable. I want to cry my eyes out, but out of anger! My jaw is in pain from clenching. It feels as if my teeth are about to break! The nails of my fingers have dug themselves into the palms of my hands. Agh, this ticking! The sound seems as if it's getting closer to my ears, just louder and louder!

"A nikah can only happen between two Muslims. She will be living a life of sin with this marriage!"

Tick. Tick. Tick.

"Amna, her parents are already living a life of sin and hell for raising a disobedient child like that."

Tick. Tick. Tick.

"I would rather have no children than to have one who goes against MY wishes and our religion. Shame on this girl and her parents for not raising her right!"

TICK...TICK...TICK.

That's. It.

"BAS!"

The timer on my phone goes off, blaring throughout the silenced dining room! Did I... just yell...'enough'?! And in Urdu?! Oh, shit. Zara, breathe! Gosh, I don't know where that came out of, but it's an itch that keeps...itching!

"What...did you just say?" Uncle Ahktar squints his eyes, nostrils flared as the timer is still going off. My mom grabs my phone and shuts it off while pinching my leg under the table that's stopped shaking. I've had...enough. These people are not the elders we've been told to respect! Respect is earned, and they haven't earned it! Speak up, Zara! Speak up!

"I'm so sick...and tired...of hearing you two talking AND talking."

"Zara!" My mom screams my name.

"You two should be ashamed of yourselves, not Noor or her parents!"

"Zara, chup!" Mom yanks my hand.

"Mom, I'm not done!" I feel bad for saying that, but I'm ALL IN to be the 'batameez' child until I set these rotten butter chickens straight.

"So what if she's marrying someone who's not Muslim? Did Allah come down and tell you heathens personally that it's a sin? What gives you the right to judge her? For loving a human being that Allah made?! At least her kids will be raised in a loving, respectful environment...seeing love and affection rather than fights, which is what I've seen in our family and it's far more traumatizing!"

I see my parents' gasping eyes, which is making me feel ashamed for a slight second...because ultimately this outburst is a reflection of them in others' eyes. But I'm just...I'm SO mad! I'm frustrated! I'm frustrated with these stupid outdated beliefs and values!

"It's because of people like YOU that parents feel the need to be ashamed of their kids for choosing their happiness! This world is divided because of people like YOU who hold such intolerance in their hearts. You consider yourselves as Muslims?! Ha! Isn't Islam based off of unity and peace? Something you two CLEARLY don't believe in. You go around claiming that you love ALLAH, but really...you're doing the one thing that the God you believe in despises! Hurting people! It's all I've seen you guys do for as long as I can remember!"

"Zara, bas!" Mom yells, but I act as if she didn't just damage the hair cells in my ear.

"It's so sad you can't see that there's more to life than what you two talk about. If you truly love Allah, talk about how we can change our minds, our thoughts, our behaviors to make this world a better place for the people that Allah created! But, NO! you want to talk about things that keep the world more divided than it already is!"

"Chup, Zara!" I hear my mom yet again call my name with great anger in her voice, but I choose to ignore it.

"You think Noor will be living a life of sin? No, no. It's YOU guys who are sinning every second of your life by gossiping about other people, without knowing what they might be going through AND judging them as if you're so perfect! She's happy, but you two...ARE CLEARLY NOT. If you were, you wouldn't spread so much hate. You have hatred in your hearts, not love! You are no Muslims in my eyes, let alone decent human beings!"

"ZARA!"

I gasp, choking on my own breath. My blood turns cold. The room becomes silent.

The only sounds ricocheting throughout are the echoes of Uncle Ahktars voice, my breathing and the ticking of the clock. And just like that...I'm eight years old. Afraid and scared. His voice... makes me feel sick to my stomach. My eyes are on the verge of tears. I can't explain the anger and hatred his voice possesses that could make even the strongest person shiver from fear. My hands tremble, just like they did when I was younger but this time...they're touched by something that calms me down this very second. A warm hand, squeezing mine under the table. It's Arsalan's.

"Adil, control your daughter! Sonia, what have you taught her?! To be disrespectful to her elders?! Raising her voice...at us?! Batameez! You should be ashamed of yourself, Zara! Girls who are outspoken NEVER get married. No family will tolerate a girl like you being married to their son!"

I know hate is a strong word...but I HATE Uncle Ahktar.

"Then they do not deserve my daughter."

My tearful eyes find my dad, looking directly at Uncle Ahktar with conviction. My dad...spoke up for me against him. I never thought I'd ever get to see that.

The room is silent once again. If you could see Uncle Akhtar and Amna Auntie, you would think they're close to exploding into a million pieces from seeing the color of their faces—red as cherry tomatoes.

"Let's go, Ahktar! We've had enough of this humiliation! Your daughter will make your life hell one day if you do not control her, I tell you!"

"Well, then. I wait for that day." Dad chuckles...which brings a smile to mine. "She is not an animal that needs to be controlled. She's a human being...and I've seen more humanity in her than I have in both of you."

Oh...my...Allah. If my eyes weren't already on the verge of tears, they sure are now. My dad has never...NEVER in his life talked back to his older brother. In that moment...I forgave my dad for the times he never stood up for me against him. This is going to kill both of them inside...and from the look of their dropped jaws, it seems like it already has.

They both rise off their chairs and storm towards the door. God, I want to say one last thing but I feel as if I shouldn't since I've already said too much but...screw it! They deserve the taste of their own medicine.

"Oh, and by the way...Myra's dating a white guy. So, before you go around talking about other people's kids, look at your own."

Their eyes widen, lips separate, but nothing comes out. Uncle Ahktar stands there by the doorway like a statue, but gets pulled by the arm by Amna Auntie who's shooting her death stare at me. I couldn't care less at this point.

"Zara, look what you've done!" My mom

runs out the door after them.

"I should go after your mother, she doesn't need to stop them." Dad shakes his head as he jumps off his chair and walks outside with fast steps.

I exhale deeply, trying to slow my flying heart.

"Uh, Zara..." Jace snaps me out of my concentration, "what in your uncle's asshole was that?!" I completely forgot both of them were here, until Arslaan reminded me of his presence by holding my hand...which he's still doing! I glance down at our interlocked hands and loosen mine out of his grip. I'm just going to pretend that...didn't happen.

"I...uh—" Now, I'm at loss for words. I myself didn't know what that was. I guess I was triggered because maybe one day...I'd be in Noor's shoes.

As I'm about to open my mouth to say more, a smell catches my nose. It catches all of us.

"I think something's...burning." Arsalan sniffs the air.

"The samosas!" Jace jumps out of his chair and runs to the kitchen. Me and Arslan do the same. He opens up the oven and smoke comes rushing out. We cough as we inhale it all in. The samosas are as black as the hearts of those two devils that walked out. My mom's going to kill me, which only makes me feel more shitty. I stood up for the right reasons today but why does it feel wrong? Why do I feel guilty?

I throw my hands up and drag my feet outside to the backyard—my one sanctuary. I plop onto the outdoor couch, unwrapping my dupatta from my neck and tossing it beside me. I throw my head back on the couch, looking up at the night sky. It's clear of clouds, making the stars and the moon as bright as can be. It reminds me of the one entity that brings me as much peace as the one in the sky—my AJ. I wish he were here, holding me.

I hear the backdoor slide open, but I don't have the energy to look.

"Hey...you okay?"

It's Arsalan.

"Yeah..." I sigh, propping myself up. "I'll be okay."

"That was...a bit tense." He sits next to me, sinking into the couch.

"Well..." I chuckle, "I guess I finally released all my pent up anger towards them."

"I think they might have received ALL the pent up anger you have against the majority of desi aunties and uncles." He laughs under his breath. "But...they deserved it."

"Don't know if my mom would agree. She's probably furious with me right now."

"She might be. Your dad is talking to her in the guest room."

"Agh, I don't want to hear it." I plant my

face into my hands. "I just want to go home."

"We'll leave whenever you want to, Zara." He scoots closer to me. "But, I want you to know...I'm incredibly proud of you."

My face is no longer in my hands, but moving towards Arsalan's eyes.

"Why?"

He scoots even closer. I can feel the warmth of his breath on my skin.

"Because..." he whispers, "you spoke up for those who haven't been able to do it themselves. I think you took a step closer to making this world a better place. The thing is, you probably know you might not be able to change THEIR minds...but you can choose to not pass down that same outdated mentality to the future generation. And I KNOW you'd move stars to make sure that happens." He faces his body towards me. "Not only am I pretty proud of the present Zara...but I know I'd be proud of the future Zara as well."

His eyes are fixed on mine, and mine are trying to understand...his. That was very kind of him to say...even if I don't feel as courageous as he's making me ought to be.

"Uh...thank you." I divert my eyes from his and fidget with the corner of my kameez. "And, um...thanks for holding my hand."

"It was my pleasure." He pauses. "You were shaking...it broke my heart to see you like that."

From the corner of my eye, I see him rub

his palms together.

"Yeah...I get that way when I see them, especially when he raises his voice like that. Just...bad childhood memories." I shake my head, as if that would make them disappear. "I guess after all these years, it still affects me the same way it did as a child."

Ah...I never thought I'd be confiding to Arsalan about such a vulnerable part of my life. But I guess it's too late since he witnessed the bulk of it within a few hours.

"Well, I think you handled it all like a true 'sherani'."

I turn my head towards him, only to see him smiling at me.

"Sherani? You're calling ME a lioness?" I chuckle at his comparison.

"What's so funny?" He furrows his brows. "You totally were like a little sherani back there! You completely annihilated them! I was watching their faces the whole time and resisted the urge to burst out laughing."

He nudges me with his elbow. I can't help but smile along with him.

"Well, thanks for thinking I am."

His smile fades from his mouth, but not from his eyes.

"Zara...you have no idea what else I think of you."

I know I said he has these unpleasant eyes that seem to search for every hidden thought of mine...but it's not like that anymore. As he's staring into my eyes, I see a sort of yearning...a yearning to be understood.

Our little moment of silence is interrupted by the sliding of the door. Ah, great. My parents are probably here to lecture me. Well, mostly my mom. Arsalan scoots away from me and off the couch. He bows his head at them before making his way into the house. My mom looks...livid. Both sit on the chairs placed on either side of the couch. Here...we...go.

"Zara. I...don't even know where to start," she says with a tone oozing with disappointment. I'm not surprised.

"Mom, I'm...sorry." I'm not really sorry. I'm sorry that my mom's mad.

"You don't have to apologize, Zara." My dad glances at me.

"Adil, she SHOULD apologize. Not to us, but to them."

"Why should I?!" I guess I'm still pissed.

"Because you talked back to your elders! This is not how we raised you!"

"I was just feeding them some logic that they clearly don't have!"

If I've learned one thing from our desi culture is that your opinions to your elders DON'T matter. Your voice DOESN'T matter. If you're younger, there's no way you can ever be right to them! You cannot simply disagree with their values, beliefs, and thoughts because it will never be anything more than just disrespect in their eyes.

"Like this?! Zara, you know how they are! You could have just kept your mouth shut until after they left!"

"No, Mom! I couldn't!"

I swear a vein in my head is going to pop any second now!

"I couldn't because...if I sat there, listening to them...they'd think I agree with their damaging beliefs! And, I don't! I think two people who love each other should be together, regardless of their race or religion. It's not right and you know it!"

"Zara, they were wrong about everything they were saying..." her voice lowers, "but...it does get hard. You don't understand their culture, they don't understand yours...it can be very difficult for both to manage the differences."

Although she didn't disagree with what they said...hearing her say that hurts equally.

"A lot of things in life are hard, Ami. But you try. Why can't anyone understand that you fall in love with someone without looking at the color of their skin or the faith they were born into? Things we have no control over."

I choke on my words. My throat feels as if there are thousands of nails attached, scratching against each escaping syllabus.

"You haven't been in that situation, so you can't understand!" My emotions are taking over me.

"Well, neither have you, Zara!" She throws her hands up, but then...slowly relaxes them onto her lap. "Have you?" She asks, furrowing her brows so hard, a huge bump forms between them.

I gulp as loud as the crickets chirping, trying to hydrate my dry throat. Maybe this is my chance to come clean. Maybe she'd understand...or at least try to.

"No." I blurt out.

I guess I'm not as courageous as Arsalan thinks. Anyone would say no if they heard the way she asked. It was as if she wanted to be assured that I...I wasn't in love with someone who'd make us the talk of the community.

The muscles between her eyebrows relax as she sighs of relief. Guess I made the right choice of not telling her. For now, it will just have to remain a maybe.

"Chalo, beta. Just call them tomorrow to apologize." She calms her voice.

"I'm not going to call." I answer without moving an inch of muscle.

"Zara, please. Don't argue with me!"

Argue? I'm...not arguing, Mom. Can't you see that? I just can't do this anymore.

"Mom..." I close my eyes, "you made me do things I didn't want to as a child just to make others happy. You both neglected and overlooked MY needs as a child and I never complained."

I didn't know I was entitled to having my needs fulfilled. I didn't even know I had any.

"So, please...don't do the same thing you've done to me my whole life. Please make me feel safe, at least now."

My words tremble from my shaky voice.

"What do you mean we neglected your needs?" My mom questions my plea. "We gave you everything you needed—a nice big home, the best food, clothes, car, money. You never had to worry where any of it comes from. How many people out there have all this without having to work for it? You should be thankful you were born with a silver spoon."

And there we go again, making me question my own sanity. Are basic human necessities the only type of 'needs' required for living? Are emotional needs not as important as physical? I guess not.

I remain silent because that's the only thing I can do at this point.

"Zara..." my dad clears his throat, breaking the awkward silence, "you don't have to call them. In fact...we don't have to see them for a while."

A tear wells up at my tear ducts, but I wipe it away before looking at him.

"Thanks, Dad."

"No, um...beta, you don't have to say thanks..." he moves around in his chair, "I'm... sorry."

Anyone with brown parents knows that you'll never hear them apologize to you even if they know they're wrong. They'll probably cut up some fruit and tell you to eat as a form of an apology, but never say those two words. So, to hear him say that...I never thought I'd ever feel at peace hearing those words. I never wanted an apology. I just wanted them to ask if I was okay.

"No, um...it's okay, Dad. It's in the past." I'm not able to look him in his eyes. I feel guilty that he's even apologizing. "Anyways, I should get going. I think the boys have to go."

Before they say anything, I slide off the couch, grabbing my dupatta and throwing it over my shoulder.

"Well, the samosas are burnt but I'll pack the biryani for you guys." Mom says as we walk towards the sliding door.

Through the glass door, I see Jace holding a multipurpose spray and Arsalan cleaning the kitchen island with a microfiber cloth. I chuckle, thinking...how the hell did they find that? It was a cute sight to see though, one that made me smile.

"Oh, no it's okay! Just leave it, I'll clean up, don't worry." My mom forces the cloth and the spray out of their hands. "You both are so sweet for doing this."

"Auntie, you did so much. This is the least we can do." Arsalan smiles. He really does have his way with the aunties...or just my mom.

"Well, if you want to do something for me, eat the biryani I'm sending home with you guys." She taps Arsalan's cheek with her hand, while having the biggest smile on her face. Ah, great. I bet she's picturing him as her son-in-law.

I head upstairs to my room to grab the clothes I was wearing earlier. As I step inside, my phone dings and I see the only name on the screen that could bring a smile to my face instantly—my AJ.

I unlock my screen and click on his message.

My love, I just saw your message from earlier. Got done with practice a little while ago. It was such a long day, but guess who we met?! The Weekend! Me and Lee were fanboying the whole time, haha. Now Lee and I are in Koreatown with the other members for dinner. I wish we could come here together without anyone recognizing me. Maybe we can plan one of our secret dates again? I miss you, meri jaan. <3 How are you doing? Did you eat?

From that sweet text, all I read was 'The Weekend'. AJ and I are CRAZY about him! It's so cute seeing him fanboy over his favorite celebrities. Sometimes I think he forgets that he's a celebrity as well.

What?! The Weekend?! I'm so jealous right now!

I reply, throwing my phone on the bed to get my clothes from the bathroom. A few seconds haven't passed and my phone dings again.

It's him. This is the fastest he's replied in a while.

My love...you didn't answer my questions. Are you okay?

I'm not but...I don't want him to worry about me. There's a lot going on with him already.

Yes. :) Just on my period, but I'm okay :)

I hit send. Blame it on the period. That and a bunch of smiley faces should do the trick...I hope.

"Zara! The boys are ready to go!" My mom shouts from the kitchen.

"Coming!" I grab my clothes and purse, shoving my phone into it.

I rush downstairs and find my parents standing by the doorway.

"They're waiting in the car for you." My dad pats my head.

"Oh, okay. Well...khuda hafiz." I place my clothes and purse all in one hand to give my parents an awkward side hug.

"Khuda hafiz, beta." My mom runs her hand down the back of my hair so lovingly as if she just didn't make me feel like absolute crap. "Oh and...um. Arsalan's...a good boy."

I glance towards my dad, only to see his eyes flick from me to the floor. Desi dads are so awkward when it comes to boys and their daughters. To be fair, this is...pretty awkward. I don't want Dad to know I see boys as more than just friends!

"Uh, yeah. He's okay." I clear my throat. "Anyways, bye guys."

I turn around, heading to the door.

"Um, beta..." my dad calls out, "we...love you."

I give a weak smile and bob my head. Turning away I swallow my heart that's found its way into my throat. I hope you still do when I tell you about AJ.

CHAPTER 6:

*The Music, The Moon, and
The Man on the Billboard*

"Did Arsalan grab his food from my car before he left?" I ask Jace as I wiggle my apartment key into the lock.

"Of course he did. Why would he forget his dream mother-in-law's food?" He laughs as I push open the door.

"Ha, ha. So funny." I roll my eyes, setting the keys down on the entrance table.

"It's a little funny."

"Not really," I argue, kicking my shoes off and placing them in the corner of the entryway.

"Hold up." He waves his index finger in the air like a sassy queen, then latches two fingers onto the knob of the hallway cabinet, swinging it wide open. Rummaging through the sea of blankets, he pulls out my favorite—a navy blue, fluffy galore one.

"Here." He tosses the blanket to me. It unfolds open in the air, landing perfectly on my shoulder.

"What the hell is this for?" I brush it off of my shoulder and set it on our couch.

"Oh, I thought you might need it since you're acting so cold!"

"I'm not acting cold!" My nostrils flare on their own. Oh, shit. Okay, maybe I am.

"Yes, you are. You barely said two words to me and Arsalan in the car, especially him since he was the one actually trying to talk to you."

"Well, sorry if I wasn't in the mood to talk."

He sighs and walks towards me, wrapping his arms around my tiny, wimpy self.

"I know, bubs. I'm sorry. I was trying to make you laugh."

"You're not doing such a great job." I let out a quiet chuckle.

"Clearly, I am now."

I wiggle out of his arms.

"I'm sorry, I didn't mean to be rude. I just had a lot going through my head on the drive back."

"Yeah, I figured you did from the way you were driving like a crazy person. You kept looking out at the moon the whole time like a main character. I was afraid I wasn't going to make it back home."

"Very funny." I nudge his shoulder. "I can't

organize my thoughts. Everything happened so fast. I can't remember what I even said or what was said to me."

"Well, from where I was sitting, it seemed like you finally let out what you've been waiting your whole life to say."

"I did. There were years of pent up anger in those words. You know, I always imagined that it'd feel so good to let it all out finally, and it did...for the most part. But, I don't feel satisfied."

"Really? It wasn't satisfying seeing them almost shit their pants?" He chuckles, pulling out his phone from his pocket, glancing at the screen, and shoving it back in.

"It's...not that. I just know that my words probably didn't resonate with them. They won't change their ways or minds, just like the many others in this world who also have the same hatred in their hearts. It just makes me feel unsettled knowing this cycle of hate and division will continue from generation to generation, no matter how many of us make the effort to change it."

"Listen," he places his hands on either side of my shoulders, pulling me in closer, "as bad as this sounds, you can only do so much to change others. Rarely do people open their hearts and minds to new perspectives because if it shakes the beliefs and values that they've known their whole lives, it means they'd have to question every single thing that has been told to them. They'll be confused, just like we were when the results of the presidential election came out three years ago." We chuckle, but mine ends with a snort, which makes Jace laugh. "All you can do is stand up for what you believe in. And from the looks of it, it seems like you won't have a problem doing that, my little feisty, sexy Pakistani princess."

"I know, you're right."

"Now, is that all that's bothering you?"

He knows me too well. That isn't the only thing that's been on my mind. My mom's words keep replaying in my head, which makes me frustrated, stuck in this state of screaming internally because she doesn't understand. But I just want to move past this day and not talk anymore. There was too much of that today.

"Yup, that's all."

"Alright," he pulls his phone out of his pocket again and the screen lights up, "why don't you go into your room and freshen up."

"Agh, yes. A hot shower might wash away this day." I groan, dragging my feet to my room.

"Uh—maybe wait to take a shower." He pauses.

"Why?"

"Well—I was thinking we could go out for a drink!" Again, his screen lights up.

"Jace, it's like nine at night."

"And? Has that ever stopped us before?" He raises a brow.

"Um, yes. It has."

"Come on, okay. Just this once. Please?" Jace makes a puppy dog face. Ah, he looks adorable.

"Agh...okay, but just this once! We're getting too old for this." I shut the door behind me.

"Okay, Grandma! Speak for yourself!" His faint shout seeps through my door.

I walk to my mirror and stand there, staring at my reflection as I wipe the smeared mascara under my eyes so I look less of a racoon. As I do, I picture AJ standing behind, nestling one of his veiny hands around my waist and pulling me in closer and tightly against his body. I'd give anything to have that right this second...to feel the warmth of his skin comfort my own.

Knock knock.

Ah, shit. I got to get ready.

"One second, Jace!"

I hurry to my closet and pull out a pair of dark wash skinny jeans. I take off my 'shalwar' and force myself into each pant leg, hopping on one foot to balance myself and...ouch! What the—where did this wall come from?! Agh, my elbow feels as if someone smashed it with a hammer. Okay, that's a bit dramatic. It's more like a wooden spoon.

Knock knock.

Jesus! He's so impatient!

"At least let me zip up my pants!" I hobble towards the door, zipping up with one hand as the other twists the door knob. "Oh my gosh,

Jace! You're so freaking—"

"Hi, my love."

My stomach tumbles in excitement hearing that Australian accent coming out of his dimpled smiley mouth.

"AJ?!"

My arms open and wrap themselves around his neck, and immediately I feel a sense of relief throughout my body. The jarring day and the dull pain radiating in my elbow are all wiped away.

"Yes, my universe." He laughs, placing the unoccupied hand around my waist and giving it a gentle squeeze. "It's me, bearing treats for my little baby."

Treats? I pull back to see a white shopping bag that's holding onto dear life from ripping and a drink carrier with three In-N-Out ice cream shakes.

"What's all this?" I ask.

"Well…you texted saying you were on your period. So, I brought you a big bag of Kit Kats, Cool Ranch Doritos, a bottle of Midol, a heating pad, and socks that have the moon on it. Oh, and a chocolate shake."

My misty eyes stare at his beautiful face as I sigh from admiring this specimen of man. He makes me feel so safe and taken care of. I have a hard time accepting his love at times, especially when he's spoiling me. I know that's how relationships are supposed to be where you take care of each other, but normally in the past, the very few, short-lived 'situationships' I've been in, it was always me giving more than I received. And, I was okay with that. No one ever went out of their way to make sure I felt okay when I wasn't. AJ makes me feel seen, appreciated, and heard, even when I don't ask to be. How can I not fall in love with him, this human being with the most generous soul? How can anyone say this isn't right? How can this love built on care and respect be wrong to others? Agh, I gotta stop thinking about dinner! Stop thinking and kiss him, Zara, you idiot!

I place my hand behind the nape of his neck, feeling the coolness of his dainty silver hoop brush against my hand, and pull him close to my face. Staring into his eyes, I lean in before closing mine to kiss those plumpy, pink lips of his. If I start losing my memory at some point in my life, I feel like I'll always remember the taste of his luscious lips—minty vanilla.

I pull away, just enough to look up at his eyes.

"What was that for, love?" he whispers.

"That was a thank you kiss," I whisper back, tightening my arms around his waist and resting my forehead against his chest.

"You never have to say thank you, baby." He twirls a strand of my hair with his finger. "The moment you became my girlfriend, it became my job to take care of you no matter what.

I promised you that I always will. You're my little 'jaan'."

I giggle at 'jaan' as he brushes gentle strokes on the back of my head.

"Still...thank you, AJ. This means the world to me."

"And it would mean the world to ME if you drink your chocolate shake before it melts." He reaches around me and grabs a cup from the carrier. I unwrap my arms and pull back,

grabbing the shake while laying a quick peck at the top of his nose.

"When did you get the time to get all this?"

"Zara...I think at times you forget I'm a K-Pop star."

"Okay? That doesn't explain much." I raise a brow.

"It doesn't?" He laughs with a cocky glint to his eyes. "I got a guy. It's that simple."

AJ flicks the tip of my nose.

"Yeah, okay. It's THAT simple." I say in a playfully mocking tone. "Some of us don't have butlers. We have to drag our asses to get the things we need."

"I don't have a butler."

I tilt my head to the side, raising my brows while sipping on the shake I'm giving him shit for. I love messing with him.

He chuckles and says, "Also..." placing the shopping bag and the remaining shakes on the coffee table, "I...know what happened."

He knows what happened? Is he like Edward Cullen from *Twilight* who can read minds?

"What do you mean?" I set my shake down on the table, waiting to hear what he knows.

AJ locks both of his hands to mine.

"There was something off about your text...and I had a feeling it wasn't just because of your period." He pauses with worry on his ethereal face. "You never send smiley faces. At least not two in the same sentence. So, I texted Jace, and he told me what happened. Hence this mini surprise."

Ah, that Jace. I can't even be mad at him because he knew seeing AJ would make me forget everything. I'm kind of glad he did because I would've never mentioned it to AJ.

"Oh...that explains why he was checking his phone so much." I bob my head, laughing it off, but AJ's eyes are on me with no trace of a smile on his face.

"Zara...I don't know why you feel the need to hide things from me." He tightens his fingers around mine. "I know you try not to make me worried, but of course I'm going to worry about you. You worry about those you love, especially the person you're dating. How would you feel if I kept things that upset me all to myself?"

Fair question...and one I do not have the answer to.

He loosens his grip from one of my hands and makes a hook with his finger to lift my chin up.

"Hmm?"

Oh, he expects me to answer it.

"I would feel...like I'm not your girlfriend?"

Is that the right answer?

"Yeah, exactly." He nods with a wrinkled forehead. "I'm your boyfriend. If there's one person you can turn to, it's ME. Well, besides Jace." We chuckle at the same time. "Your worries are my worries. What upsets you, upsets me. What hurts you, hurts me more than anything. Don't you see you're a part of me?" The frustration in his voice matches his furrowed brows and puppy eyes. "Promise me you won't hide anything from me again."

"Mhmm." I purse my lips.

"No, I don't want this 'mhmm' bullshit." Still having his finger under my chin, he presses his thumb right below my bottom lip. "Say I promise." His concerned eyes widened at his request.

"I promise."

"Good girl." He exhales loudly, pulling me in for a tight hug. "We're a team, my love. We take care of each other. I'm your boyfriend and that means something to me. I don't care how busy I am, I will ALWAYS be there to listen and help in any way I can."

Not a word comes out from either of our mouths. The only sound that has my attention is his beating heart as we rub our hands down each other's backs. I can't thank Allah enough for sending this gem into my life. I thought boyfriends like him only existed in movies and books—which seem to be written by female writers, hence why they're so desirable in the first place—but boy was I wrong. They exist in the real world, too. But...only as a Korean-Austrailian K-Pop star.

Knock knock.

AJ and I turn our heads to the door. It cracks slightly open. Jace's head peeks in.

"I hope I'm not interrupting anything?"

"No, you're not." I chuckle, unhooking my arms around AJ's waist.

"Oh, okay, good. I thought y'all might be doing the nasty, so I waited a few minutes longer." He grins like the Grinch as he walks in, shutting the door behind him.

"Jace!" I snap at him, but AJ bursts out laughing.

"What?" He enunciates the 't'. "You should be thankful I'm so considerate."

"AND thank you for that," AJ says while still laughing. "Here, I got you a strawberry shake—your favorite." He takes the shake out of the carrier and hands it to Jace.

"Aw, baby boy...you shouldn't have." Jace takes a sip and closes his eyes. "But this tastes like the milky streams from heaven. Thank you."

"No problem at all. I'm happy you like it."

"Speaking of 'happy'...the car is all ready to go."

"Car?" I question Jace's lewd comment. What the hell is going on?

"Yes, car. Your little superstar boyfriend is taking you on a little adventure."

"AJ?"

"It's a surprise. We have four hours, so go get ready!" He catches a glimpse of my 'kameez' and jeans and his eyes light up like the Eiffel Tower at night. "How did I not notice you wearing this? Or your nose ring! Wow. Wow. You look like a Pakistani princess."

"Princess, my ass." I let out a laugh. "I'll change the top real quick."

I turn away from him, heading towards my room but he grabs my wrist.

"No, don't. I like it."

"Are you kidding me? I can't go out like this!" I look down at my colorful 'kameez'. "People always stare."

After the nine-eleven terrorist attacks, the few times I've worn shalwar-kameez outside of my house, I've gotten some...interesting looks from people which made me incredibly uncomfortable. Their whispers lowered my head in shame that I didn't deserve to feel. I was never sure if they were admiring the intricate designs and jewels on my clothes or associating me as 'one of them'. Dad asked my mom and I to stop wearing them outside of the house after hate crimes directed towards Muslims or anyone who fit the image became headlines of every news channel shortly after the attacks. I haven't worn any traditional Pakistani clothing in public since I was eight years old. I've had to suppress the one joy of my identity in order to feel safe in my own country.

"So? Let them. You literally look like a princess." AJ brings his palms together and rests them against his lips as his admiring eyes scan me from head to toe. "Plus, I—your prince—will protect you. You know that."

I hesitate, but a part of me really, really wants to.

"Ah, alright. You've convinced me."

"I knew I could." He kisses my forehead with those cloud-like lips.

"Ew, get a room." Jace diverts his eyes while slurping on his strawberry shake. "Anyways, have fun! AJ, there's the blanket you asked for." His mischievous eyes gesture to the couch. "Don't get caught doing the nasty in the car."

He winks at both of us, leaving AJ's face and ears bright red. Why is he blushing? I can't help but laugh at the sight, wanting to see more of it.

Jace prances past us to his room with a delinquent smile.

"Stop laughing." AJ covers his ears.

"Okay, okay. I'm done." I smack my hand over my mouth, holding in my escaping laugh.

"Anyways..." AJ plucks my hand off of my mouth, spins me around and hugs me from behind. "Ready to go?"

"Yup." I run my fingers along one of the sleeves of his black hoodie. "AJ, it's spring in California. People leave their countries to vacation here just so they don't have to wear these."

"Oh, should I take it off?" he asks, burying his face in the nape of my neck.

"Yes, unless you want to sweat through your hoodie."

"I have no problem taking it off..." he whispers, brushing his lips along my neck, "but the problem is..." I feel the corner of his soft lips come to a rest against my ear, exciting goosebumps throughout my skin, "I'm not wearing anything underneath."

When I say my jaw dropped open, I don't mean it figuratively. I mean it...literally.

I clear my throat and reply with almost a whisper, "Well, then you should definitely keep it on."

"Alright, my love. Whatever you say."

Even though I can't see his face right now, I know he said it with his unforgiving eyes and cocky grin.

"I'm gonna go get some shoes." I untangle his arms off of me and slip into my tan Tory Burch sandals that I got on sale from Nordstrom last month, conveniently sitting by the entrance table.

He digs through the white shopping bag and pulls out a disposable camera.

"Wow, I haven't seen one of these in ages." I handle the camera out of his hand as if it were a delicate artifact. "Why'd you buy this?"

"Because..." he takes it from me, "it's going to capture our little adventure in more of an aesthetic way. I don't know, I always liked the quality of these over our phones. All my pictures from my childhood seem so classic because of these bad boys. Plus, it captures the moment without giving us the option to go back and alter it. Kinda cruel, huh?" He winks. "Here, smile!"

Click.

"AJ, I wasn't even ready!"

"Baby, I'm sure you look beautiful as always." He caresses my face with his warm hand. My, my. They're always so warm. "Okay, we gotta go, baby. We're losing time!"

"Okay, okay!" I grab the blanket off the couch.

"Um, excuse me. What do you think you're doing? I'LL carry that."

He snatches it out of my grip.

"You can carry the camera and our shakes." And hands it to me.

"Alright, so are we taking Jace's car?"

"Yes, I asked if we can borrow it since it's bigger."

"Okay, I'll drive."

"Uh, no. I'LL drive."

"Um—are you sure?"

"Yes, Zara. I drive in Korea, too...sometimes."

"I know that. But you've never driven in America."

"Zara." He responds in a frustrated tone. "Just trust me, okay?"

If anyone were to see him this second, you'd think he's a little child convincing a parent they're old and smart enough to handle big tasks.

"Alright, my dear. I trust you." I tiptoe and pat his head. "You can drive, but if at any point you feel scared, you let me know, okay?"

"Yes, Mom." He rolls his eyes, shooting me a look of annoyance. "Let's go."

I grab the shakes and gently place the camera inside my purse. L.A. isn't ready to handle the cuteness of my little surprise adventure with my K-Pop prince.

◆ ◆ ◆

"You did really well, AJ." I rub the top of his thigh.

"Yeah, I was until you yelled at me." He parks the car with a pout.

"I didn't yell."

I totally did.

"I just...stopped you from making a left turn when the car was coming from the other side with...a slightly loud tone."

I feel so bad.

"I yelled at you for YOU."

"For ME?!" He rotates his body towards me, crossing his arms.

"Uh, yeah." I elongate the 'yeah' to buy time to think of a good reason for brutally yelling at this little teddy bear. "A K-Pop prince is in this car, and I did NOT want to be the girl who gets killed by one, since I'd probably be the one that dies on impact. Do you want to get arrested for manslaughter? And then you can say goodbye to K-Pop! Do you want that?!"

Still having his arms crossed, he squints his eyes at me and purses his lips, as if he's trying to understand this totally unnecessary dark explanation.

"My love, I love you, but...you come up with the strangest stuff at times. I don't know what goes on in that gorgeous head of yours." He chuckles, which makes me feel better.

"You don't want to know." I reach over and plant a kiss on his freckled, supple, bare cheek. I didn't notice before, but he looks different—he looks...tan. Are my eyes playing tricks on me? "Also, why are we at Rodeo Drive? All the shops are closed."

"I know. That's exactly why we're here." He peeps out the window.

We're parked beside Lacoste, across the street from Valentino. All of Rodeo is lit with fluorescent lights, making the glittery luxurious brand names pop out more. The swaying palm trees on every side are adorned with amber colored string lights which look like fireflies. There's no one else, not a single being in sight.

I reach for the handle to open my door.

"Zara, what are you doing?" He gasps as if I've done something terribly wrong.

"Uh, opening the door to get out? Unless you much rather prefer having our little adventure in the car."

That sounds...wrong. So wrong.

He smirks, which quickly slips into a scowl.

"I'm glad you didn't or else I would have shoved your head back in and then opened your door. That's MY job. You know that. Just...let me be your boyfriend, okay?!" His theatrical cry makes me throw my head back in laughter. He's the walking definition of funny and cute.

"Okay, okay! Sorry, jeez!"

And they say chivalry is dead. Well, it is but men like him are keeping it alive...thank god.

He sticks his tongue out at me, shining his dimpled smile, and hops out of Jace's 2009 Jeep Wrangler while pulling out the black beanie from the pocket of his hoodie. Then he skips to the passenger side, gathers his purple hair into the beanie, and opens my door like a true gentleman.

"Milady." He offers his hand.

"Thank you, my dear." I grip onto his soft

veiny hand—which also seems to have a tan—for support and leap out.

"You're welcome. Now, we need the camera."

"Oh, it's in my purse."

"I'll grab that for you, love. Can you check if there's a bin around so I can throw away our cups?"

"AJ, the 'BIN' is literally right behind us." I point at the trash can that is visibly in the perimeter of our sight.

"Okay. Damn, girl. You're so cheeky today." AJ laughs, reaching over me to pick my purse from the seat and the empty shake cups from the cup holder. "I like it."

"Well, that's me. Cheeky Zara." I wink, which probably looks like a sad eye twitch.

"Okay, Ms. Cheeky," he mocks, throwing away the cups in the trash can, "can we go on with our little adventure?"

"Lead the way."

He lifts my arm and slides it through the loop of the handle of my purse, adjusting it on my shoulder.

"So, the purpose of this little escapade is to be silly."

Uh, come again?

"Be silly?"

"Yeah, be silly. Laugh. Sing. Dance, I don't know!" He shrugs his broad shoulders. "Let's just pretend we're in a poorly written rom-com movie."

"Okay...and what does a poorly written rom-com entail?"

"Playing a game."

"Uh-huh, go on."

"I'm going to say one of the shop's names around here and the first person to find it wins."

"That sounds...horrible. I LOVE it." My eager hands make tiny claps, exactly the way he does. Jesus, he's definitely rubbing off on me.

"It does, doesn't it?!" He chuckles, pulling out his phone and clicking on the search engine with his boney finger. "Okay, the first shop on the list is...Tiffany & Co., do you know where that is?"

"No." I act naive. I totally know where that is.

"Good, because if you did that wouldn't be fair." He squints, assessing if I'm telling the truth or blatantly lying.

"Oh, I completely agree. It wouldn't be."

"Alright, ready?"

"Ready." I raise a confident thumbs up.

"Okay, I'm gonna count in Korean."

He clears his throat.

"Hana."

I take a step backwards. His eyes land on my feet and his head tilts in suspicion but doesn't say a word.

"Dul."

Another step back, but this time he steps forward. He knows. My roguish smirk completely gave it away. But, I don't care.

He licks his bottom lip and chuckles, shaking his head in disappointment with a glimmer of playfulness in his eyes.

"Set!"

And Usain Bolt's spirit has entered my body. I turn around and bolt past some shops I occasionally window shop since I can't afford some of them just yet.

"Zara, you little liar!" I hear him behind me. "I knew it!"

The blinding lights reflect off the windows, making me partially dizzy and slowing my pace. Agh, these damn sandals! I know I have an advantage over him by knowing where the store is, but he has one on me, too! He's running comfortably in his gray Prada sneakers, while I look like I have something stuck up in my ass.

"I'm gonna get you!"

Shit, it didn't take long for him to catch up! I turn my head around and catch a glimpse of him practically gliding down the sidewalk. He's running so fast, it seems as if he's flying! My god, my weak ass legs are already giving up on me. Gah! No, keep running, Zara! He doesn't know his way around. Well, neither do I really, but I know way more. I sprint ahead, dashing across the crosswalk. He catches up to me and slows to my pace, running side by side. Smirking, he races straight ahead, but he's going completely the wrong way! Ha! I turn left, galloping past the famous landmark of Rodeo Drive—the silver lady who has no limbs or a face.

"Zara!" I hear his distant cry.

"Suck it!" Although I'm huffing and puffing, that managed to still come out of my mouth.

"Ha, you thought!"

His voice seems closer. I turn my head back, only to see him a few feet away from me! I run faster, exerting my wonky knees, but before I can take my next breath, he's speeding past me with a stupid grin on his face. He's not even out of breath! I know K-Pop stars have a lot of vigor but how the—

"Ah!" And in a blink of an eye, I trip over my own feet! My arms fly open but I hold onto my purse as if there were thousands of dollars stashed in it.

"Zara!" AJ stops his tracks, spins around in a panic, and dives down to catch me before I even hit the sidewalk. His arms take a hold of my waist, supporting me up as we fall down—me on his body and him on the concrete, right in front of Stefano Ricci. "Ah!"

"AJ, are you okay?!"

"Uh—yeah." He moans in pain. "My bum broke the fall, but I'm fine."

"Good thing you have a nice big one."

I wait for his reaction.

There's a moment of silence, but then we both burst into uncontrollable laughter in each other's arms.

"All thanks to my wide pelvis."

He scoots me closer to him, positioning me between his legs as we stay sitting there. He locks me in his arms by tightening them around me, propping his warm face between the nape of my neck.

"This is so nice." His warm breath grazes my skin as he whispers. "Oh and uh—I did something slightly cheesy."

"Cheesy?"

He reaches into his pocket and pulls out his phone.

"I think it's cute, but I think you might think it's cheesy."

AJ unlocks his phone and opens Spotify. A playlist pops up titled with a capital 'a', heart emoji, and a capital 'z'.

A <3 Z

The first song in the playlist is called "Moonlight" by Chase Atlantic—one of our favorites.

"What's this?"

"It's our playlist."

He scrolls through. There's a wide spectrum of genre here, from Ed Sheeran and Paul Anka to Usher and The Weekend. "I added some songs that remind me of you...of us."

"Oh yeah?" I glance intently at each and every one of them, but my eyes come to a halt at a particular one: "Head In The Clouds" by Joji and

88rising. "Head In The Clouds, huh?" I giggle.

"My favorite...probably because a beautiful memory is attached to it." He lays a lingering kiss on my tan, blushed cheek.

"A beautiful one indeed." I smile, thinking of that very unforgettable moment back in Korea.

Setting his phone on my lap, he pulls out a white AirPod case from the other pocket and pops it open.

"Here." Handing me an earpiece. "Put this in your ear."

"Oh, in my ear? I was gonna put it in my mouth." I wiggle the Apple creation into my ear while proudly smirking at my snarky comment.

"You know," he clicks his tongue, "you're lucky you're having a bad day or else..."

"Or else what?" I hold my gaze at him.

His stunned eyes are always so rewarding to my inner demon.

But I'm not the only one who has a devilish grin right now. He places his thumb on one side of my face and tightens his fingers on the other. With a gentle squeeze, he turns my face away from his gaze towards the intersection of Dayton Way and Rodeo Drive. He lowers his lips, hovering perfectly above my ear and grunts, "You're gonna wish you kept that sassy mouth of yours shut."

What the—what in the Christian Grey was that?! I gulp, choking on my own saliva like a starstruck teenager. Till this day, I'm always amazed at how quickly he can change his whole demeanor within seconds apart, keeping me on my toes. Funny and cute? No, no. Those aren't the only two characteristics that define this reincarnation of Apollo. Add in seductive and slightly domineering, respectfully. He's the epitome of both sweet and spicy.

"Anyways, princess..." he rasped, pushing my hair back so tenderly with the same intimidating hand that just held my dazed face, "let's sit here, in the middle of L.A.'s greatest tourist attraction and travel back to 1959."

He pushes the other AirPod into his ear, picks his phone off of my lap and scrolls through the playlist.

"When I'm stressed, sometimes I listen to this song and imagine you and I slow dancing at some fancy 1950s bar looking all dapper."

Scrolling all the way to the bottom of the playlist, he clicks on "Put Your Head On My Shoulder" by Paul Anka. As soon as the song starts, I lay my head on one of his broad shoulders. We both giggle at my cheesy gesture. Figured since we're already way past the cheesiness, might as well go all the way.

But, my god. This moment, this sight, this warmth—impeccable. My flushed skin is kissed by the cool, crisp California breeze. The balmy night of spring is decorated with faint stars in the sky. And the moon...she's glowing, peeping through two swaying palm trees that seem to be dancing to Paul Anka's famous tune.

"Zara, let's take a picture. Can you take out the camera, please?"

"Oh, yes." I unzip my little Longchamp and hunt through my Mary Poppins bag. "Here." I fish it out from a sea of random crap and hand it to him.

"Alright." He flips the camera with the flash facing us–the original way to take a selfie. "Ready?"

"Ready." I pat down my hair.

"Hana, dul, set! Cheese!"

Click.

"It sucks we can't see it right away," I complain.

"That's the beauty behind it, baby girl." He sets the camera beside him on the ground.

"So, who won the game?" I ask, slowly rocking side to side to the song.

"Hmm…" he takes a moment to think, "you did."

"I did?"

How?!

"Yes, because you knew where the store was. I'm sure you would have won despite me being faster than you." He teases with a chuckle.

"So…do I get a prize?" My eyes light up like a kid getting candy.

"Well, what do you want?"

Oh, AJ. What a dangerous question you've

asked my yearning soul. What do I want? Isn't it obvious? It's you. You now, you tomorrow, you every day. Could you possibly give me that?

"A new memory with you." My eyes return to his adoring gaze.

He stares back at me with one of the warmest half-smiles one could ever see.

"That can be arranged." Without another word, he jumps up onto his feet. "Princess." He extends his hand to me.

Holding onto his hand, I stand up, smoothing out the wrinkles of my 'kameez'. He takes my purse off of my shoulder, and lays it beside the camera. He grabs my hand and places it on top of his shoulder, giving it a gentle tap. Placing a hand behind my waist, he pulls me close to his body. I feel the roughness of his hoodie and taut muscles through my thin 'kameez'. Taking my other hand, he positions it comfortably between his thumb and fingers. We're perfectly in a closed dance hold as they say.

"What are we doing?" I ask, even though I have a tiny inkling of what's about to happen.

"Making a new memory."

He kisses my forehead, slowly swaying his body to the song just like the trees. Mine becomes in sync with his, and suddenly, I'm in a 1950s bar with him. He's in a black suit, hair slicked back, playing with a curled strand of mine. I'm in a red swing dress, rocking a red lip. Now, if only we could travel back in time to live this little realm of fantasy. But, that's the thing about how he makes me feel. I don't need a time traveling machine to feel completely and absolutely out of my own little world—I have him.

Our eyes are glued to each other, refusing to look away. There could be a meteor shower going on but it wouldn't tempt me to avert my eyes from his wanting, alluring stare. I don't need to look up at the night sky to be star lost—I can just stare into his twinkling eyes. I see a whole galaxy in them. When he looks at me with his soulful eyes, I can't help but to forget every worry that keeps me up at night. They speak without expressing a single syllable. His seeking eyes ask if I'm feeling the depth of each and every word of the song that fills our ears. I reply with a simple loving smile as confirmation. We chuckle as we exchange shy glances—this very moment has become a scene in a K-drama. The dazzling lights of the shops have blurred. The light kiss of the temperate breeze on my skin is replaced with the warm touch of his hands. The desire to continue dancing with him grows each fleeting second. I guess this is the euphoric feeling directors and writers try to show in movies and books when the characters are dancing carelessly under the moonlight, getting completely drenched in the rain with their lover. It's not meant to be awkward or uncomfortable. It's supposed to make you feel young and alive. You may think you're in love with someone, but…if they don't make you want to dance under the rain with them, then they're simply not the one.

"I want to dance in the rain with you," I blurt out without blinking.

He smiles, showing his sparkling pearly whites and deep dimples.

"That's what was going through your head for the past few seconds?"

"Mhmm." I nod with googly eyes.

"I promise you, my love…one day we will. Okay?"

He kisses the top of my head and lays me against his chest, tangling his slender fingers through my raven black hair as we continue to sway to the music

"Oh, aren't you two the sweetest!"

I hear a faint shriek of a woman. We jump out of each other's arms. I pull the AirPod out from my ear which promptly stops the music. There's an elderly interracial couple—probably in their seventies—standing a few feet away from us with the friendliest smiles on their faces. The fair petite woman is dressed in a long, emerald green summer dress, jeweled with a pearl necklace and earrings, topped off with a black Chanel bag. The tall, slim gentleman is wearing a crisp white button-down styled with shiny silver cufflinks, and tucked in black slacks—all complimenting his deep brown skin tone.

Hopefully, they don't recognize him. I mean, they're old. I'd be surprised if they knew who Justin Bieber is.

"Oh, hello, ma'am." AJ switches to his American accent. He places his hand on his chest and slightly bows to them out of respect. God, he's such a man with exquisite grace.

They walk towards us hand in hand.

"Hello, dear," she replies with an endearing smile.

"So sorry to bother you kids." The gentleman apologizes with a soft-spoken voice as he places his wrinkled hand behind the woman's waist. "My wife and I were on a stroll and saw you two dancing. She insisted on coming over to talk to the beautiful couple."

"Oh, I couldn't help it!" She brings her excited hands together. "Seeing you two reminded me of when WE were young. Remember, Will? We used to sneak out late at night and meet at the park around the corner of my old middle school?"

He smiles ear to ear recalling the memory —must be a really nice one from the look of it.

"How can I ever forget that, my love?" He strokes her cheek, making her blush as if she were still a teenage girl.

AJ and I eye each other hearing him say 'my love', giggling under our breaths. Mr. Will seems to be an older version of my sweet, sweet AJ.

"We fell in love because of music." Ah, there's that smile of his again. He has this smile

I'd imagine Santa to have—warm and jolly. "I was walking to this ice cream shop with my friends one summer afternoon, cracking jokes about something you would expect a stupid teenage boy to make...when I heard this angelic voice singing my favorite song."

"Be My Baby by The Ronettes." She adds with a twinkle in her eyes, "It was a very popular song back in our day."

"And it deserved to be." My little musician agrees.

"Oh, my dear. That song lit up the world. It played at every corner of Los Angeles. My friends and I would sing at the top of our lungs everywhere we went. And, I remember that day I met Will. I was singing along with my friends and caught him staring at me with his mouth wide open."

"Yes, and I'm not ashamed of that one bit, my beautiful bride." He tosses a tender smile at his wife. "It's beautiful what music can do, isn't it?"

"It certainly is." I give AJ the same smile as Mr. Will. It IS beautiful how music has the power to bring people together and my AJ gets to be a part of that.

"You two truly took us back in time tonight. We didn't get to see each other as much because our parents didn't approve of us dating, so we had to meet in secret. Things were a lot different back in our time, as I'm sure you can imagine." Even though it's been years, you can still hear the sorrow in her voice.

"People believed you could only fall in love with those who have the same skin color as you." Mr. Will scoffs. "Our parents held the same belief, but...Mary and I didn't."

"We knew if we got caught, our parents would go to the extremes to make sure we didn't see each other anymore. And at times for Will's safety, I'd think maybe it's best if we went our separate ways, but the thought of being apart from him...oh, it brought me nothing but great sadness."

As both glance at each other with the pain they must have felt back then, I feel AJ's hand find mine, squeezing tightly. Is that how he feels about us? Does the thought of us not being together bring him intense agony? Because it does to me. More than I can even imagine.

"But I guess we were written in the stars, weren't we, Mary?" He tries to bring a smile back to her face. "So, whatever time we found to be together, we'd just dance to our favorite songs and talk the night away. Nothing mattered during those moments. We'd forget about everything—everything that was happening in our lives."

"Is that what you two are trying to do?" she inquires with a teasing smile.

"You could say that." AJ replies, smiling...though it seems like he's hiding a million thoughts behind it.

"Is that your camera on the ground, son?" Mr. Will points.

"Yes, sir." AJ nods, turning around to catch a sight of it.

"Oh! Would you like us to take a picture of you two? This is the perfect view!" Mrs. Mary asks, bringing her eager hands together.

Mrs. Mary sounds awkward. Should I call her Mrs. Will? Or just Mary? Ah, Mrs. Mary is fine. I'm always confused as to how to address the elderly without an honorific. It just sounds so disrespectful calling them by their name, which is why I have so many 'aunties' and 'uncles' even though I'm not related to them at all. Okay, completely off topic, Zara!

"Actually..." he glances at me with questioning eyes but then answers, "that would be amazing, thank you."

AJ walks over, picks the camera up and hands it to Mr. Will.

"Wow, I haven't held one of these in forever, son. I forgot how to use them." He laughs while keenly admiring the relic. "Okay, you two kids ready?" He levels the camera to his eyes and looks through the viewfinder.

"No, Will! Go around them, get the moon and the trees behind them!"

"Oh yes, if you could do that please, that would be awesome! My girlfriend LOVES the moon!"

AHK, my heart! Girlfriend? He called me

his girlfriend! I know it sounds stupid, but hearing him say that in front of someone else leaves me giddy and warm. I don't get the pleasure of hearing it often.

"Not a problem!" Mr. Will and Mrs. Mary bounce around us. "Okay, ready now?"

AJ places his hand around my waist and brings me close to him, leaning his head on top of mine.

"Ready." AJ shoots a thumbs up.

"Oneeee, twooo, three!"

Click.

"Kids, okay, now look into each other's eyes!" Mrs. Mary squeals like a cheerleader.

AJ and I glance at each other awkwardly, blushing as if we were being teased in middle school.

"Oh, come on, kids! You're young and in love! Let the camera capture it, too!" Mr. Will supports his wife.

With a loud sigh, AJ and I look into each other's eyes with the utmost shyness. It's a bit awkward since we have two pairs of eyes on us, but it's a little funny—a moment I don't think we'd forget.

"One, two, three!"

Click.

"Beautiful!" Mrs. Mary shouts as AJ and I look away, blushing with a sheepish smile.

"Here, son." Mr. Will hands over the camera to AJ with a smile which fades into a tilted head with squinting eyes. Shit, he doesn't recognize him, does he? "You look familiar."

No matter how many times I've heard people question AJ the same thing, it never fails to make my teeth grind in worry.

Mrs. Mary stops and stares at AJ in the same way as her husband, but unlike her husband, a light bulb goes off in her head from the way her jaw drops.

"You look so much like the cute boy on the billboard down the street! Oh, he's in this band, I can't remember the name. Our granddaughter pointed them out the other day. She's a HUGE fan."

"Oh, I get that a lot." AJ hides his nervousness behind a laugh, but his ears reveal how he's feeling.

It's funny how many have noticed that he looks a lot like himself, yet no one has ever questioned or thought it might really be him. Probably because they wouldn't think that the man from the billboard would be dating someone like me—a girl who will never get to be on one.

"Well, you're very handsome, dear." She pinches AJ's cheek, radiating a grandmotherly aura.

"You're too kind, ma'am. Thank you so much." His ears turn more red than they already are.

"Anyways, you kids go on with your night." Mr. Will shines that jovial smile that matches his wife.

"Thank you for letting us be a part of it." Mrs. Mary steps closer to AJ, giving him a hug which makes her seem so small in his arms.

"No, thank YOU for being a part of it," I thank the spirited woman who just made our night. "I'll never forget you two." Shit, I'm about to cry. AGH, my period blues are going to flood Rodeo Drive with my tears.

"Oh, my dear! We won't forget you either!" She leaps out of his arms and wraps hers around me. Her affectionate hug is warm and homey—like a hot cup of cocoa with marshmallows. It's the hug you'd want after a heartbreak from your grandma. "You are a beautiful couple. And you, my dear, are so incredibly gorgeous…along with that outfit. I was admiring it the whole time."

My outfit? She likes MY outfit—the one ensemble that I was ashamed to wear because of a demeaning stereotype others created out of ignorance. But, at this moment, it wasn't seen as that. It was appreciated—a joy I didn't think I'd ever experience.

"Thank you so much. You have no idea how much your words mean to me." I smile as I hold back the impending waterfall from my eyes.

"You're most welcome, my dear." She pats my back. "Please take my phone number and keep in touch."

Her ring grazes against the Chanel stamp made of gold hardware, making a scratching sound as she opens her bag.

"Here you go, dear." She unlocks her iPhone X and hands it to me. I save my number under 'Zara' and call my phone to leave a missed call to save hers later.

"Alright, done." I hand it back to her.

She squints at the screen.

"Zara—wow, that's a beautiful name. And what's yours, dear?" She turns to AJ, waiting for a response. Ah, shit.

"Felix." He replies with his fake name as if it's second nature to him.

"Well, Felix. My handsome boy, take good care of this gem." Winking at AJ, she lays a light stroke on the side of my arm.

"I intend to, ma'am." He glances at me with this glint of admiration in his chocolate brown eyes. How is it that he has the power to leave me breathless just by one look each time?

"Zara, Felix—you lovebirds have a great night." With his Santa Claus smile, Mr. Will locks hands with his wife as AJ and I wave goodbye, both disappearing behind the little walk up to the rest of the shops.

"I'll miss them." I let out a loud sigh.

"Yeah...me too." His Australian accent is back. "But at least you can keep in touch with them, love."

"You're right." I nod, already missing the two. "Alright, what's next on the agenda?"

"Hmm...you're gonna like this one, baby

girl." He lowers himself to my ear to whisper, "I'm taking you to the stars."

"The stars?"

"Well, more like a place above the Hollywood Bowl. Apparently, the view of the city is phenomenal and it's the one place where you can see the stars better."

"Oh, I may have heard of that place."

"Have you been?"

"No." I answer.

"Well, what are we waiting for, baby girl?"

"Lead the way, my little K-Pop prince."

"Wanna race to the car?" he asks with a devilish grin that doesn't suit his angelic face.

"Yeah, sure. If you want my legs to break into pieces." My knees are still recovering from what seemed to be a game between the tortoise and the hare.

"Oh, Zara." He clicks his tongue. "Guess I just gotta take ya."

"Wait, what?"

And before I can even think, his hands are around my waist, lifting me up effortlessly, as if I weigh nothing and throws me over his shoulder!

"AJ! Put me down!" I ordered the K-Pop prince, hitting him on his back.

"Shut up." He smacks my ass, not fazed at all by my protesting hands. "A baby could hit harder than you, my love."

"Agh, whatever." I groan as I relax my arms and legs in defeat. And let's be honest, this is kind of hot.

He opens the passenger door with the same hand he smacked my ass with, chucking me onto the seat.

"Now, princess." He levels his eyes to mine, staring intently with a smug face. If he didn't have the kindest eyes, I would have smacked the smugness off his face. "Ready to see some stars?"

"Ready as I can ever be." I roll my eyes, sounding more sarcastic than I ever have.

"Good." He kisses my forehead, his eyes drenched in mischief. Closing my door, he goes around the car, climbing into the driver's seat. "To continue our little adventure, I'm taking the liberty of starting the drive with a song from our playlist. I think you might like this artist." He taps on his screen and looks at me from the corner of his eye to see my reaction as the song plays.

A smile blossoms on my face as soon as I hear the voice of the artist. It's PLVTINUM, the same artist whose song made me mindlessly grind on AJ at the bar in Korea—a day I will never, ever forget.

"'Champagne & Sunshine'—this song reminds me of you, my little L.A. girl."

I turn the volume up and roll down the window. Sticking my head out, I allow the vibrations from the loud music to pulsate through my chest and the wind dances in my hair. As every passing fluorescent street light touches my skin,

I soak in the feeling of being young and alive. It's simple moments like these that make you feel as if you're in a movie—one that you wish to watch for a lifetime.

◆ ◆ ◆

"God, this is beautiful." I look out at the city, admiring its lights that twinkle like the stars. The buildings seem small from up here, but not too much. I never noticed how congested L.A. is until now, but regardless, this is a sight worth seeing especially at night when it's pitch black, with the only source of light being the illumination of the moon.

"Are you talking about me?" AJ jokes, still adjusting the blanket we're sitting on cross legged, right on top of the hood of Jace's car. He's been trying to smooth it out for the past five minutes since we've got here.

"You wish." I elbow the side of his rib. "How'd you find out about this place, by the way?"

"Uh—" he clears his throat, though he totally didn't have to, "a friend of mine told me about it."

"Which friend?" I ask curiously. Which friend of his would know about the ins and outs of Los Angeles?

"Um—The Weekend," he says with a proud smile.

"The—The Weekend?!" I try to talk in a hush tone, but The Weekend is the reason why we're here! Who can say that?!

"Yes, my love." He places a finger over his lips and makes a 'shh' gesture. "He was asking if I've done any sightseeing yet, and I said I haven't but I really wanted to take you somewhere with a nice view of the stars. So, I asked and he told me about this place. Neat, huh?"

"Very neat." I reply, still in disbelief.

"Okay, this needs music." He whips out his phone from his pocket, and scrolls through our playlist. Still can't believe he made one for us. "Zara, do you want to add some songs to it?"

"Um, sure." Damn, I can't think of any at the top of my head.

He hands me his phone and I take a few moments to think. Oh! Let's start with Lana Del Rey. I tap on the search engine and as soon as I start typing, AJ scoots closer to peep at the screen.

"Hey, hey! No looking." I turn the phone away from his gaze.

"Ahh, fine." He elongates his words, pretending to look up at the sky but I can see his lurking eyes.

I added four songs: "Young and Beautiful" by Lana Del Rey, "Everyday" by Ariana Grande, "Collide" by Justine Skye, and "Heaven" by Julia Michaels.

"Here." With the screen unlocked, I hand

back his phone.

Just like I did, he scans the new songs attentively.

"'Heaven' by Julia Michaels reminds you of me? Isn't that a song in *Fifty Shades Freed*?"

I'm surprised he even knows that. When did he get the time to watch *Fifty Shades Freed*, let alone any other movie?!

"Exactly." I toss a flirty wink, hoping he'd catch the reference to Christian Grey— the sexy side of Mr. Grey, not the toxic one. From that shy smile conjured on that ethereal face, it seems like he caught it.

"Anyways..." he licks the corner of his mouth, confidence in his eyes. I don't mind stroking his ego a little if it means he'll stop thinking so low of himself. "I'm going to put this playlist on shuffle and listen to the songs." He taps on the green circle with a sideways black arrow.

"Vibes" by Chase Atlantic plays. We stay quiet, listening to each word of the song while gazing at the city lights. The melody is so inspiring. I don't know what it is about music, but it makes you fall in love with a variety of emotions—happy, sad, romantic, bliss. It allows you to feel each one even if you haven't before. It enhances any experience—big or small. But I never thought music could feel so exhilarating listening with someone—someone who makes you happy the way your favorite song does. That experience is the one that doesn't require an exchange of words besides listening to the ones in the song.

"I like this song," I say, humming to the tune.

"It's nice, isn't it? You can actually hear their Australian accent. Can you notice mine when I sing in English?" he asks, genuinely curious.

"Hmm...I definitely remember noticing a hint of it in one of your songs."

"Interesting." He strokes his chin like he's thinking about whether or not it's a truthful observation. "Let me know if you hear it at the show. I wonder if you can when I sing live. Oh! Speaking of the award show...when you see me making finger hearts during the performance, just know that those are for you."

"For me?" I look at him, doe-eyed.

"Well...yeah, princess. Let's just say it's code for 'I love you and I'm thinking of you'. Cute, no?" He scrunches his nose at me like a little boy at his crush.

"It's cute for sure...but also kind of hot knowing it's JUST for me." I flirt with the K-Pop star.

"Oh yeah?" he whispers, seduction in his eyes. "Does that...turn you on?"

"No..." I gulp as those words go straight into my stomach, waking up the butterflies. "Not at all."

"Not even a little bit?" There's that cocky smile of his, just filling that mischievous face. I don't even know why I instigate, knowing damn well I cannot take the heat.

I shake my head...and the naughty thoughts that begin to cloud my mind.

He laughs off his smugness, giving me a kiss on the cheek. I know we flirt a lot with each other, but most of the time it just ends there. Besides at the party, he's never asked for anything more than just a kiss. To be honest, I think it might be because of me.

"Hey AJ...can I ask a question?"

"Yeah, go for it, baby girl."

"Um—does it bother you that we...don't have sex?"

He turns his head towards me so quickly, his earrings jiggle as if a gush of wind just passed by.

"What?" Confusion drips through his furrowed brows. "Where is this coming from?"

"I mean...after what happened that night."

We've never talked about this since that night he surprised me in L.A., nor have I ever mentioned it to Jace.

"Zara..." He reaches out to hold my timid hand, eyes full of concern. "Of course not."

"Are you sure? I know we haven't talked about it since, but...I'm really sorry we had to stop." I talk fast without catching a breath. "I just...tensed up! My mind was racing with a million thoughts and I felt like I was doing something wrong. It was hurting me, I couldn't—"

"Zara, shh. It's okay. Look at me." He places both of his hands on either side of my face. "I'm not dating you for your body. You understand that, right?"

I say nothing.

"There's more to a relationship than sex. You're not ready, and I completely understand that. I'll wait for however long YOU want. In fact, we don't ever have to have sex!" I let out a quiet laugh, calming me down. "I would never, EVER ask you to do something you don't want to. I would rather die than for you to ever feel pressured into doing anything you feel uncomfortable doing. Even at the party, I just wanted to kiss you, even if it seemed like I wanted more. You just let me know when you feel uncomfortable, okay? Whether it's something I say or do. I'll stop immediately."

"Thanks, AJ."

"Thanks for what?" He scoffs as if I've said something offensive. "There's nothing extraordinary about what I've said. Making you feel safe is a priority—it's a basic standard of being in a relationship. Don't ever apologize over something like this. It hurts me, baby."

He pulls me in for a hug. I feel the muscles in his arms flex as they tighten around me.

"You do make me feel safe, AJ."

"Good. That means I'm doing my job."

He lays several kisses on my forehead and as he continues, I slip into a daydream of being at Daniel Caesar's concert with AJ when his song "Get You" starts playing.

"Man, I love this song!" he howls, tapping his thigh along to the tune. "God, music was the best thing humans have ever created. That and spaceflight." We chuckle. "But, Zara, I love music so much. It's more than just entertainment to me. I think it's more of a tool for me to understand how and what I'm feeling. It helps to bring out these emotions we can't seem to understand and place a meaning to. It inspires the world. It inspires ME. Every. Day."

You can hear the passion in his excited voice and see the glimmer of love for music in his eyes.

"I really am the luckiest guy in the world, Zara." He says in a low, soft tone, staring out in the distance, "I get to do the one thing I love every day. How many get the chance to do that in their lifetime?"

"Not many, I'll tell you that," I respond, laying my head on his shoulder as he skips to the next song.

"Get You The Moon" by Kina plays.

"But, AJ..." a thought comes to mind, "isn't it hard being a K-Pop idol sometimes? I mean, I understand you get to do what you're passionate about, but at what cost? Your privacy is gone, the whole world knows you and you have to hide so much of your life from everyone in order to have one."

He stays quiet but lets out a weary sigh.

"I guess that's the price I just had to pay, love. But...I'm okay with it. Especially if it means that somewhere out there, our music made someone smile. I still remember that point in my life where smiling started to feel like a luxury." There's a half smile on his face, but his eyes seem to be reliving the past. "So...if losing my privacy means I can make someone's day better in any way, it's worth it to me." He strokes the side of his index finger with his thumb. "Though, at times...I do wish I could disappear to a place where no one knows me at all. I think that might have been a reason why I was so drawn to you."

Whipping around to face him, I ask—perplexed by this discovery, "Really? Why?"

"You didn't know who I was...I guess I wanted to know what that was like," he confesses, gloom taking over his eyes. That's another thing about those chocolate candies—his smile may show one thing, but his eyes...his eyes can never lie.

"And...did you like it?" I try to raise his spirits back up, perking up the tone in my voice.

"More than anything in this world." Ah, there are those deep dimples I love so much. "You kissed the sadness away."

I'm speechless, yet again. I shouldn't be surprised anymore, but I always am.

"And you, my little K-Pop prince, kissed away the cynic in me." I smile at him, placing a soft kiss on his shoulder as he pushes back my hair behind my ear. "Now, you make me feel like I'm living in a 60s romantic song."

"Starlight" by Jai Wolf plays next.

"Oh yeah? Well maybe...I want you to feel like you're stuck in a symphony." He taps the tip of my nose with his boney finger, making a 'boop' sound. "I want to make you feel the euphoria when listening to a new song on repeat. Each time you listen to it, it's never enough. Maybe... just maybe I want you to get addicted to me."

Too late, AJ. I'm pretty sure I already am.

"But, really..." he grabs the palm of my hand and brushes it against the side of his face as if it were a comfort toy, "I want to see you smiling. All the time. Just the way you've made me. I was happy, but you've made me happier. I know they're nothing but simple words, but Zara...I—I can't describe how much meaning and love is behind each one of them."

How do you possibly respond to something as loving and heartfelt as that? Sometimes I can't believe he's actually mine. Sometimes...I can't believe he loves me as much as I love him. And sometimes that scares me because I have never wanted someone so badly and never have I been badly wanted by someone.

"I believe you, AJ," I whisper teary-eyed.

"Do you trust me?" he whispers back, his

eyes fondling mine.

And without any hesitation, as always, I answer, "I do."

Without saying a word, he shows his affection by kissing the palm of my hand.

"My baby," he says, continuing to kiss and brush his lips along my hand.

Bing, bing, bing!

"Ah, shit." He groans, grabbing his phone irritated.

An alarm on his phone goes off, putting the music on pause.

"AJ, why'd you put an alarm?" I ask as he shuts it off.

"So we don't lose track of time. I tend to when I'm with you." He titters, playing the next song—"Paradise" by Chase Atlantic. "But we still have thirty minutes before we have to get going."

"Wow, okay. You'd think thirty minutes isn't enough—which it isn't—but weirdly enough, I feel like it's a lot."

"What do you mean?"

"I mean…" I gather my thoughts, "when I was in Korea with you, time seemed to fly by. I didn't even have the chance to really think about anything at all. But, here in L.A., oddly enough… time seems to have slowed down. It's obsolete. I'm more aware of it and of what I'm feeling. I hope I'm making sense."

"It does, actually. Because I think I felt the same way when we were back in Korea. I don't know, maybe when you're on vacation, time goes faster because so much is going on."

"Ha—" I scoff, "I guess that happens when you're trying to escape your reality."

"Are you still trying to escape reality?" He questions with an inquisitive tone, wanting to know my thoughts.

"Um...I think I still am, but only when I'm with you." I pause again, trying to find the proper words to explain something I'm still trying to figure out. "When I'm with you, I forget about our worldly responsibilities—our identities. I forget that I'm Pakistani, a Muslim, a graduate student, a daughter who has to uphold certain expectations. And...I also forget you're a K-Pop star. Like what Mr. Will and Mrs. Mary said, when they were together, it was just them in those moments. Nothing else mattered. I never appreciated the value of time until I met you. When we know that we have so much time to spare, we become careless with how we spend it. But...when it becomes limited, I think that's when we start to live in the moment. I count every second that passes by when I'm with you because it's one second less being in your presence."

"That reminds me of this word in Japanese. It's called 'ukiyo', which means living in the moment without worrying about the troubles of the world. I guess I've never really been in that state of mind before until I met you." He exhales a sigh, staring into my eyes.

I will never get over the way he looks at me. It's hypnotizing, and not in the way where you mindlessly listen to whatever he says. But, in a way which made me question how a person like him actually exists in my world. His one gaze, one smile, makes me forget there's something called time. It doesn't feel real but also does at the same time. He makes me feel so alive, out of this world. Slowly, but surely he has become one of the worlds I pictured as a kid. I used to imagine inconceivable ones with beautiful fairies and talking dragons, but never thought one would have a K-Pop star with a microphone and a stage.

"Well, what can I say...I'm just THAT amazing." I flip my hair over my shoulder like a sassy queen, which makes him laugh as if he were trying to save me the embarrassment.

"God, I love you."

Like I said, hearing that never fails to give me butterflies.

"I love you, more than anything." I bring my lips close to his until I feel his warm breath on mine, before pressing into his cloud-like pillows.

"Moonlight" by Chase Atlantic ques next. It seems like this playlist just consists of their songs.

"We are like those obnoxious couples now who constantly say 'I love you' like a million times in a row," he says as I separate my lips from his.

"I'm okay with it, as long as it's not in front of others. PDA is not my thing." I make a 'no' motion with my finger. I don't mind telling him how much I love him, even if it means I say it a million times in a row.

"What? You don't like feeling like a teenager madly in love?" He teases as if he's baffled by my statement.

"It's all I feel when it comes to you." I say, noticing how the moonlight touches his smooth skin. He looks godly, descended from the heavens. "You completed my teenage dream."

He really did. I didn't know what that song by Katy Perry meant until I met him.

"Do you think we fell in love too quickly, like teenagers?"

What is up with all these questions today?

"Umm..." I glance at the moon as if it would whisper an answer. "I think I thought I was in love with you back in Korea."

"You thought?" He asks quizzically.

Shit, did I say it the wrong way?

"I meant that when we met, it was probably infatuation. We both felt these intense feelings we hadn't before, and sometimes we confuse it with love because that's what it feels like —exciting and thrilling. When teenagers first fall in love in high school, it's so passionate and potent because it's a new feeling. Perhaps that's what we were—just teenagers but in our mid-twenties." I laugh in hopes to remove the confused look on his face. Thankfully, it worked. "But, I didn't fall in love with you until we started dating. I think love takes time. You know you're in love with someone when you can love their flaws as much as you love the best parts about them."

"What's my flaw?" he asks with a slight hesitation in his tone.

"Hmm…" I pause for a dramatic effect, "I think your flaw is that you're incredibly unkind to yourself. And, it can be so frustrating and painful to watch you treat yourself the way you'd never treat someone else."

"I'm…working on that." Scratching the back of his head, he nods while letting out an 'oh you caught me' laugh. "So…are you in love with me?" He waits patiently, a worried look on his face as if there's a chance I might say no.

"Falling in Love" by Dennis Kruissen and Drew Love plays next.

Slowly, I lean in…my face lingering right in front of his.

With a smile, I mutter, "Indefinitely."

You can see the relief on his face visibly. I don't understand why he'd even question it.

"Well, whatever you say, I think I fell in love with you the moment I met you."

"Oh come on." I give him a little nudge.

"No, really. I'm telling the truth." He convinces me, but I widen my eyes to emphasize my little point. Why am I trying to work against my own benefit right now? "Okay, fine. Maybe it wasn't love—though I'm still positive it was—I just knew you were going to be special."

"Oh really?" I raise a brow, a flattered smile on my face.

"Yes, if I didn't think that, I wouldn't have practiced learning your favorite song by Nusrat Fateh Ali Khan," he blurts out, his eyes widening like this was supposed to be a secret.

Awe, what?! He took out his time from his busy schedule…to learn a song that's not even his language? Who does that these days?

"You did what?" My smile keeps getting wider and wider.

"Yeah…" He laughs nervously, "obviously my pronunciation is terrible, but Urdu is hard. And it's not exactly the same song sung by him, it's a remix I found by The Yellow Diary which is much easier. I just couldn't get the god-like vocals like Mr. Khan."

"Korean is hard too."

"I guess learning another language is hard on its own."

"I just can't believe you'd do that."

"Zara, why do you get surprised? This is nothing. I'd do anything to make you happy."

There is no doubt in my mind that he wouldn't.

"Alright, then stay true to your words. Sing the song for me."

"Um, I don't know…I'm not that great."

"Please?" I make a puppy dog face.

"Ah, alright."

See, it works every time. He pauses the song on Spotify, then clears his throat and starts singing. Oh mere allah, his voice—it's like this song was meant to be heard through his vocals. The raspiness in his voice makes the song even more unique. I can't even imagine how long it must have taken him to practice. His willingness to tackle a language so foregin to him...what more could I ask for? I would never have any expectations from him to learn Urdu. But, hearing him sing in my language...I can't think of a more beautiful thing than this right now. My body is filled with goosebumps and my eyes with tears.

I jump onto him, tightening my arms around his neck.

"That was beautiful, AJ." I sniffle, trying to suck back in my tears and snot. "Thank you so much. I don't know how to tell you what this means to me."

"Meri jaan, are you crying?" He lays his hand on my cheek, forcing me to meet his eyes.

"No." I lie, hiding my shaking voice with a stern tone.

"You are crying!" He laughs at my emotional wreck. Screw you, period. "Awe, my baby girl."

He cradles me in his lap, like a mother does her baby.

"Okay, I'm done." I wipe the tears from my

eyes and my nose with my sleeve.

"Are you sure?"

"Yes." I say with assertiveness, assuring him that I'm a big girl who can control her emotions. Well, maybe not today. "I just got emotional, thanks to my period."

"You can get as emotional as you like, my love." He kisses my forehead, stroking my hair. "I want to give you something."

He reaches around me and takes off his favorite silver bracelet he always has around his wrist.

"This bracelet..." he dangles it in between his fingers, "it means a lot to me. I bought it when I debuted. It was the first present to myself. I want you to have it."

He slides it through my hand, and gently places it on my wrist.

"AJ, I can't accept this." I try to pull it off, but he stops me.

"Please keep it." He pleads. "You already know you have all of me. But you can have this part of me while I'm gone. Reminding you of me."

"I don't need a reminder, AJ." I lay a kiss on his cheek. "You've touched every part of my life, that no matter where I go, what I do or what I see...I'll always find you. And that, is enough of a reminder."

Silly boy, thinks I need an object to remind me of him. Little does he know, he's always in the back of my mind, reminding me that there's someone who loves me unconditionally.

As he kisses my forehead with those warm, plumped lips of his, I take a deep breath in and exhale out so loudly, it echoes through Mulholland Scenic Parkway.

It's quiet without the music playing. The only other sound I hear besides the crickets chirping is AJ's breathing. It's peaceful—it's comforting, just like when I look up at the moon, soaking in its light.

"Seems like a full moon tonight." AJ breaks the silence, pulling out his phone and plays "City of Stars" from the movie *La La Land*.

"Not yet. Full moon is on Thursday—the day of the K-Pop award show," I correct.

"Well, to me it looks like a full moon. Oh, look!" He points to the sky. "A shooting star! Make a wish!"

We both close our eyes and I take a breath in.

"Done?" He asks. That was quick.

"Almost." I reply, slowly opening my eyes back up.

"So, what'd you wish for?" He brings his face close to mine, and asks in an excited way like a child would.

"I can't tell you that. It won't come true." I push him away. I won't even dare to utter my own wish to myself. I want it that badly.

"Lame…" he makes an 'L' on his forehead

with his thumb and finger, "by the way...why do you like the moon so much?"

Another question I've never answered. But, this time, I know the answer.

"Because...it's a constant reminder that there is more to the world. We get so caught up with the little problems in our lives, we fail to see there's so much more out there. The moon is always there, shining its light, making its presence known to us. Every single human being on this planet—regardless of what language they speak, where they are in the world, the color of their skin, gender, or identity...have seen the moon. We're all different, but we share one same experience—looking up at the sky and seeing her."

"You're my moon," he says with a pep in his voice.

"What?"

"You said the moon is a reminder that there's more to this world. You're my reminder. When I look at you, I see there's more to my life than being me—being AJ."

"I thought I was a star?" I ask in a playful tone, curious as to how he'd answer.

He laughs quietly, pulling me in close with a single swift motion and staring into my eyes.

"You're my whole universe, Zara."

Oh, AJ. You're my everything. I couldn't picture this before, but I can now. As much as others might say that it's too soon in our relationship to think about the future, I'd say I really don't care. The truth is…I DO see us getting married, buying a home together, raising a child with him and growing old blissfully. I'm not sure if it will happen, but I'm assured that I can imagine it without a single doubt.

I lay a tender kiss on his cheek, trailing kisses down to his jawline.

"The way I feel about the moon is how I feel about you," I whisper, as I continue kissing.

"Which is?"

I stop, and gaze into those chocolate brown eyes I love so much.

"Every time I look at it, it feels as if I'm seeing it for the first time. Enamored by its beauty. And, that's exactly how I feel about you—it's like I'm seeing you for the first time."

He smiles, doesn't say a word. But his eyes speak on his behalf. I guess I'm not the only one who gets speechless.

"I love you, Zara. I will always love you."

He places a passionate kiss on my forehead, and brings me in for a hug. My head lays against his hard chest, feeling the warmth of his skin seep through my own. I inhale the smell of his cologne that bounces off his hoodie—I'll never forget the smell of his skin. He's my happy place—he's become my home.

Some people make us feel a certain way we haven't before. At times, we don't even know where to begin to describe that feeling. We use words that can somewhat explain the phenomenon, but there seems to be none in any human language to express how he makes me feel. I guess these feelings are ultimately left as definitions with no words attached to them. And, I find that incredibly beautiful. Maybe these feelings don't need a word as a form of representation. They are just simply meant to be felt.

CHAPTER 7:

What Lies Beneath The Star

"Zara, hurry up! We're going to be late to your precious boyfriend's event!" Jace hollers from the living room.

"Just one second!"

He's so impatient. We're early, if anything, but now I feel rushed. Though, I understand since we also wanted to see him on the red carpet. I wiggle my dainty silver 'jhumkhas' into my ear in a hurry, and run a hand down my outfit. My black 'churiyan' and AJ's bracelet rattle as I do. Seems like I look…pretty good. I straightened my hair, wore a black flowy blouse with a v-cut neckline and white flare jeans, finishing it off with my black doc martens. I push in my nose stud and assess my makeup—black liner inside my water line actually makes me look pretty edgy but the pinkish-brown lipstick adds in a hint of femininity.

"Zara! If your ass isn't out here at a count of three, I will drag you out myself!"

Oh. My. God! He's so irritating at times! Catching one last glimpse of myself in the mirror, I sprint out of my room and find him in the living room, dressed in a navy blue button down and dark washed jeans, his curly hair slicked back.

"Okay, I'm here." I gather my phone and some breath mints from the kitchen counter and chuck them in my black clutch with gold embellishment that my mom bought from Pakistan.

"We'll leave in five minutes, just gotta check traffic real quick," he says, eyes locked to his phone.

"And you made me rush out like we were leaving already." I roll my eyes, setting my clutch on the entrance table.

"Well, it's better to be ready. Anyways—" he breaks eye contact with his screen, "you—oh, my god." His jaw drops, removing any sort of annoyance that was on his face. "AJ's going to die seeing you."

"I know." I shoot a confident wink, "I wanted everything to be on point, especially my contour since it normally looks like I slathered shit all over my face."

"Well, it doesn't look like shit today. You look more chiseled than Adriana Lima."

"Okay...let's not go there. But, thank you." I show my gratitude with a smile.

"You ready, bitch?" He swipes the car keys off the table.

"Ready!"

Can't wait to see my K-Pop star strut his talent today.

◆ ◆ ◆

"Where is he?" I grunt to Jace, irritated at him as if he's in charge of AJ's life.

"How the hell am I supposed to know?" He scans the sea of photographers who are trying to salvage every shot of K-Pop stars on the red carpet. "I can't see anyone past these vultures."

They really are vultures, screaming frustratedly and shouting at the stars to look here or there. I mean, I get it, it's their job but...gosh, do it in a more kind way! They're only interested in getting the best shot compared to their rivals. If I were in AJ's shoes, I'd get so overwhelmed and anxious by the chaos.

"NOWus are next! Look!" I overhear a photographer standing a few inches from Jace and I.

My face lights up, excited to see the boys—especially my AJ.

"AJ! Look over here!" A photographer shouts from my left.

"Lee! Smile!" Another from my right.

People crowd in, pushing me and Jace towards the back. It's so loud from everyone shouting and chattering, trying to get the boys' attention. I tiptoe, hoping to see a glimpse of AJ. Ah, and once I do...I find peace. He's radiating, dressed in a pinstripe black blazer with a Prada belt cinched at the waist—nothing underneath—topped off with black slacks and shiny black boots. His ears are jeweled with black earrings that have Prada written out, and his neck has a silver weaved choker.

There's someone interviewing the group. AJ's speaking but I can't make out anything he's saying. He looks so composed—so professional—gesturing with his hands as he replies to the interviewer. Completely different from how he normally is. The interviewer gestures for the eight members to stand against the backdrop that says 'K-Pop Fusion Award Show 2019'. One by one, they line up, AJ being the last, overlooking all the members. They stand there, posing for the photographers and looking like gods paying a visit on earth to bless us mortals. Flashes from the camera reflect off their faces per millisecond. I can't see anything from the secondhand flashes attacking my eyes. I don't understand how they can stand there without blinking violently or having their vision impaired. They're completely unfazed by the blinding lights.

"I can barely see AJ." Jace says, tiptoeing like me, placing his hand on the photographer's shoulder—who is engrossed in taking pictures—next to him for support.

"Agh! Me either!" I finally let out a groan. Being pushed around by these vultures only stirred a pot of immense frustration. Why do I—his girlfriend—have to see him from all the way here?! If only I can scream that to each and every one who's here. That's it. I'm moving towards the front.

"Follow me," I blurted, determination in my eyes. The front has now become my Mt. Everest, and I plan to climb.

"What do you mean?" Jace asks, but without saying a word, I grab his arm and push through people.

"Excuse me!" I make it past, trying to add some softness in my voice.

"Hey!" One photographer complains, but I chose to ignore it.

"Sorry, my friend's crazy—" Jace looks at him timidly, apologizing as if the photographer were his mother. Why is he acting like me when I need him to act like HIM?

"Sorry, excuse me!" Just a few more people, and I'll be standing there in front of him.

"Zara! What the hell are you doing?" Jace says in a hushed tone, tugging my arm.

"Getting to the front," I reply, not caring about the annoyed faces surrounding me.

As I push through, AJ and the boys become more visible to my sight. Just one more person, and I can see AJ up close.

"Excuse me!" I say and the photographer

steps to the side without an eye twitch. And there he is—my AJ, a few feet away from me.

As he's scanning through the sea of photographers, his eyes land on me. He blinks quickly, and several times, as if he couldn't believe I'm standing there, right in front of his eyes. I smile, trying to minimize the excitement of seeing him, but I allow my eyes to communicate how I feel. There's a glimmer of joy in his eyes and just as his coy smile is about to turn into one that would deepen his dimples even more, he looks away... acting like I'm not even there. My own smile fades away. I don't know how to feel, but I know one thing...this didn't feel good—not one bit.

"NOWus, you can walk on over." The event coordinator points in the direction of the entrance to the award show. Lee leads the way, and the boys follow, AJ being the last as always. I wait to see if he'll look back. Look back, AJ. But he's walking away—away from me like I'm just another person in the crowd. At this moment, I realize that this is what our reality will be like. A single rope separating us—his world on one side, and mine behind a stanchion.

◆ ◆ ◆

"Oh my god! Of course they won song of the year!" Jace catches his breath from screaming the entire time Got7 were receiving their award. "It was only the catchiest song that made me want to dance all the way to Korea. Ahh, man... Jackson is such a sight to sore eyes." He places his hand over his heart in admiration for the star.

I nod, anxiously waiting for AJ to come on stage. I still feel a bit weird about what happened earlier, but since the show started, I've been trying not to make it a big deal. Instead, I sang along to some songs I know by the talented K-Pop groups, even though I had no idea what I was saying or if anything that was coming out of my mouth was actually Korean. I swayed to the songs with Jace, feeling like an ant in the front of the stage of the Staples Center that holds twenty thousand seats. The stage itself must be half the size of a football stadium, with big screens right above, shaped like a pentagon box with a screen on each side.

"Up next, we have the ones that bring RnB into a whole new light. WON's, get ready because here is none other than our very own kings—NOWus!"

Ah, finally! The crowd goes wild. The arena echoes with what seems like a million screams. The lights cut off, making everything pitch black, but the big screens. A video plays, showing an animated navy blue night sky. Stars twinkle beside the moon, with the focus moving in on a mountain cliff, showing a shadow of a wolf howling to the moon. If I saw this anywhere else besides here, I'd think it's a scene from an anime show. The music in the background is a symphony of one of their songs, but a piano version. You'd think Mozart composed the piece for the wolf gang.

Lights above and around the stage, as well as throughout the arena, flicker with fluorescent lights, looking like shooting stars. There's a box in the middle of the stage, as big as a small building. It lifts up as the lights continue flickering, only to show the boys standing, earpieces attached, ready to perform. AJ's in the front, facing my side, microphone in his hand. They look absolutely ethereal, dressed in navy blue velvet tops that sparkle with glitter as if they were wearing the night sky. Every one of their outfits are different from one another, and have intricate designs made with what seem to be diamonds resembling the constellations. Each one of the boys have tiny clear jewels glued above their brows all the way to the middle. AJ's hair is slicked back with a strand falling in front of his forehead. He is wearing a bedazzled choker with one earring that has the Chanel logo, and on the other a diamond stud. He looks like Prince Eric, just with a microphone in his hand. From the big screen, I can see he's wearing gray contacts, which makes his smokey navy eyeshadow pop.

As if the crowd couldn't get any wilder, they do. They cheer and scream, girls crying as they dance and sing. But, I'm not paying attention to any of it—I'm hypnotized by the performance. I cannot explain the gravity of their presence, the way they can make the whole arena become so captivated by their movements, their lyrics, their enchanting voices—connecting thousands of people as they all sing their song in unison. The arena rings with the voices of each person there. The flickering lights, the dance team, the harmonies that bounce off the walls—all make for an experience that would make anyone feel alive. I understand why so much time and effort goes into this. It's an escape from the world for a moment—a moment that will be remembered forever.

I will never understand how the boys and the dancers can manipulate their bodies in such a way to make those quick, smooth movements so pleasing to the eyes. Or how they can perform with these lights that can easily make a person dizzy. I mean, I'm standing still in front of them and I'm ready to fall over to my side. Yet, they're all doing all sorts of stunts and AJ is showing off his godly backflips, while also looking at the moving cameras. I can barely walk properly, and here they all are showing the world their skills that took years of practice and precision.

As the performance is coming to an end, the dance team and the boys all come to the center for the final few seconds of the song. If anyone in the crowd was sitting, they're all now standing. People pulled out their lightsticks, making the arena literally look like it's filled with glistering stars. Lights flicker more as if they couldn't go any faster, which comes to a rest as the performance ends. The crowd's cheers bring smiles to the boys' sweaty faces—which makes their skin glisten as if it's made of glass—as shown on the big screen. And as promised... there's AJ, lifting up his hand and making a finger heart with the biggest smile on his face—the smile only I get to see. That makes me feel better—I still feel seen.

As the crowd continues to cheer their lungs out, all of the lights on the stage and around the arena shut off abruptly. Before I can take my next breath, there's a scream. And it's a raspy one—one that is ingrained in my head.

"AJ!" I scream instinctively while the crowd gasps. I start pushing the people standing in front of me to the side as if that would be of any help. His scream went straight into my stomach, making me sick.

"Zara, calm that dramatic ass down!" Jace tugs on my arm, keeping his voice quiet as possible. "He's fine, but people are looking at YOU!"

I come out of my worry trance, and find the 'this bitch is crazy' glances on me, illuminated by their lightsticks. They can judge all they want, they're not the one dating the person who just screamed as if he got impaled by a knife.

But, to my dismay, the lights on the stage shot right back up and the judgy glances have averted from me and onto...a shirtless AJ?! My jaw drops, but not in the way you'd think. I'm shocked to say the least. He's never been shirtless on stage. And he's not completely shirtless...he's wearing a mid-size cape—ones that royals wore —made from the same material as his shirt in the previous performance. To top off the look, he's wearing a black crown covered with jewels, all colors of the night sky. His abs appear more defined, more prominent...more tan. That explains the diet he was on and why he looked so tan the other day. He looks amazing...but I feel so uneasy seeing him this way.

"Damnnnn..." Jace has a similar reaction. "What in the bedazzled ass crown jewels is that?! Did you know about this?"

"No." I shake my head, still shocked at the surprise. Why wouldn't he tell me? This is kind of a big deal.

He starts singing in Korean. It's a slow song, with the only instrument being a piano. But his voice isn't the only one ricocheting throughout the arena...there's one of a girl. The spotlight follows to an entrance.

"Oh, shit! There's Rose Lin!" Jace exclaims, cheering as she struts towards the stage to...AJ. Her long, wavy jet-black hair and silk dress flow behind her. The colors of her dress and makeup matches AJ.

The lights have turned amber, embracing a romantic mood. They're singing to each other, looking into one another's eyes as they walk in slow circles—it's incredibly intimate. If someone who isn't a K-Pop fan was to see this, they'd think the two are in love from the chemistry that's so potent between them. Those around me chant their names together...making me feel even more uneasy. Why do I feel this way? It's just a performance...but seeing AJ shirtless, around her, singing in this intimate, sexual, yet romantic way—I'm jealous. I thought only I got to see AJ's body, but now the whole world has... especially her. I'm sure they practiced like that, too. Gosh, I'm thinking nonsense. But, are my feelings valid?

"Rose Lin! AJ! Rose Lin! AJ!" The crowd continues to chant as the performance seems to be coming to an end. They stand still in front of each other, singing harmoniously. Their voices do sound great together. Both hold their note, and with one final stretch, their song finishes, but each has their gaze on the other. The crowd claps, cheers, and continues to chant both of their names together. This feels like hell. I don't want to hear his name attached to some other girl, especially when this girl looks like a Greek goddess of K-Pop.

"That. Was. Brilliant." Jace says, stunned by their performance, just like everyone else.

I nod and clap, supporting my shirtless boyfriend.

The lights cut, making the stage pitch black. After a few seconds, they turn back on but instead of AJ and Rose Lin, there's the host who I know is famous, but I still can't figure out where I know her from.

"What a beautiful performance by NOWus and our gorgeous Rose Lin! I know we all have been waiting for them the whole night. And now, as the show is coming close to an end, it's time to announce the artist of the year. I have been given the honor of announcing the winner, and I couldn't be more excited!" The crowd 'whoo's', and she waits for them to stop cheering. "And the artist of the year award goes to…" She opens the envelope and pauses dramatically as she sees the name, "None other than, NOWus!"

Screams and cheers send vibrations through the arena. The boys step onto the stage, one by one in a line, AJ at the end wearing the velvet top from his first performance. The host hands the mic and golden award shaped like a star to AJ as his face shows up on the big screen.

"Hello, beautiful people!" He smiles as the arena screams in their honor. His dimples appear deeper than ever and his glossy eyes speak his gratitude. "Thank you so much for giving us this award. We are truly so humbled, and honestly we couldn't have done it without our WON's! Without your unconditional love, we wouldn't be standing here on this prestigious platform. You are…priceless and we can never, EVER repay you for all the support. This is for you, WON's!" He raises the award and with a popping sound, confetti falls like raindrops on the stage, making the crowd go insane.

"Whooo! Go, sexy thangs!" Jace claps violently, compared to my silent ones.

I'm truly happy for the boys though, they've worked so incredibly hard. They deserve this.

"Hey, so Ari told me we need to go to that security guard in the corner." He points at a gentleman wearing a black and yellow shirt, with 'security' spelled out across the chest. "She said she'll be there and we can meet up with AJ backstage."

Although I am still feeling a little…well, whatever I'm feeling, I'm excited to see him and congratulate for this accomplishment.

◆ ◆ ◆

"There's our superstar!" Jace's arms fly open, picking up AJ as he gives him a celebratory hug. "You killed it, as always. I was screaming my vocal cords out, louder than those teenyboppers."

"Thank you, thank you! I don't doubt that one bit." AJ replies as Jace puts him back down in this tiny hallway. It's lit with a few fluorescent tube lights which give off a greenish tint.

"I was watching all of it on the T.V. backstage and let me tell you, I swear I heard Jace's voice blaring throughout the arena," Ari says, winking at her beau.

AJ's eyes find me as I stand there quietly.

"Hi, my love." His arms loop around my neck, bringing me close to his body. My blouse brushes against his velvet top. "Did you like the show?"

"Yes, I did. You were amazing. Congratulations, AJ." I say as I pat his back, and he strokes my hair.

As we pull away, we lock eyes. I try to bring a smile to mine, but his are concerned.

"You okay?" he asks, squinting at me.

"Yeah. Why wouldn't I be?" I laugh it off. I might just be making it all a big deal. It was JUST a performance. That's his job. But I just can't shake off this uncomfortable feeling. I can't seem to explain it. Just seeing them on stage, with such chemistry...it was like the greatest acting performance, unless...it wasn't.

"Zara!" And there's that deep voice that has made the world fall in love with it's uniqueness. "Ah, I missed you!" I got grabbed from behind and spun around.

"Lee!" I jump into my Aussie brother's arms and give a proper reunited hug. "I've missed you, too."

"Oh, it's been too long." He pulls away, picking at one of the jewels on his forehead that's about to fall off. "Did you enjoy the show? Especially hyung's finger hearts? He told me about them." Lee giggles, glancing over at AJ who has a shy smile on his face.

"Yes, I enjoyed everything," I say vaguely, patting his pale cheek that has little crease marks from his makeup.

"Good. Now hyung's ALL yours." He winks, turning around to talk to Ari and Jace.

As AJ pulls me in again for a hug, I stand there awkwardly thinking of things to say without making it seem like there's something bothering me. I'd talk to him about it, but this just doesn't feel like the time nor the place. AJ just looks so happy, I don't want to take him away from his victory. But, as AJ slowly pulls away from me, I catch a glimpse of his face. It seems as if something else has taken away the joy that was in his eyes and replaced it with an intense glare at something behind me.

"Oh, hello." I hear a soft-spoken voice with a British accent. Instinctively, I turn my head towards the direction of the voice, which turns out to be...

"Rose Lin!" Jace shouts.

She glides past me and stands next to AJ, who has this look on his face as if he had just seen a ghost.

"Hello, how do you do?" She speaks so eloquently, towering over all of us in her six-inch heels. Her skin is so smooth, butter could slide from it. She not only looks like a goddess on stage, but off as well.

Jace and Ari are both completely starstruck, unable to conjure any words to come out of their mouths. Lee's face resembles his hyung's—serious and severe.

"AJ…" She says his name, stroking the side of his arm, which makes him jump like a startled cat. "Aren't you going to introduce your friends to me?"

"Um, yeah…" He shoots a side glance at Lee, "This is my sister, Ari, and her boyfriend Jace." He gestures towards the two who still look as if a cat got their tongue. "And this is…Jace's friend, Zara."

Jace's…friend?! That's how he introduces me as?!

"Oh…" she trails me with her eyes, but comes to a stop at my wrist, "well, nice to meet you all." Still having her eyes on my wrist, she says, "AJ, you should invite them out to karaoke with all of us in Koreatown."

"Uh—yeah, I was just about to," he says, clearing his throat, and unable to look me in the eyes.

"Great, I'll see you all there." And with a smile—which totally seems fake—she waves goodbye with her perfectly manicured hand, phone in her hand. "Ciao!" She glances at AJ with a flirtatious smirk, and walks past me.

Ciao yourself, buttface. No one can tell me that wasn't weird!

"Well—" Lee claps his palms together, "hyung and I will get changed and take off our makeup and meet you guys there?"

"Yeah—just text me the address," Jace says, finally breaking free from his trance.

"Will do." AJ gives me a quick glance, then looks away with a thin smile on his face. I feel too...weird—for a lack of a better word—to even look at him.

What in the world was all of that about? Why is he so uncomfortable next to Rose Lin when he just did such an intimate performance with her? And why—why is he acting so strange?

◆ ◆ ◆

It's been almost an hour since we've been at this karaoke bar. We were placed in a private room once we arrived, further away from the rest of the crowd. The buttface was the first one there to greet us with her perfectly long hair and toned legs. She kind of gives off the Regina George vibe from *Mean Girls*.

Other than AJ and the members, there are a few other K-Pop idols here, all taking turns to sing and drink soju, besides AJ. He's been sitting next to me and Lee, while Jace and Ari mingle with others as the social butterflies they are. You'd think AJ would do the same, but surprisingly enough, he's not. The moment he arrived, Rose Lin's face lit up as if she'd been waiting for him for years. But he's ignored her and has been with me the whole time, with the exception of talking with the other idols for a couple minutes.

It would explain why she keeps shooting me a disgusted look every chance she gets, which I don't understand—I haven't done shit to her.

"So, Zara...how have you been holding up?" Lee asks, talking over the noise of the music and singing.

"With what?"

"You know..." he says, leaning in closer to me, "with the whole K-Pop thing. I know it's been quite a lot having to deal with the secrecy. And, I'm sure besides that, you have your own worries when it comes to how your family might react. I can't imagine it being easy." There's so much concern in his deep brown eyes.

"Um...it hasn't." I let out a defeated chuckle. "But...I love him, Lee. I guess that makes all the hurdles worth fighting for. Plus, I think it might be too soon to be bringing family into this." I act as if I haven't even given any thought, even though that's ALL I've been thinking about.

"Oh, come on. He's gonna marry you, noona! You're all he ever talks about!" He chuckles, running his fingers through his silver-colored hair, cut in a way that accentuates his heart-shaped face. It's cute he calls me 'noona', even though I'm only a year older than him. "You're already my sister-in-law in my mind, so... you both better get married."

"Maybe one day!" I brush it off with a clumsy laugh. When it comes to the topic of marriage and AJ, for now...it will always have to remain a maybe.

"What are you two talking about?" AJ chimes in, turning his head away from one of the idols he was speaking to.

"Oh...nothing." Lee says as if he was deliberately trying to spill a secret. "Just talking about Zara potentially joining our little family someday."

AJ's smile transforms into an awkward one, laughing it off as if he wanted to change the topic immediately.

"Zara, do you want anything to drink?" he asks with a red cup in his hand filled with water.

And before I can reply, Rose Lin slides in next to him.

"I'll have a drink, AJ." She glances at me with this evil smirk on her face, trailing a finger down his arm, which makes him take a step away from her. Why does she keep looking at me in such a way when I'm just 'Jace's friend'? What the hell did I do to her? And why does she keep touching AJ in such a teasing way?! It's starting to piss me off seeing that.

His ears turn as bright red as the cup in his hand. Both his and Lee's faces dramatically change to how they were backstage. What is up with that?

"I was asking Zara." AJ replies, no emotion in his voice.

"And? You can't grab me a drink while you get one for her?" She hisses like a jealous girlfriend.

He says nothing. His eyes refuse to look at her. Is he mad at her? What's their deal?

"I—I'll be right back." AJ shoots the same glance at Lee as he did backstage.

"Yogurt soju for me, please!" she requests the pop star.

"Zara, you want soju, too?" Lee asks in a rushed tone.

"Uh—no. Water's fine." I reply, confused at the atmosphere.

With a quick nod, Lee follows AJ to the table full of soju, a water jug, and some soda.

"Ah, isn't he just so scrumptious?" she asks, checking out either AJ or Lee, I can't tell.

"Um, who?" Trying to see which direction her eyes are pointing at.

"AJ, of course."

Excuse me?!

"I mean..." She plops down on the chair Lee was sitting on, crossing her moisturized pale legs. "We've been friends forever, but I've always thought he's such a sight. Don't you think so?"

With a thin smile, I nod uncomfortably.

Before another word can come out of her round, plumped, cherry lips, AJ and Lee come back, each one carrying a drink.

"Here's yours." Lee hands a red cup to her, but her eyes are glued to AJ.

She watches him intensely as he hands me mine.

"Thanks...Lee." She emphasizes his name while having her eyes on AJ. It seems as if she's a bit angry that he wasn't the one to hand her the drink. "Well, I'm going to go sing. I mean, after all...that's what I'm best at." She winks at me, getting off the chair. Taking a few small steps forward, she stumbles on her heels and...

"Whoops!" Her drink slips out of her hand, and lands on me. "Oh, I'm so sorry, Zara!" She apologizes, but there is no remorse in her eyes. In fact, she has a stupid, visibly apparent smirk!

This...BITCH! She totally did that on purpose!

"What the hell, Rose Lin?" AJ leaps towards me, assessing the damage done as I sit there, drenched in soju.

Lee bolts to the table and grabs all the napkins, catching the attention of the whole party. Jace and Ari rush to my side, their mouths wide open, while the rest of the members crowd behind them.

"Are you okay?!" Jace asks, glancing at Rose Lin, as Lee hands me the napkins, which are quite useless at this point since there's no way it can soak up all of it.

"Yeah, I'm fine." I reply, dabbing the napkins on my wet clothes.

"Here, I'll take you home." Jace slowly pulls out his keys, squinting at Rose Lin as if he caught the same smirk that I did.

"Uh—Jace, I'll take her home and then

come back," AJ interjects.

"Yeah, that's fine. Just stop by my hotel. Jace and I will head there after. You sure you'll be okay, Zara?" Ari asks with a worried tone.

"It's just soju, not acid," Rose Lin growls, rolling her eyes as AJ helps me off my chair.

My clothes are starting to give off the stench of soju, thanks to your stupid ass, bitch. I refrained myself from calling her by any names, but it's clear she has something against me and I just don't know why. But I do know it most definitely has something to do with AJ.

◆ ◆ ◆

"She totally did that on purpose!" I throw my clutch on my bed, letting out all the anger that's been marinating for the past couple of minutes with one swift motion. I didn't say a single word to him, though he kept making sure I was drying up—which I didn't. I'm still wet as a dog.

"No, she didn't, my love." He defends her with a soft tone, setting his phone down on the bed. He probably doesn't want to aggravate the situation even more.

"Yes, she DID!" I enunciate 'did', which makes him worry from the way he keeps following me around in the room, until I gesture to stop. "Turn around."

"What?"

"Turn around, I have to change."

"Oh, okay." He doesn't argue, and puts a hand over his eyes as he turns away from me.

I lift up my arms, forcing myself out of my blouse that feels like it's glued onto my skin. Same with my pants. Agh, this is the worst! Now, I feel all sticky and gross, but I'll shower once he leaves.

I'm still bothered—pissed, mad…whatever you wanna call it! There's something going on and I need to know. But, am I making it a big deal? No, I'm not! This whole night has been throwing me off, especially when it comes to her! Just keep your mouth shut, Zara. It's best if I do. But, no! Why should I push down my feelings? I'm gonna say something. I'm gonna—

"AJ!" I blurt out as I push my arms through the sleeves of my oversized NASA sweatshirt.

"Yeah?" He jumps to turn back around, but then stops once he realizes I'm still not done changing.

"There's something bothering me," I say with a dauntless tone, forcing each leg into my gray sweatpants. I'm done trying to protect him with how I feel.

"Okay, what is it?"

"You can turn around now." I fix my sweatpants as he does, stalling to buy some time to figure out how to ask him about Rose Lin. With a deep breath, I say, "There's no better way to ask this, so I'm just going to say it."

I see his Adam's apple make a conspicuous up and down motion as he gulps and nods. My boldness has subsided seeing him nervous. Now...I am, too.

"Did something happen between you and...Rose Lin?"

His face turns white, despite having a tan. His ears shoot red and his eyes—his eyes widen like a deer in headlights.

As each second passes, I feel sick to my stomach. You never really feel like time has stopped completely until you ask a question to which you secretly know the answer to.

"Zara..." he whispers guiltily.

He didn't have to say anything else but my name to make my blood turn cold. Sometimes our gut warns us with the truth, but our hearts refuse to listen.

"Something did...didn't it?" I question with a calm tone as a lump in my throat begins to suffocate me. My eyes forget they need to blink, but it seems like shock has paralyzed us both.

"Zara, I can explain." He leaps forward, reaching for me, tears welling up in his sorry eyes.

"No, stop." I make a barricade in front of my chest with my arms.

"Zara, please! Just listen!" he begs, regret in his voice.

I can't think straight nor can I stand on my feet. It feels like my brain and body has been drained of every drop of blood.

"Then talk." I reply with no emotion in my voice, my eyes unable to meet his.

"Zara—I" he stammers, "it happened once! We got caught up in the moment during practice and she kissed me, but...I kissed her back for just a second! It was just a second!" He places his cold hands on either side of my face, hoping I'd look him in the eyes. "But, you have to understand, it meant nothing to me! It didn't mean anything at all! I've been feeling so guilty ever since."

"When?" I ask, putting all the weight of my face in his hands as it feels like life has left my body.

"Zara, please, don't—"

"When!" I raise my cracked voice, looking straight into his eyes.

"A month ago." He confesses as a teardrop trickles down the cheek I kissed with so much love. You can see the hatred for himself in his eyes as he closes them shut—regret has taken residence in those deep brown eyes I stared into like they were the only ones in the world.

"Why?" I whisper, not allowing myself to shed the tears that blur my vision.

"Zara, stop, please!" He begs as if it's physically hurting him to answer my questions. Once, his plea would have softened my heart immediately, but you can't do anything to something that feels like it's been broken into a million pieces right before my eyes.

"Just...answer." I relax my clenched jaw, breathing slowly to calm my beating heart.

"I—I don't know. I wasn't thinking. It happened so quickly but I stopped it! I told her I didn't feel anything for her anymore!" he says, hyperventilating.

"Anymore? What do you mean anymore?"

I feel like puking every organ out of my body to make room for my lungs! It's getting harder and harder to breathe.

"We liked each other for a bit before I debuted, but it wasn't anything, Zara! She means nothing to me!"

I plop onto my bed while he towers over me. His teardrops fall on my carpet. I feel so dizzy —so lifeless.

"Does she know who I am?" I ask, barely able to breathe, but curious to see if he's mentioned me to the one who wants his heart.

"No, I couldn't risk exposing you." He shakes his head. "Listen, Zara, I know you're mad —"

"AJ, I'm not mad," I interrupt. "I'm disappointed." I say, swallowing my hurt. "I never thought that YOU of all the people in my life would ever look me in the eyes and lie straight to my face."

"Zara, you have to believe me, I wanted to tell you about what happened when you asked me the night of the party, but I thought it'd only hurt you!"

"And this didn't?!" The tears I tried to hold back finally escaped my eyes. "Finding out this way is ten times worse, AJ, because I—I had to ask!"

God, this hurts so much! It feels like a jaded knife ripped me into half! It hurts that he lied but it hurts even more to see his eyes turn bloodshot red from shedding so many tears, despite the fact he just made my world stop spinning.

"There's already so much working against us, but the one thing we had was trust and you—you broke it! And, I gave you all of it! I feel like a fucking idiot—loving you unconditionally, looking at you as if you were the most beautiful, perfect person I've ever known!"

"Zara, I'm not perfect—I'm far from it!" he falls on his knees and wails, nestling his face into my lap.

"No—no, you're not perfect, AJ." I finally break down, tears stream down my face and neck. "But you made me feel perfectly loved."

His phone screen lights up. I catch a glimpse of one notification after another.

"Zara, I—I'll always love you! I can't breathe without you! I—" he looks up at me with repentant eyes, sobbing profusely, "I'm in so much pain. I'll have to live with this forever, knowing how much I hurt you! I hate myself more than I already do!"

I don't want him to hate himself. I should, but I don't. I could never wish that, no matter how hurt I may be.

From the corner of my eye, I see his phone light up again, but he doesn't. His devastated eyes haven't moved from mine.

"I—I love you so much!" he takes my hands into his, pressing his cold palms to mine. "Do you trust me when I say that?"

At least once in a person's life, they're faced with a question which puts them at odds with what they want to say versus what they should. This is that question for me. I never imagined that I would ever have to answer his question with one painful yet simple syllable...

"No."

An aching silence fills between us, two heartbroken lovers. There's no sound but the buzzing from his phone on the bed that once witnessed such loving and caring conversations... which is far from what this is.

I don't know what's more agonizing—having answered a question I'd always say yes to, or seeing the world shatter in his eyes.

"You should get that." I break the excruciating silence.

He stays in place, slowly placing my hands back on my lap and reaching out for his phone.

As he scrolls through what seems like thousands of notifications, his eyes widen.

"Zara..." His chest rises and falls. "There's a picture of us going viral."

How—how is that possible?

He hands me his phone, showing a picture of me hugging him, my back facing towards the camera, but you can only see my hair and the side of my earrings. It's taken from a distance.

"What are you going to do?" I ask as I hand back his phone, trying not to show any hint of worry, which I am feeling despite everything.

"I'll—I'll figure it out. I don't care anymore," he says with whatever strength is left in his voice.

I remain quiet. Hearing him say he doesn't care goes against everything he's worked hard for. I mean, the reason why he snuck around in the first place was because he valued his career so much. Everything we did was for that responsibility he has. Despite how I may be feeling about him right now, I do hope he doesn't get in trouble or have people create countless rumors and stories. How silly of me to still care.

"So...what do we do, Zara?" His eyes stay fixed down on my carpet as he throws his phone on the floor, still sitting on his heels.

Normally I'd spare talking about how I feel to not worry him. But, I don't have the patience nor the strength to put an iron shield over his feelings right now.

"I don't know. But...what I do know is that this changes everything."

"I know." He says it softly, almost a whisper.

"You know what's funny, AJ? I thought the

reason why we'd ever break up in the first place would be over things we can't control. Whether it's K-Pop, our parents, the cultural differences—distance. I never imagined it'd be…"

I can't even bring myself to say the word 'cheating' nor do I think he has the gut to hear it from the way he's crouched beside my legs.

"Why'd you kiss back, AJ?" He runs his hand over his face as I ask. "Although it pains me to ask, I have to know what it was that made you risk what we have? Was it not enough? Was my unconditional love still not enough? Or was it me—was I not smart or pretty enough for you?"

I feel this burning ache inside my chest which no medicine could mitigate.

"Zara, that's far from what it was." He sniffles, as tears flow down his cheeks. "If anything, I didn't feel enough for you."

"Don't use that as an excuse for what you did."

"I swear, Zara. It's not an excuse." He finally looks up at me, eyes and cheeks more red than before. "I can't explain what happened, but I guess a part of me wanted to like kissing her back. Because at least then…I could leave you to a life of normalcy. I mean, just now, if your face would've shown in the picture, your life would change forever! There'd be reporters, paparazzi at your door, people stalking your every move! You'd never be left alone! Everyone would know who you are! The guilt would have eaten me alive, knowing that happened because you're with me! I thought for a split second, maybe it'd be easier to date someone like her, even if I'm not as happy as I am with you because at least you wouldn't have to deal with all of the countless repercussions!"

"You think that's supposed to make me feel any better?" I say with the utmost confusion. "If I wanted to be in a relationship with someone it'd be easy with, I'd be dating Arsalan. But, he's not who I want! I wanted to fight for you! You, AJ! Not anyone else! It just hurts to know that you ended up not feeling the same way."

"No, Zara. That's not it!" He weeps, "I do want to fight for you! More than anything, but I get so scared. I'm scared, all the time! I've been far too selfish. You think I don't know that I could never give you the life that Arsalan can? I hate the fact he can fulfill every need of yours that I cannot. I hate that he can give you the life you deserve. How long can I possibly ask you to keep loving me the way you do—so selflessly? With him, you wouldn't have to go against your parents or have to sneak around just to see him for a few hours. You can build a home, a family—a life with him. And, I don't know if I can ever give you that, even though every part of me wants to give you the world!"

"And look what you've given me instead! You ripped the little world I had right out from under my feet!"

"I know, Zara. I know! I'm so sorry I'm selfish. I only thought about what made me happy—and that's you! Kissing her felt like nothing—nothing like how it feels when we do. It only reminded me what we have is real and rare—worth risking everything for!"

"And you couldn't talk about this before having your tongue down her throat?" I say with my wounded soul, nostrils flared. My emotions are all over the place. I'd get sad, but then I'm fuming with uncontrollable anger the more he talks.

"Zara..." gasping sobs escape his mouth as he holds onto my legs. "I'm so sorry! I—I just can't live without you! Knowing what I've done is a punishment for a lifetime. I'm so sorry, I'm so fucking sorry! I love you, Zara. I—"

"You keep hurting me, AJ." I let out a little whimper as he continues to cry as if someone he loves has died. Though, it does feel like something has.

"I know, I'm so sorry, Zara!" He unwraps his arms from around my legs, and holds onto my hands, staring at me with pleading eyes as they well up with more tears. "Just tell me what I can do to fix this, please! I'll do anything!"

"No, AJ—stop." I look away from the eyes that I'd give my life to in a heartbeat. "You're not the AJ I fell in love with, you are someone I can't recognize anymore."

Although he is right in front of me, I have

never felt so far away from him.

"Zara, I—I can't imagine never holding you again. I can't imagine not being in your arms anymore—these warm arms. They're my safe haven." He kisses the top of my wrist, leaving teardrops on my sleeves. "Zara, you're my everything, my life, my oxygen!" He bawls, hopelessly trying to salvage our love. "You're—you're my whole universe."

There are words that can hit you like a car going at the speed of light. Words that can melt stones without any source of heat. That's the thing about words, whether they're good or bad—you never forget them. For me, those four words will forever remain the ones that can soften my heart, no matter how hard it can get. But the difference this time is what I promised myself—to have the courage to walk away when I need to, regardless of the words that have seared into my heart and soul. It still doesn't make it easier to utter the next few words that I have to say, though every cell in my body begs not to.

"I'm not anymore."

His lamenting eyes pierce into mine one last time, desperately hoping I'd change my mind, but ultimately looking away like he knows there's nothing more he can do. He loosens his grip on my hands—the hands that love being held so tightly by him. Grabbing his phone, he pushes himself off the floor back on his feet. I keep my eyes away from his, as I don't dare to look into them for they might tempt me to jump off my bed, hug, and forgive him. Without a single fight, a single word, a single noise, he drags his feet out of my room, closing the door behind him.

I slide off my bed and onto the floor where he left drops of his tears, reminding me of what just happened. I wrap my arms around myself, and finally let out a cry so loud, the echoes bounce off the walls. These same walls that once heard me declare my love to him, now have heard the disownment of the same love.

As I look around—my eyes drenched with tears that hold the memory of the moments passed—I find him in every corner. The first flowers he gave me that have withered and dried, the ticket to his concert back in Korea secured into the wall with a thumbtack, the first picture we took, captured as proof of our love, in a frame sitting on my dresser—all left as reminders of the times I was unequivocally happy. How do I just forget them now? How do I get over the times he's made me smile when I needed to most? How do I remove them from my collection of breathtaking memories—memories that will constantly remind me of what I've lost?

Did I make the right decision? He apologized, was remorseful—should I have forgiven him? Given him a second chance? Have I driven him into Rose Lin's arms? Is he going to be okay? Am I—am I going to be okay?

My heart cries—throbs in unbearable pain because regardless of the mistake he made, I still love him. And I realize at this moment that no matter what happens, he'll always have a hold over me.

CHAPTER 8:

Zara's Night

"I'm so glad you left her." Rose Lin sits on AJ's lap, latching her long legs to his.

"She left me," he says with a frown, looking at the palm of his hand. "But now that means you and I can be together." That frown transforms into a menacing smile.

"Yeah, exactly. Plus, it'll be easier being with me. You can have me at your disposal at any time of the day…if you know what I mean," she says in her stupid British accent, winking at him as he looks at her with a lustful stare.

Effing assholes! He really couldn't wait to crawl into her toned arms, now could he?! How can he do all this—right in front of me?! Wait, where am I? Am I…in a closet?! Jesus, these clothes dangling over me is making it harder to see through the crack.

"And…you're prettier. I always had to lie

and say she's the most beautiful girl I've ever seen, but really...it's you." He 'boops' the tip of her nose, just like the way he did to me. God, I can't tell if that hurts me or infuriates every particle in my body!

"Oh, I know I'm prettier than her. Have you seen me? I have the body and face of a goddess. I'm the Aphrodite of K-Pop." She flips her long, flowy black hair over her shoulder. Aphrodite, my ass. She's more like the ostentatious wicked witch of K-Pop.

"Yes—yes you are...my love."

My love? MY LOVE?! Is he just recycling everything he used to say to me?! He really is a piece of shit, isn't he?!

He caresses her face, looking into her eyes JUST the way he did with me. Leaning in, she gets closer to his face, and he with her. They stare at each other, glancing at one another's lips.

Are they going to kiss? God, it's going to kill me if they do. They get closer, and closer. Their lips lightly brush against each other. They breathe heavily, chests rising and falling rapidly. No, no, no! She can't kiss my boyfriend! Not this time!

And right before their lips press together, I jump out of the closet, and roar, "NOOOO!"

"Zara!" Jace barges through my door, waking me up from my nightmare.

I'm laying on the floor, the same place my former lover cried his eyes out just hours ago.

"Are you okay?" He comes to my rescue, pulling me into his arms.

"I'm fine, just living a nightmare." I push him away, acting like my heart wasn't torn apart last night.

"So I heard." Jace flops next to me against the bed. "He broke down crying in mine and Ari's arms when he came back."

"As he should." My nostrils flare the more I think about my dream, which doesn't seem far from the truth...though it is far from the truth, but I just want to be angry—I'm entitled to be.

"Zara..." he brushes back my hair, "he was pretty broken up."

"Yeah, well—so was I. Do you even know what he did?"

"Yeah, he told us. I won't lie, there was nothing I wanted to do more than to punch every singing note outta him when he was telling us about what happened, but I didn't have to do anything at all. I think he's already beating himself up from the way he was bawling his eyes out. I can tell he hates himself more than you do."

"I don't hate him. I just wish he could choke on his own tears." I mumble, grinding my teeth to the thought of him kissing her with the same lips he kissed me.

"You don't wish that, let's be real." He crosses his arms.

"Then what do I wish, Edward Cullen?" I mimic his movement.

"You wish you could run up and hug him."

"No, I don't." I argue with the fake mind reader.

"Yes—yes you do." He argues back.

"No, I don't, Jace. I won't want to hug the person who lied to my face and made me look and feel like a complete fool—repeatedly." Even though I was thinking I made a mistake last night, I'm burning with fury over what he did.

"I know, bubba. I'm so sorry." He kisses the top of my head. "If it makes you feel better, after you and AJ left, I 'accidentally' spilled a drink on her. She was pissed at me." Thinking of the sight actually makes me chuckle. "I do think she has an inkling you and AJ are—I mean, were together."

Ha, 'were'—what a taunting word, reminding you of things that are now forever remaining in the past. The only way it's less gibe is if the word is attached to memories less happy. Unfortunately, I'm not that lucky.

"Well, he's all hers now."

"Don't say that, Zara. Do you want to talk about it?" he asks with a gentle tone, rubbing my thigh to comfort me.

"No—I'm done talking."

"Then what do you want to do?"

"I want..." I contemplate the cure to a broken heart, "I want to not think about anything at all."

"And how do you do that?"

I glance at Jace, malevolence in my eyes.

I jump to my feet, plucking my purse off of my bed, and fish through the sea of crap to find my phone. Scrolling through my list of contacts, I click on the one name I never thought I'd ever call when in desperate need of some reckless fun. I press on the telephone icon, calling...

"Hello?"

"Arsalan." I answer back to the one and only savior who can guarantee a roguish night out. "Are you free tonight?"

"I can be for you. What do you have in mind?" he asks flirtatiously.

Good, I'm in the mood for some of his sleazy medicine.

"Take me out dancing tonight," I demand the desi Damon. I see Jace's jaw drop from the corner of my eye.

"Wouldn't your K-Pop boyfriend mind?"

"What boyfriend?" I reply, scoffing at the sound of that title. "Be here by eight. Can't wait to see you...doctor." I end the phone call before he can ask the 'who's', 'what's', and 'where's'.

"Zara, what are you doing?" Jace's face exudes immense confusion, but I couldn't be more certain of my actions.

"Having fun, what does it look like I'm doing?" I toss the phone on my bed.

"Like this? Are you sure you want to cope with a painful break up like THIS? There are other ways, like finding what's at the bottom of a Ben and Jerry's and watching slasher movies," he advises, but I could care less about caring at all.

"Yes, like THIS. I don't want to stay home, eat a bucket of sugar, and cry myself to sleep after watching innocent yet dumb people get murdered brutally. Either you join in, or you're more than welcome to watch me from the sidelines because I'm going out tonight whether you like it or not."

"It's not like you, Zara." He steps forward, attempting to feed me some valid logic, but I'm really not in the mood to listen.

"Maybe I don't want to be, Jace! Maybe...I just need to tend to my own heart and ego in my own, unconventional way. Just let me not be me for one night. That's all I'm asking."

"Alright, fine." He surrenders his hands in the air. "I'm in."

"Thank you, I appreciate it." Well, that didn't take much convincing. "I just can't stand being in the apartment right now, having every corner filled with memories of him."

"Whatever you need. It's Zara's night."

"Zara's night it is."

I'm ready to not be Zara. Not for forever—but certainly not for tonight.

◆ ◆ ◆

"Zara! Arsalan's going to be here in five minutes!" Jace hollers from the kitchen.

"Okay!" I reply, curling the last strand of hair.

Setting down the curling iron on my sink, I stare at my reflection, making sure my makeup looks okay. I decided to go with something different—something bold. I never wear shimmery eyeshadow. Normally I'd go for neutral matte. But today, I wanted something that catches people's attention. I went with a potent gold shimmery shadow, accentuating the black specks in my brown eyes. I part my hair to the side, giving myself that vintage Hollywood hair.

Shit, I'm still in my towel! I hurry to my closet, sliding each hanger one by one to find something—still don't know what I'm exactly looking for. But then one dress catches my eyes—one that I'd never wear. A little black dress. I rip the towel off of me, and slip into the most revealing dress I've ever worn. I don't even know why I bought it in the first place. Maybe I thought that one day I'd have the courage to wear something as tight as this. Today seems like the perfect occasion. I run back to the mirror and fidget with my dress. It's tight alright, hugging every curve of my body but…I like it. I want to be looked at. If any auntie from the community saw how short this dress is, they'd immediately call my mom and tell her it's way too above my knees, to a point my ass and shame hang out. I mean, it's not even that short but it surely feels like it. I find matching strappy black heels to finish off my outfit, praying I don't trip and fall tonight.

All that's left is jewelry. I reach for my black 'churiyan' and find AJ's silver bracelet next to them. Ah, shit. I forgot to give it back to him. Do I give it back to him? Or do I keep it? A part of me wants to keep it, but the other part wants to toss it out. Eh, I'll ask Ari to deal with it. But, no churiyan for me today—too Zara-ish. What about my nose ring? It looks good but... reminds me of my little adventure with AJ. Nope, taking this out. Alright, earrings—ah, my silver 'jhumka' earrings I wore yesterday would go perfect with this but...now it's attached to one of the most terrible nights of my life. Screw it! I'm wearing these. Time to make more memories with them to replace the old ones. One Zara ensemble won't do much harm for the night.

Ding dong!

Ah, that's him! I smooth down my dress, fix my hair, and wink at myself in the mirror—I'm ready for Zara's night.

Opening my door, I see Arsalan and Jace both in the kitchen with songs playing, blasting through Jace's speaker. Arsalan's setting up three shot glasses on the counter while Jace is carefully pouring the liquid courage.

"Hey, Arsalan." I greet the desi Damon with a flirtatious smile like the one that's always on his face. His lips part and his eyes cannot believe what they're seeing.

"Wow," he blurts with his unfiltered

mouth.

"What?" Jace's focus is interrupted by Arsalan's screech, but then looks in the direction of his eyes. His mouth drops. "Wow, that's a short tight dress." You'd think he'd be proud I'm embracing my insecurities, but I can't tell how he feels from the shock on his face.

"Yeah, I know." I agree with confidence, skipping to the kitchen.

"You look...different." Arsalan observes, lips still parted.

"And...is that bad?" I get close to him, looking deeply into his eyes without blinking.

"Not at all. Just, different." He replies with a nervous whisper, making the inner flirt push the old Zara completely away.

"Well, I have the shots ready." Jace interrupts Arsalan's and my playful staring contest, placing three shot glasses right in front of us three.

"Oh, I'll take that—" Before they even reach to grab their respective glass, I pick one up and chug it down immediately. Then, continue to pick the second, gulping it down without making a face or gagging. Then the third...leaving the boys stunned, yet again. "What? I was thirsty." I wipe the corner of my mouth with the edge of my thumb, licking the faltering drop of the vodka off of it while looking at Arsalan teasingly.

"I'll just...pour more." Jace says with his brows raised high.

"I'll take care of this, Jace. You can go use the restroom since you've been waiting for a while. I just ordered an Uber, so it should be here soon." Arsalan takes the bottle from him.

"Uh—yeah, thanks." Jace walks past me, patting me on the back with worry in his eyes. I don't know why he isn't encouraging me like he normally does. I'm finally having fun.

As Jace shuts the door to his room behind him, Arsalan turns to me, locking eyes with mine.

"Are you okay?" he asks, squinting his eyes at me.

"Yeah, why wouldn't I be?" I bite my bottom lip, doe-eyed.

"Because you just gorged down three shots, when the sight of one makes you puke." Wow, I didn't realize he was that observant. "Does this have anything to do with AJ by any chance?" he inquires. Compassion in his voice doesn't suit him at all.

"No." I growl, snatching the bottle of vodka out of his hands. "Not at all." And swig the potion in large gulps to forget last night while staring straight into Arsalan's concerned eyes.

"I'm just having fun," I assure him, wiping my mouth with the back of my hand.

"Alright, you're cut off for the night." He seizes the bottle out of my hand with one quick motion, taking away the chance to wrestle it back.

"No, I'm not," I argue, annoyed by him treating me like a stubborn child.

"Yes—yes you are." He gestures to stop with his finger.

"I can drink however much I want. Who the hell are you to stop me?" I complain, visibly clenching my jaw to show I'm blatantly annoyed.

"Someone who gives a shit about you." He steps closer to me, his eyes switching from looking into mine, one and then to the other. "You can get VERY sick," he warns, furrowing his brows to emphasize his concern. Arsalan's actually really worried about me.

"Well...then you can take care of me," I say with a low tone, a smirk on my face, confusing him with my unusual behavior.

He stares into my eyes as if he's trying to figure out what's gotten into me. Then, his eyes land on my nose.

"Where's your nose ring?"

"I took it off," I say with a spunky tone.

"I said it looked nice on you."

So did AJ.

"Well..." I click my tongue, trailing a finger down his tan bare chest that's peeking through his v-cut gray shirt, "I think I'll let myself be the judge of what looks nice on me and what doesn't."

As we eye each other—me with uncareful flirty eyes, and him with care—Jace swings his door open, making Arsalan step away from me but I remain standing, eyes still on him.

"What about those shots?" Jace asks, rubbing his palms together.

Without moving his eyes from me, Arsalan says, "Coming right up." He pours the vodka in two shot glasses.

Jace picks one of them up and raises his glass. Arsalan follows.

"To Zara's night." He cheers, looking at me with a hint of worry but covers it with ingenuine excitement.

"To Zara's night," Arsalan repeats, and clinks his glass to Jace's, both gulping down at the same time.

I grin to the sound of that—to Zara's night indeed.

◆ ◆ ◆

"I.D., please." The exceptionally tall, stoic security guard of this nightclub—my tipsy ass already forgot the name of it, even though Jace mentioned it only a hundred times in the Uber—stops and asks me with such a threatening tone. God, why do they have to always look like there's something stuck up their asses—who pissed them off?

"I.D., please." I mock him mimicking his facial expressions, drunkenly attempting to unzip my purse.

"Excuse me?" he snaps, voice deep and

raised but I couldn't care less at the fact he has the authority to not let me in to dance my heart out.

"Haha—please ignore my friend, she's drunk," Jace says with a nervous laugh, yanking my purse out of my hand and swiping my I.D. out.

The security guard shakes his head and rolls his eyes as he flashes his light on my driver's license. Oh, hell no! No one, and I mean NO ONE rolls their eyes at someone who just had her heart ripped into shreds!

"Excuse me, mister…I do not appreciate—" I step forward to give him a piece of my mind, and before I can finish my sentence, Jace pulls me back by my wrist.

"THANK you, sir." He widens his eyes at me as the guard hands back my I.D., telepathically telling me to shut the hell up before he kicks us out, and Arsalan who's patiently waiting at the entrance for us. "Let's go!" Jace scolds me in a hushed tone, gesturing with his eyes to move forward.

"What took you so long?" Arsalan asks, looking behind us at the security guard.

"Little Miss. Grumpy was trying to start a fight with the security guard," Jace says with a disappointed head shake.

"He was being rude!" I defend myself, stomping a foot on the ground, which leaves me unbalanced, but Arsalan grabs onto my arm before I tip over like a cow. Crap, the alcohol is starting to hit more and more by the minute.

"We could have totally taken him." Arsalan winks at me, still having his hand around my arm like a mother on her out of control child.

"No, we couldn't!" Jace glances back at the security guard. "He's like a giant! He would've cut off both of our beanstalks, and then hurled Zara violently across the streets of West Hollywood."

"Okay, I don't care." I roll my eyes, swaying back and forth. "Can we go inside now?"

"You two go on, I have to wait for Ari," Jace says as he scans through the line behind us.

"Ari's coming?!" I groan. God, I don't need any reminder of AJ.

"Yeah, why?" Jace questions, puzzled by my complaint. "I told her about the whole 'Zara's night' and she wanted to be a part of it, so I told her to come. She just wants to make sure you're okay."

"Okay, wait. Let me get this straight. You wanted me to feel better. So you decided to invite the SISTER of the one who broke my heart? Yeah, that makes total sense." I articulate my frustration by crossing my arms. "Arsalan, let's go."

I storm inside and Arsalan follows.

"Hey, wait!" Arsalan shouts, stopping me in my tracks by hooking his hand onto my elbow. "That was pretty harsh, Zara. Jace is just worried about whatever's going on with you."

"Okay, then maybe everyone needs to stop

worrying about me! I haven't compelled myself to shut off my human emotions. I'll deal with it when I need to." I brush his hand off of my elbow, and march towards the bar.

I just wanted one night to not think about anything! Is that too much to ask? Agh, Jesus. I need to snag myself a drink before I pop a vessel.

❖ ❖ ❖

After convincing the fun police, aka Arsalan, I bought and slurped on my delicious Moscow mule that seemed to have the answer to my problems at the bottom of it. I feel so amazing—so worry-free! Exactly what I wanted. Sorry—needed.

"Zara, can you come with me to the restroom?" Ari asks, trying to talk over the loud music. "Old Town Road" by Lil Nas X plays in the background.

"Yeah, I need to pee!" Thank god she reminded me, or else I would have held it in and risked getting a urinary tract infection.

We both exit out of the circle us four made by the bar, and head towards the restroom. There's not a long line, thank god! We immediately get escorted to the bathroom stalls by two attendants.

Gosh, peeing while your world is spinning is the most challenging thing any sane person can do.

"Zara, you done?" Ari asks through my bathroom stall. Music from outside trickles through faintly.

"Yeah," I say as I flush with my heel, then pull my door. "All done."

We both hobble to the sink and the bathroom attendants smile at us, turning the lever for us and dispensing soap onto our hands.

"Thank you!" I shoot them a friendly, drunken smile. Then both leave to help a girl puking on the bathroom floor.

As I'm washing my hands with the warm water gushing through the faucet, Ari finishes first and reaches over me to grab some napkins.

"Hey, Zara...how are you doing?" She asks, softness in her tone. Agh, not this. Not now.

"Ari, I don't wanna talk about it," I say, waiting for the water to become clear of soap.

"Are you sure?"

"Yes, I just don't want to think about it."

"Okay, yeah. That's totally fine." She gets closer, cuffing her hand over my ear to whisper, "But, AJ wanted me to tell you not to worry about the picture. He cleared that up by saying the girl in the picture was me." She steps away after finishing her sentence. "Thank god our hair looks the same."

God, can she not say his name? It's making me sick.

"And I just want to say that I yelled at him a lot. I'm so disappointed in him. How could he do that?! And that bitch is SO not my bias anymore." She wipes her hand forcefully with the napkin as the remix version of "Bad Guy" by Billie Eilish plays.

And I just don't care right now. Jesus, I was having such a good time, and now I'm getting pissed because I'm picturing AJ and that bitch kissing. AGH!

"Look, Ari. I appreciate it but I really just don't want to talk about him."

"I'm sorry, I won't push it. But you know he does love you, right? I hate him right now, and totally on board with that, but I hope you don't think that he did it because he didn't love you. I don't know what the hell was going through his stupid head."

"Ari...please, I don't care." I turn off the faucet.

"Alright, but just know you can talk to me about it. I just want to help, Zara." She hands me a napkin.

Well, this isn't helping shit! The more she talks and defends him, the more I think about how he single-handedly broke my trust, made me insecure, and didn't fail to make me feel like a complete idiot!

"You wanna help me?" I turn to face her, I'm boiling! "Then maybe stop trying to convince me that your lying, cheating ass of a brother actually loved me." She looks around nervously as I catch some attention from girls walking into the bathroom stall. I should stop, but she doesn't get it! "He never did, okay? Get that through your head. If he did, he wouldn't have gone and stuck his tongue down some bitches' throat." I wipe my hands off the paper towel once more and toss it in the trash can. "Stop lying to yourself. Leave the lying to your brother."

Her eyes widen like a baby who just got spooked by a loud noise.

"Oh, I'm sorry—" She stammers, turns around and sprints out of the bathroom. I remain standing there, holding onto the counter, trying to breathe to cool my anger. I know I said more than needed to, but I just don't care.

Two girls walk up to the sink next to me, giggling drunk.

"Yeah, he said it on his v-live that it was his sister. I don't buy it!" One girl says to the other. Are they talking about AJ?

"There's no way! But I read it's some girl from here! Lucky ass girl, wish it were one of us!" She holds her phone screen to her friend's face. "But look at her earring? It's actually so pretty. At least she's got taste."

As I'm staring at my reflection, I notice my earrings—the same as last night. God damn it. I didn't realize anyone would care enough to notice them that closely. Immediately, I rip them out of my ears, chuck them into my purse and strut out of the bathroom.

I guess no matter what I do, I just can't get

away from last night, AJ, and freaking K-Pop—not even for one night!

As I'm turning the corner out of the restroom, I find Arsalan standing there.

"Hey, where's Jace?" I ask, looking around the premises to see if he's there.

"He ran after Ari. She looked pretty upset, saying she should go home."

Ah, shit. Remorse creeps up my conscience, but I need to push it back down. I don't want to feel that right now. And before I completely push it all away, I see Jace storming towards us.

"What did you say to her?!" he shouts, but in a way so no one around us could hear.

"Nothing," I answer calmly.

"So, she's just upset for no reason?" He asks like he doesn't believe me.

"Seems like it, doesn't it?" I cross my arms as he looks at me with pissed eyes...which lowkey is making me a tad bit anxious. I've actually never seen him mad at me before. "Okay, I barely said anything to her. She kept bringing up, you know who, and I didn't want to talk about it."

"Okay, well, whatever you said made her feel like a shitty person. She wants to leave because she said she ruined your night."

"Well, she did," I say with certainty, pushing away the shrivel of anxiety. She did ruin my night defending her stupid brother.

He looks at me with disappointed yet

angry eyes. If I saw those eyes any other day, I'd melt with shame and guilt, but I genuinely don't give a single shit. It's my day to cope with MY breakup, not worry about anyone's feelings.

"I'm...going to take her back to the hotel. I think I'm gonna spend the night there." He turns around to leave, but stops his tracks to turn right back around. "You know, I love you so much, Zara. And I'm there for you with whatever you need. But you and I both know you're not being yourself right now. And in the midst of that, don't end up hurting someone else who actually cares about you...like you just did with me." And with one last look of disappointment, he walks away.

I thought hearing AJ confess his crime was painful, but hearing Jace say that feels ten times worse. No, Jace...I—god, I feel so shitty! But, no... why should I feel shitty at all? I'm the one who's going through a heartbreak. At least Jace and Ari are happily together—not me! You don't have to feel bad. YOU got hurt. YOU got cheated on over a stupid excuse. YOU—you had your heart ripped out of your chest by that stupid K-Pop star. Not anyone else. You're entitled to cope however you want to deal with your breakup, even if someone doesn't approve of it. Screw this.

"Arsalan, dance with me." I grab his hand, locking mine to his. Whoa, this feels...strange. His hands are soft and rough at the same time —strong. Though they're just hands, they feel different. Maybe because the only ones I'm used to belong to someone else.

I guess the touch of our hands not only surprised me, but him. He grips on to mine tightly like I'm about to fall over a cliff, glancing at me and then at our locked hands with a look on his face I can't recognize. There's this gloominess to it.

I lead him, pushing through the crowd to the dance floor as the Gryffin remix of "Desire" by Years & Years starts playing, filling the club with the most upbeat atmosphere—one that's lifting my spirits back up. I place his hands on my waist, wrapping my arms around his neck and pulling him close to me—feeling his rock-hard abs against me. His eyes are accompanied by slightly furrowed brows as they're glued onto mine, but still no smile on his face—far from what my face looks like. I'm drenching myself in the flickering neon lights that are moving to the beat of the song—my body joining in, but Arsalan's as stiff as a log. And...one by one, everything's escaping my mind—Jace, Ari, Rose Lin, K-Pop, and AJ. I'm indulging this totally normal moment. And, I'm not complaining about the company either.

As I'm fully drowning myself in the music, forgetting about the world and everything around me, I'm feeling a sort of deja vu—like I've done this before. Remembering the feeling of dancing with a man...dancing with AJ, at that small bar in Korea. And just like that, he's intruded on my mind. I see AJ and Rose Lin kissing in front of my eyes. I see his hands all over her body. I see his eyes looking into hers. My blood churns, filling my stomach with the same feeling you feel when you're on a rollercoaster. A part of me wishes he could see me right now, dancing with Arsalan. But I'm gonna break free from him in this temporary euphoric moment with the help of the desi Damon.

"Arsalan, thanks for being here for me," I say with a mindless flirty smile.

"No problem." He replies, clearly not reciprocating the flirtiness. What is up with him? You'd think he'd be enjoying this, but it just looks like he's just here as my own personal bodyguard and not to have any fun.

"You're so handsome." I bite my bottom lip, fondling his with my eyes.

"Thank you," he says with a thin smile.

Um…okay?

"Aren't you gonna tell me I'm pretty?" I need my ego stroked right now, even if I have to be forward about it. Thanks, liquid courage.

"I don't have to tell you that. You already know you are."

"Well, hearing it won't hurt." I draw closer to him, enough to feel his warm breath on my skin.

With a sigh, he says, "You're pretty."

"That didn't sound genuine," I scoff with a

brow raised.

"It is."

"Then prove it." His infamous devilish grin manifests on my face. "Kiss me."

His lips part, and eyes slightly twitch as if he couldn't believe I just said that. I mean, a part of me doesn't either but I'm going to go along with it.

"No, Zara."

Ouch. I'm just getting rejected left to right, aren't I?

"Why not?" I ask, enunciating the 't' angrily to hide my hurt ego.

"Not like this." He shakes his head, and I lock eyes with a guy behind him with blue, lustful eyes.

"Fine, if you won't, I'm sure someone else will." I give a bitchy smile, and loosen my arms around him, then march towards the one who seems to be interested in kissing me.

"Hi." I give an inviting, promiscuous smile. He seems like someone who was definitely in a fraternity back in college.

"Hey there, beautiful," he says in a sleazy tone but totally reciprocates the vibe I gave off. Sliding his hand against my back, onto my waist, I jump from his touch. I know I'm still getting used to the touch of another man, just didn't feel this way with Arsalan. But, I ignore it with a laugh.

"Zara, let's go." I hear Arsalan's voice from

behind me. He sounds like a pissed dad.

I turn around, looking up at Arsalan and see his eyes dark with anger.

"Excuse me, who the hell are you?" The guy raises his voice at him, still having his hand around my waist.

Arsalan plucks his hand off my waist, setting the guy off from the way his eyes widen.

"None of your business." He replies, clenching his jaw. "Zara let's go."

"Um—okay." I comply with his command as people stop dancing to stare.

"I asked…" the guy pushes me to the side, and steps towards Arsalan, "who the hell are you?"

Oh, shit. I hope I didn't cause this soon to be fight.

"Zara, let's go." Arsalan says with more force, ignoring the guy as if he didn't just ask him a question.

"She's not going anywhere," the guy says with a threatening tone, springing towards Arslan, but he doesn't even flinch.

"Back off," Arsalan says calmly, though the way his hands are turning to fists clearly shows he's not calm at all.

"No–no, I don't need to back off." The guy laughs, "But, you need to…you freaking terrorist!"

What in the name of Uranus did you say, you little piece of—agh!

The few paying attention gasp. Arsalan—he's not even fazed at all. But, unlike him...I'm livid! I thought my blood boiled at its finest during the dinner fiasco, or when I think of AJ and Rose Lin kissing...but no, no—those don't even compare to this. This is the moment my inner Hulk had been waiting for so patiently.

As blood rushes to my head, my breathing becomes as fast as the music in the club, and my hand turns into a fist and...

"Oomph!" The guy grunts at...my punch to his gut! My punch?!

"Zara!" Arsalan calls my name in surprise.

I stand there, staring at my fist, trying to comprehend the fact that I—Zara Shah, a pacifist—just punched a guy who's wailing in pain, lowkey sounding like a seal.

And if that weren't enough for my inner Hulk, I open my mouth, not knowing what I want to say and blurt out, "You're a bad...BAD person!" Bad person? That's what I decide to go with? What am I—two?!

"Zara, let's go!" Grabbing my hand like a mother to her unfiltered two-year-old, Arsalan drags me out of the crowd, laughing, and we sprint through the doors, out of the club.

Zara's night wasn't going as planned, but that—that made up for it.

◆ ◆ ◆

"Arsalan, please hurry and open the door. I'm gonna throw up!" I cry out as Arsalan struggles to insert the key into the lock. He's not even drunk like I am!

"Okay, okay. I heard you a million times in the Uber. Just give me a moment—" he pushes the key harder into the lock and twists the knob, successfully opening the door. "Anddd, there we go."

Without thanking him for the simple task, I toss my purse on the floor and bolt through the entrance all the way to my bathroom.

I hunch over my toilet, my hair sliding to the front but I could care less if it gets vomit on it as long as it means I get the relief.

"Oh my god!" I gag as the taste of vodka surfaces, "I'm wanna kill myself."

"Zara, here—" Arsalan walks in to my rescue, placing a Pedialyte from the fridge on the sink's counter. Then, gathers my hair from the front and holds it back. "Take your time. I'm here." Gently rubbing my back with quick strokes.

"I promise to Allah I'll stop drinking if it means I could throw up right now."

Arsalan laughs, "I don't think you should make that big of a promise just yet."

I wait to see if Allah can grant my wish right this second, but it seems like I'd have to suffer through the nausea.

"Arsalan, I don't think it's coming yet."

"Okay, how about we sit down here until you do. First, drink this." He twists the cap off of the Pedialyte and holds the mouth of the bottle to my lips.

"Mhmm, okay." I take large sips, then gesture to stop once my stomach starts to feel like it's going to explode from liquids.

He helps my drunk ass to lay my back against the wall beside the tub. Pulling down the towel that's hanging on the curtain rail, he folds it into a little pillow, placing it on the butt of the tub.

"Here, put your head down on the towel. I bet it is spinning." He holds onto my head.

"It is—it totally is." I put all my weight into his hand as he places my head down. Then, he sits in front of me.

As I close my eyes to make my world stop spinning, I jump from the sound of his laugh.

"I can't believe you punched a guy." He continues laughing.

"Yeah, me neither." I let out a little chuckle, but then the dull ache in my knuckles reminds me of why I got angry. "He totally deserved it."

"Ah, it's fine." He brushes it off with a laugh like it's no big deal.

"No, it's not fine," I say defensively. "I don't know how you just stood there not saying something back."

"Eh, it's not the first time someone's said that to me. And, I can assure you it's not the last."

"But, doesn't it make you mad? It makes me mad."

He pauses, looking out at a distance as if he were seeing a reel of his life events.

"It did make me mad. At least it used to." He shrugs it off, "I'd get frustrated, a lot. Especially when they'd bring up nine-eleven in history class and all eyes would be on me—the brown, Muslim kid. But, they thought saying, 'Oh hey, don't worry, you're one of the good ones', would make me feel better. But…it only made me feel worse." He scoffs, shaking his head. "Every time someone compared Islam to a terrorist religion, whether it was at school or in the news, I'd get so confused—doubting the religion that only taught me about peace. I'd question, how—how can those people claim themselves as being Muslim but commit such an inhumane act? How can Islam allow that?" He lets out a loud sigh. It vibrates through my bathroom. "But, they weren't Muslims—they weren't even human beings. Yet, they managed to taint our religion, making it hard for the rest of us to constantly prove to others we aren't one of them."

"And sadly, people believe that we are."

"We can't blame them, Zara."

"Why not? Don't they have common sense?" I argue.

"You'd think, right? But…I think it's all because of fear." He points at his thin beard. "Fear breeds ignorance, and ignorance breeds hatred.

When they're constantly seeing on the news or watching movies and T.V. shows that have this narrative of Muslims being the enemy—of course that changes the way people look at us."

"If only they'd see Muslims like us—" I gesture to myself with a finger, "they'd see how harmless we are. I can't even lift my head up right now."

"Okay, my little drunken punching star. I don't think we're the best examples to broadcast to the world." We both laugh, which hurts my head even more as it slightly bangs against the tub.

"Ouch." I rub my head. "Oh mere khudaya, I think I'm getting punished with this headache and this tub is making it worse."

"Ah, come here, sparky." He scoots to my side and extends his arm around me, placing the other hand on the side of my cheek that's on the towel, and moving my head against his chest. "Is this better?"

"Hmmm…much better." I nestle my face into his shirt, pretty sure I'm rubbing off my makeup on it but…it's so soft.

"Are you cozy?" He asks, running his fingers through my hair.

"Hmmm…so cozy." I drag my hand—which feels like a thousand pounds—to rest it on his chest.

"Good, good. I'm here for you."

This is so nice right now. Though my head

is spinning, this feels like the cure for it. He's warm. He's comfortable to lay on. And he smells amazing. He smells familiar. He smells just like… AJ—Armani. Ah, great. Funny how scents can spark a memory or the thought of a person. I didn't need this right now. The smell is making me sick, when once I couldn't get enough of it.

"Ah, hey, you're kinda pressing on my bladder and now I have to pee," he says, laughing carefully so he doesn't pee his pants right there and then.

"Go pee in Jace's room. This is occupied."

"Gotcha, boss. But, um…in order for me to do that, you gotta get up just for a few minutes. Promise you can rest on my chest after. Okay?" I feel his breath on my forehead as he lowers his face a little down, his lips hovering above my forehead.

"Okay," I agree, slowly raising my head off of his chest.

"Careful, careful." He says while positioning me back against the wall. Then, he walks hurriedly out of my bathroom.

The smell of his cologne still lingers in my hair, reminding me of AJ. I think for a moment there, laying on his chest and smelling the scent…it felt like I was laying on AJ. And honestly, despite how much I want to hate him or how much I dreaded anything that had to do with him today…I miss him. I miss him a lot. And more than anything, I wish he were here instead. Call me dumb, or a masochist. My drunk ass self wants him to take care of me.

Ding dong!

Did the doorbell ring or is it in my head?

Ding dong!

Okay, I'm sure that's not in my head.

Ding dong!

That is the doorbell. Why isn't Jace just using his keys? Agh, now I gotta figure out how to get up.

Ding dong!

Oh for freaking sake, I'm coming! I reach out to hold on to the counter and push myself off the floor with whatever strength I have. Oh my god, I'm going to fall on my ass and probably choke on my own vomit. Just take a small, slow step, Zara. Right foot, then left. Right foot, then left. Okay, great. I'm out of my room.

Ding dong!

Oh my god, I'm coming! Right foot, left. Right, left. I got this, I'm almost there.

Ding dong!

Jesus, why the hell is Jace ringing the doorbell like there's a murderer after him! Oh, shit... what if there is!

Ding dong!

I'm coming, Jace! You won't be murdered on my watch! I clasp onto the doorknob, holding onto it for support and twist it open.

"Zara?"

Oh, fuck. That voice. That face. Those deep

brown concerned eyes. All good enough to make the butterflies in my stomach fly up to a point they come out as...

"Blaargh!" I hurl everything in my stomach into the kitchen's trash can. That's going to leave a beautiful stench from the Thai food I ate earlier today.

"Zara!" He leaps forward, holding my hair back.

"AJ..." I say weakly, "what—what are you doing here?"

"I had to see you before I leave tomorrow. But first, let's take care of you." He grabs me by the waist, holding me up as I can't feel my legs right now. Though I'm drunk, I'm aware enough to notice him eyeing my outfit, prompting a quick eyebrow raise as if he were surprised.

"You shouldn't have come. We're broken up," I reason, still confused as to why he's acting like last night never happened.

"Zara, don't exert yourself too much." He picks me up in his arms, as mine cling onto his neck and he carries me to the couch, laying me down as if I were dead—which isn't far from what I'm feeling right now.

"Why are you here?" I ask with a slurred speech, "Are you even here or am I too drunk that I'm imagining you?" I examine his face with eyes that feel like they're moving in all sorts of directions to verify he's really here. His hair is slicked back, a touch of brown shadow on his eyelids.

He's probably coming back from an event.

"I'm here...Zara." He pushes a strand of hair out of my face with his boney finger, staring at me with admiring eyes. It feels like that one stroke just gave me peace, which it shouldn't. Not even one bit.

"You hurt me." I push his hand away, hoping that'd also push away what I'm feeling right now.

"I know, Zara. And—I'm sorry. I don't even know why I'm here. I just know I had to—"

"What the fuck are you doing here?"

Oh my god, just...kill me right now. I forgot he was here! I didn't even hear Arsalan open the door to Jace's room! Unless he didn't close it in the first place. Has he been standing there the whole time? Oh, Zara, you idiot! That's what you're worried about?

Though my body feels like it's under a sleep paralysis, I'm still aware enough to witness how pissed both AJ and Arsalan look right now.

"Why are you here? Where's Jace?" AJ asks in a speculating tone, like if he were trying to find out if we both are alone...together.

"I'm taking care of the mess YOU made." Arsalan walks slowly into the living room, AJ still standing beside my dead body. I look like Snow White when she's in that glass coffin. Except she looked radiating even in death, while I look like a raccoon on meth.

"Arsalan, I just want to have a private conversation with Zara, if you don't mind." AJ voices his intention, but that doesn't seem to convince Arsalan.

"No, I do mind. She's had enough of you tonight. Besides, don't you have somewhere to dance and sing?" Arsalan glowers at him as he stops by the coffee table, a few feet away from AJ.

"I'm not gonna fight you. But, I do prefer you minding your own business," AJ says with contesting eyes and firm tone.

"Oh, who said anything about fighting? But besides, what are you gonna hit me with? Your handy dandy microphone?" Arsalan says with a mocking tone. I see AJ cracking his index finger with his thumb. Oh, shit.

"Arsalan, I'm trying really hard not to start anything right now for Zara's sake." AJ's voice may seem calm, but from the look of his ears turning red…he's most definitely not.

"Oh, for Zara's sake?" Arsalan scoffs at his statement while taking a step closer to AJ. "I highly doubt you care…for Zara's sake. I don't know what you did, but I know for a fact it was bad enough to make Zara want to forget your existence."

AJ's jaw clenches as he cracks his middle finger with his thumb.

"If I were you, I'd run along back to your little K-Pop life. Oh, and on your way there, stop by Maybelline. They called asking for their eyeliner back." Arsalan's ridiculing tone and remarks are making me anxious, seeing AJ's distended vein in his forehead pop out.

Arsalan takes another step forward, now he's inches away from AJ's face. I force myself to come out of my body paralysis lifting my head up with the support of my arms.

"You just couldn't wait to make a move at Zara, could you?" AJ speaks up and moves closer to Arsalan. They're so close, they could kiss! Oh, shit, this isn't good.

"Well, a *man* had to step up—or just someone who doesn't have to hide in the shadows to date Zara."

AJ's chest rises, breathing heavy. He's fuming but Arsalan has that Damon Salvatore cocky smile on his face. AJ's hand turns into fist, just like mine did at the club. There's no way AJ would ever—-

POW!

I guess I spoke too soon. AJ punches Arsalan...right in the face! What the hell is going on? What is in the air today—rage?!

"AJ!" I scream, wobbling my way to Arsalan to assess the damage. His lip is busted, slightly bleeding, but Arsalan has a manic grin on his face. "AJ, you need to leave."

AJ stares at Arsalan with murderous eyes I've never seen before.

"Yeah, AJ. Double knot your way outta here, superstar." Arsalan riles him up as if he couldn't get any more furious.

With one last glance of fury at Arsalan, AJ turns and long, angry strides take him to the door. His hand rests on the knob, but he stops before twisting it. His shoulders are rising, I hear a shuddering sound as he breathes in.

"Zara…" he says without turning completely around, "I'm…sorry." Then, he opens and closes the door behind him.

Sorry? For what, AJ? There's so much you need to be sorry for…but still, despite everything…it's not me I feel sorry for, it's you. I know how even in this glamorous looking life, you have so little…and now it's one thing less.

CHAPTER 9:

A is for Arsalan

D id last night happen? Did AJ show up and punch Arsalan? Did I—I punch a guy, too? Ouch, my knuckles—yup, I certainly did. Ah, I still have my makeup and clothes on from last night. But, at least my head's not pounding as much thanks to the Pedialyte Arsalan made me chug for the sake of my life. That said, I probably deserve the pain for hurting Ari's and Jace's feelings—having a conscience is such a bitch. I'm overwhelmed with guilt. Caring really does take a lot outta ya, doesn't it?

Bing bing bing!

My alarm goes off, with a reminder that says 'volunteer with Dr. Johnson today'. Ah, crap. It slipped my mind that I signed up to volunteer today. Maybe that would help me to feel a little better about myself—feeling less shitty about my actions last night.

Knock knock!

The door cracks open slowly. Jace peeks inside with a thin smile. Oh, I missed him.

"Good morning." He walks inside, closing the door behind. "Um—how're you feeling?"

I push myself up to sit against my headboard.

"Better than I should." We both let out a chuckle.

He sits at the corner of my bed after smoothing my blanket out while I fidget with the corner for I cannot meet his eyes.

"Well, I'm glad you're feeling better." He nods, throwing me an awkward glance. There's this awkward silence in the room, and if it were a person, it would be someone wearing the flashiest, most obtrusive outfit. It's like one of us is waiting to start a conversation, but stays quiet in case the other speaks first. I should say something.

"Listen, Jace—"

"Listen, Zara—"

We both speak at the same time. Funny how we started out the same way. We really are best friends, aren't we?

"You go first," I say, smiling anxiously.

"No—no, you, please." He has that same smile as me.

"No—no, you." I try to convince, looking away to hide the shame I feel.

With a sigh, he parts his lip to say, "I'm

sorry I said what I did before I left!" He let out a guilty cry.

"No, I should be the one who's sorry—not you!" I rip the blanket off of me, and run to hug him, wrapping my arms around him as if we were reunited after eighty-four years.

"No, I should apologize, too." He rubs my back. "I didn't mean what I said. You didn't exactly hurt me…"

"I understand if I did. I was way too harsh with Ari."

"Well…what I said wasn't really about that. I mean, it was a little but I guess…" He sighs, gently pushing me off of him, "It hurt me to see you NOT be…you."

"I wasn't myself at all, that's for sure."

"And, normally, I'd encourage that." He chuckles. "But, it seemed like you were being more self-destructive, not caring about anyone or anything. It's the opposite of who you are."

"I know—I know, trust me. I woke up with nothing but guilt."

"Me, too." He squeezes the hand that went through a great ordeal.

"Ouch!" I yelp.

"Damn, what happened?!" He notices the slight bruise on my knuckles.

"I—uh…punched a guy." I say in a hushed, embarrassed tone. His eyes and jaw drop like my dignity did last night.

"YOU WHAT?!" He screams, throwing his

head back in laughter.

"Yeah...but, this doesn't hurt as much as seeing you disappointed in me."

He stops, pulling me into his arms yet again.

"Well, just make sure that's the last time, bitch." We both laugh, tightening our embrace.

"It will be. And, please tell Ari I'm sorry."

"You can tell her yourself at her birthday dinner next week." He pats the back of my head.

"I will. You better marry that girl, Jace. The fact that she's still with you after the crap I pulled last night just shows how truly incredible she is. Wait—you guys are still together, right?"

I will literally bury myself in guilt right now if I ended up breaking them up, but from the way he chuckles, I think I don't have to resort to killing myself.

"Yes—we're still together, don't worry. Maybe one day, I will marry her. Okay, wait—" He unwraps his arms, and faces me, "You need to tell me every detail of last night!"

"Oh, my god...where do I begin!" I plant my face into my hands, "So, I punched this guy because he called Arsalan a—"

Bang!

I get interrupted by a loud noise coming from the kitchen like someone dropped a plate in the sink.

I turn to Jace, a puzzled look on my face.

"Who is in—"

"Arsalan—I saw him sleeping on the couch when I walked in this morning. Now, he's making breakfast for you." He laughs, shaking his head.

"What?" I say with a puppy look on my face. That's...so sweet of him. "I should go see if he needs any help." I stand on my feet, but notice I'm still in my clothes from last night. "Once I get out of these clothes and take a shower."

He nods, glancing at my wrinkled little black dress, pinching his nose and airing out the slight stench coming from me. "That's probably a good idea." And, with a pat on the back, he walks out of my room with a pep to his step. I know he feels better just like I do after talking things out.

◆ ◆ ◆

"Hey." I step out of my room, pushing my wet hair away from my face.

"Hey." Arsalan sets his coffee mug down on the counter, a smile on his face. Walking towards the kitchen, I notice Jace isn't in the living room. "He's showering." Arsalan figures out I'm wondering about him.

"Oh, okay," I say as he hands me a mug.

"Black coffee—just like you like it."

"Thank you." I accept the desperately needed caffeine from him, when I notice his lip. "Oh, is it better now?" It looks less swollen with just a tiny cut.

"It'll be okay. Don't worry." He winks, "Here—have some breakfast." He hands me a plate with seasoned scrambled eggs and a side of toast.

"Wow. This looks good." I rip a piece of toast and gather some egg, tossing it into my mouth. "Tastes good, too."

"All thanks to your well-organized rack of masalas." He points towards the cupboard filled with the spices.

"More like all thanks to my mom." I chuckle as I take another bite. "Did you eat?"

"No," he says, picking up his cup and taking a sip of coffee. "I'm not hungry."

As I'm about to rip off another piece of toast, I stop. "Then I'm not eating."

"No—you have to."

"Nope." I cross my stubborn arms. "Not until you eat as well."

He stares at me with a slight head shake, letting out a defeated sigh.

"Alright, fine. But…" he steps closer, "only one bite."

I glare at him with disapproval. "Okay, fine." As long as he eats something.

Arslan leans in, opening his mouth. "Ahhh." He makes a sound, like a child would to their parent, ready for a bite.

"You want me to feed you?" I ask with squinting eyes.

"Ahan," he says, nodding his head.

I laugh at the sight, ripping off a big piece of the toast and gathering the egg. "Here." I place one hand under the other in case the crumbs fall. "This is for taking care of me last night." I carefully hold it against his lips until he bites on to it.

"Thank you," he says, chewing the big bite. It looks like he has a golf ball in his mouth. "And, you don't have to thank me at all." He cuffs his hand over his mouth as he chews and swallows. "It's the least I can do after all that I've pulled."

"Last night included." I raise my brows, leaning my forehead at him.

"Yeah, I'm not sorry about that." He says with no remorse in his eyes or voice, "He deserved it...for whatever he did."

"Hm." I give an ambiguous nod. Though I feel bad Arsalan got punched in the face, oddly enough I also feel JUST a tiny bit bad for AJ, too. I know I shouldn't—I know I should revel in the fact that AJ got his ass handed to him...but, Arsalan wasn't the only one last night who got hit where it hurts. "Anyways..." I say, changing the subject, while placing my plate in the sink. "I have to go volunteer at the homeless shelter, so I should get ready."

"Oh...okay, I'll just...leave." He places his cup as well.

"Or..." I press my lips together, "You can come with me?"

Eh, why not. He's not the worst company.

He tilts his head to the side, looking out

into a corner contemplating.

"Alright, but...I need to go home, shower, and change."

"That's fine, I'll pick you up from your apartment on my way there. Wear scrubs."

"Alright, boss." He winks, shining his pearly white teeth.

Let's see what a day with Arsalan is like.

◆ ◆ ◆

"I'm going on a break!" Walking out the back door towards the parking lot, I holler over to one of the other volunteers from my class. It's been a fun hour so far, not gonna lie. Arsalan has been cracking jokes with the volunteers. The girl volunteers and Dr. Johnson swooned over him. And, he is so sweet and tending to all of the people coming in for their little wounds. I would have NEVER guessed that he'd be as compassionate as he's turning out to be.

I lean against my car, putting my hand into my pocket to pull out a small bag of carrots. Ripping open the plastic, I toss one baby carrot into my mouth.

"Hey, there!" Dr. Johnson shouts, waving at me as I turn to her. She walks towards me, a coffee cup in her hand. "Your boyfriend is so cute!" She laughs, making her tight short curls bounce as the sunlight makes her medium tone skin glisten.

"Oh...no! He's...not my boyfriend."

Well, he's not really a friend either...or is he? Are we considered friends?

"Oh, I'm sorry. I just assumed—"

"No, it's fine." I assure her I'm not offended. Though, I shouldn't be considering he was so good with the ladies.

"He's cute." She winks, cracking open the lid of the cup and taking a sip.

"I guess." I shrug, crunching on the carrot as quietly as I can.

"You guys have some chemistry," she teases, tapping her elbow to mine.

"Nah, he finds that chemistry with every girl."

"Um, no, sweetie. Did you see him all googly-eyed at anyone else? No. He wasn't. He would glance at you every chance he got."

Beep beep!

She slides her hand inside of the pocket of her white coat, pulling out her pager.

"Ooo, I gotta go, sweetie. But I'll see you inside." She tosses the pager into her pocket. "Give that boy a chance someday. He's adorable." Patting my shoulder, she skips with long strides back inside.

Give Arsalan—someone I disliked from the moment I met him—a chance? That's a concept. It hasn't been even a week since AJ and I broke up...can't even think of another boy right now, cute or not. It hasn't been enough time to stop missing him either. A part of me wants to forgive him but then the other part tells me I shouldn't. I wish I could talk to my mom about this to get some sort of insight, but I might get my ass beat with shame.

Bing bing!

Who's FaceTiming me right now? I pull my phone out of my scrubs pocket and glance at the screen.

Mrs. Mary?! What—how random? I slide across the screen, accepting her call.

"Hello, my dear!" She greets with a glass of wine in her hand, a pool in the background.

"Oh my god, hello! What a nice surprise."

"I hope I didn't catch you at a bad time."

"No, not at all. How are you? And your husband?"

"I'm good, and so is he. He's out with his friends, and I'm enjoying this weather along with a glass of pinot noir."

"That sounds like a great time." I let out a laugh, supporting her decision.

"It is! How are you and that sweet, sweet boy Felix?"

Ah...man. That boy.

"Oh—uh...we broke up." I give a thin smile, sighing like I had been holding it in.

"Oh, my dear! I wish I was there to give you the biggest hug!"

Funny how I thought her hugs are the ones you'd need after a heartbreak. I could definitely use one of hers.

"What happened? If you don't mind me asking?"

I should badmouth him, tell her he cheated but…my heart still doesn't have it in it to say anything bad yet. I still care about him, even if I'm mad.

"Well…he did something that I never thought he would."

"Oh, my dear…I'm so very sorry."

"It's okay." I shrug it off, acting like it doesn't bother me but she doesn't buy it. She is a grandma, after all.

"You're not okay, sweetie. I know that face too well. Reminds me of mine when Will and I broke up."

"Broke up?" I ask, confused. She and Mr. Will—the most perfect couple who should be the poster child for love—once broke up?

"Oh, yeah. We had a lot of ups and downs. I mean, besides our parents, we had our own personal issues with each other. I hated him smoking—he would smoke two to three cigarettes a day. We used to have so many arguments because of it. One day, I had enough of it. I told him I didn't see us getting married if this continued because I wanted him healthy and alive for the kids that we always talked about having. So, he promised he was going to quit. And, he did, but his withdrawals were so bad. Regardless, we worked through it together, even if I had to put in extra work sometimes. But then, I started noticing his withdrawals got better. He wasn't moody anymore—in fact, he was in a good mood all the time! Then, one day I found a pack of cigarettes in his leather jacket he gave me to wear on a cold night. And when I confronted about it, that's when he told me how he'd been smoking again. He cried, begged to have a second chance, but he broke my trust. And that was unforgivable in my eyes. We didn't see each other for about a year."

"A year?!" I gasp, unable to wrap my head around that.

She nods, "Hardest year of my life. I lost my best friend, my soulmate—so abruptly. See, the thing is…even though I was so mad at him, I still wondered if he was doing okay. I felt so stupid for caring about him. But I realized that was okay, I did love him even though he hurt me. So I forgave myself for missing him, but I still didn't think I could ever give him a chance. Then one day, I ran into him at a record store. You'd think it was a scene out of a movie. It felt so nice to see him—so, so nice. He apologized again, said he didn't have to continue smoking to have difficulty breathing—he said stopped breathing the moment we broke up."

"So…what made you decide to give him a chance?"

"He said he had quit smoking. He didn't ask for a second chance because he thought I deserved better, but we continued to stay friends. I saw how he genuinely tried to continue not to smoke. He made a mistake, an unforgivable one, but...I loved him, Zara. I told him I'd give him another chance, but if he broke my trust again, I would leave him without looking back. And, he hasn't broken it ever since."

"But, how could you ever trust him again? How did you forgive him?"

"I didn't know if I could! I just had to take the chance that he was truly remorseful, and he was. I asked myself, how do I value this mistake? Is it completely unforgivable or can I work around it? So, when I decided to give him a second chance, I took him back wholeheartedly, without any judgment or fear."

"What if his mistake was completely unforgivable? Then what would you have done? Even though you loved him?"

"Then I wouldn't even think about a second chance. If it was something I couldn't move on from, then pretending to be okay when I'm not...I guess then he wouldn't be the only one who made a mistake. If you give someone a second chance, do so by forgiving them with all your heart, or else the relationship will be bound to end. But, if they make the same mistake again...leave forever and never turn around."

Is what AJ did forgivable? Would I be able to let it go? Trust him? I'm not sure.

"Zara! Dr. Johnson's asking for you." Arsalan's half way out from the door, a sweet smile on his face.

"Coming!" I holler back.

"You go on, dear. I have to go anyway."

"Thank you so much for calling. You really made my day."

"It was my pleasure! If you ever need to talk, I'm always here, sweetie. But, Zara..." She sets her wine down on the outdoor coffee table, "If you ever decide to give him a chance...think about yourself first."

I give her a nod with a thin smile.

"Goodbye, dear. Take care!" She blows a kiss.

"Goodbye, thank you again!"

And I press the button to disconnect the phone call I didn't think I'd need. How could I ever give AJ a chance after what he did? But...I love him. I still love him and I wonder if I could ever stop.

◆ ◆ ◆

"Did you have a fun time?" I ask Arsalan, buckling my seatbelt as he stretches his legs out in the passenger seat.

"I had an amazing time. I love Dr. Johnson! She told me I should come again." He reaches over to his seatbelt, pulling it in front of him to buckle.

"You should. I'm sure the girls would love

that." I wink at him, putting the key into the ignition.

"I just cared about if one girl loved me there."

Oh, I wonder who that can be. Can't be me—no, not me...not the one who he took care of last night.

Ignoring the comment, I change the subject, saying, "Everyone else who came in loved you, too."

"Oh, yeah?" he asks, smiling ear to ear.

"Yeah." I turn the key, starting the car. "You're actually so sweet. Who would have known?"

"I'm the sweetest. You just haven't given me a chance to see that side of me."

"Well, I'm giving you a chance right now. We still have some time before getting to your apartment."

"Alright, well...what do you wanna know?"

What do I want to know? Do I want to know him?

"Hmm, let's start with your family. Tell me about your mom."

The smile on his face vanished as if he just received some terrible news.

"My mom...passed away when I was eight."

My heart drops into my stomach.

"So...I don't remember much of her, but

my last memory of her was at the airport when she was going back to Pakistan. I never saw her again."

"Why did she go back to Pakistan?"

Am I being too nosy?

"For work—she was a doctor there, but only my dad could practice here in America. But, besides that…my daadi didn't allow her to work. She said good daughter-in-laws stay home, taking care of her husband and kids." He scoffs, the green hue from the traffic light casts a shadow on his face. "So, she suffered through depression, taking care of the rest of us, not having the time to even think about herself. Until the day she found out she had cancer. That's when she decided she wanted to go back and work, as her last wish. It's just been my dad and I, but we've barely said two words to each other since the day she left. He's barely ever looked at me."

"Oh, Arsalan…I'm so sorry."

God, my heart is breaking for him. I park the car in front of his apartment.

"Nah, it's okay." He shrugs off the pain in his voice. "Anyways, we'll talk later. Oh, and also…you might wanna check that service light. When was the last time you got an oil change?"

"Uhh—" I don't freaking know. "Not sure. My dad takes care of it."

"Okay, don't worry. I'll take your car one of these days to get an oil check. Thanks for today, Zara." Smiling, he pulls the door handle and hops out of my Volkswagen. AJ would have never been able to do that normal thing for me.

"Bye!" I wave as he leaves.

Now, I recall every mean thing I've ever said to him. Oh, man. I was too harsh. I thought I was a nice person up until now, but knowing I hurt someone who was secretly hurting all along? Now, everything makes sense. It makes sense why he wanted to try my mom's cooking, why he loved being around her and the home setting. I wonder if Jace knew, and that's why he wanted me to be a bit nicer to him. I would have never guessed that this would be Arsalan's life. I assumed too much—too quickly.

CHAPTER 10:

Happy Birthday

Jesus, my heart is going to explode. I bet Gigi, Alyssa, and Jace could hear it as well, especially since the only voices around the private room of the restaurant are ours. But Jace seems a bit preoccupied by being on the phone on and off and then having mini panic attacks each time he touches his pocket, immediately followed with a look of relief. He probably doesn't notice me fidgeting with my dress, but I also have convinced him very well that I'll be completely fine seeing AJ, just so his and Ari's night isn't ruined. I don't want him walking on eggshells because of me and AJ.

"Zara, Jace told us you and AJ broke up." Gigi reaches over the little candle that separates me, her, and Alyssa and rubs the back of my hand as condolence.

"Yeah, we're so sorry, Zara." Alyssa joins in,

eyebrows furrowed with concern.

"Oh…it's okay." I brush it off with a smile. I'm really not okay. I haven't seen him in a week since he punched the desi Damon. And now, both rivals will be sitting next to each other for the next god knows however long this birthday dinner will last.

"Did he do something to hurt you? Because Gigi and I will get our guns ready." Alyssa slides back the sleeve of her dress and flexes her bicep.

"No—no, you can put those away." I laugh it off like the break up wasn't a big deal. I don't think I'm going to end up telling the girls what he did—just don't want to keep explaining the painful ordeal.

"Okay—perfect. We're inside." I catch Jace saying that to someone on the phone. Crap, is it AJ? He's supposed to be bringing Ari to the restaurant. The butterflies of anxiety flutter inside, making my heart pound even harder.

I hear the door crack open behind me as my back is facing it. God, I don't think I'm ready to see—

"Arsalan!"

"Hi, ladies!" He greets the swooning girls as he fist bumps Jace.

"Thanks for comin', man." Jace says as he gestures for him to sit.

"It's my pleasure," Arsalan says, taking the chair right next to me. Oh, boy.

"Hey, Zara," he says with a shy smile you'd

give if you have a crush on someone.

I turn my head towards him to reply and say, "Hey."

He looks really nice—dressed in a white crisp button down and black slacks.

"Okay, both are on their way in," Jace says as he glances at his phone screen. "Zara, you good?" That concerned look is back on his face—something I've been seeing occasionally throughout the week.

"I'm good." I give him a reassuring smile.

As the anticipation grows second by second, I fidget with the tablecloth under the table. But then, I feel the coolness of a hand on top of mine—Arsalan. Reminds me of the dinner at my parents, except this time the person causing me anxiety is a K-Pop star, not a pretentious uncle. I glance at his hand, then at him. He gives me a comforting thin smile, looking into my eyes like he's trying to say, 'It'll be okay'. And oddly enough, it's working.

"Baby!" I jump from the sound of Ari's screech, hugging Jace. When did she get in?! I guess I didn't hear the door open because I was distracted by Arsalan's hand that I pushed off when I heard Ari's cry.

As both lovebirds continue with their public display of affection, my eyes dare me to take them off of the couple…and onto AJ. No, don't look at him yet. You're not ready. But he's there —I see him through my peripheral vision, standing there in all black, with his hair covered by a beanie. I just can't see his face.

"Happy birthday!" The four of us sang, having our eyes only on Ari.

"Thank you!" She says with her spirited smile, thanking everyone one by one with her eyes and then meets mine. I give her an apologetic smile and her smile grows wider, tossing me a slow, gentle nod. "Alright, let's get this party started!" She sits next to me, turning around to give me a side hug.

"Ari...I'm so sorry—" I whisper an apology.

"I know, love. I know." But she stops me in mid sentence, squeezing me so tightly.

As I'm pulling away from her, my eyes catch him—staring at me as he pulls out his chair next to Gigi. My brain screams at my eyes, telling them to look away, but they refuse. They're not being disobedient—they just missed seeing him. AJ gives me a half smile, but then that disappears once he glances next to me—at the person he punched so mercilessly. There's this eerie silence in the room, provoking the tension even more. Eyes flick towards AJ, then to me, and over to Arsalan, while fingers fidget nervously with glasses of water, invisible lint on clothes, and stray hairs.

Oh, god. Just please help me get through this. Just one last time and then...I'd probably won't see AJ again.

◆ ◆ ◆

"Thanks for dinner, Jace!" Gigi says as we pile out of the restaurant one by one. I made sure I wasn't anywhere near AJ. Though, dinner actually wasn't too bad. Jace, Ari, and the girls did their best to defuse the impending tension. AJ and I would steal a few glances at each other here and there as we pretended to be listening to the multiple conversations happening. AJ barely talked, but Arsalan—Arsalan didn't fail to strike up conversations that had to do with me and him together. I saw the way it made AJ's jaw clench with irritation each time Arsalan opened his mouth. I'd be lying if I said I wasn't a little anxious, but I think AJ knew he no longer has a right over me—which slowly was killing him inside.

"No, thank you all for coming to celebrate my queen's birthday." Jace holds Ari's hand as we all gather in a circle to say our goodbyes. AJ is right in front of me, but I'm making sure I don't even look in his direction. "I'll miss this girl." He kisses the top of her head.

"Don't worry, she'll be back soon." I wink at Ari, smiling at the most amazing girl.

"Jace, why don't you spend the rest of the night with her. I'll drop Zara back home." Arsalan offers, which raises some brows around the circle —except AJ. He gulps with anger.

"Oh, no it's okay." Jace says, attempting to mitigate the awkwardness in the air.

"No, it's not a problem. You two enjoy your last night together." Arsalan turns to me. "Ready to go, Zara?"

Instinctively, I glance at AJ, as if I wanted him to speak up and say no. A stupid, stupid part of me wants to stay longer just to be around him, even if we don't exchange a single word. How foolish of me?

I grip the handle of my purse tight, forcing myself to do what I should instead of what I want.

"Um—yeah, let's go."

With a quick glance towards AJ—who seems like he's close to crying as his eyes glisten under the lamppost—I say my goodbyes to the girls and Ari one at a time, giving each a hug. Then came AJ. We stand in front of each other, everyone's eyes on us. What should I do? Do I give him a hug? I do want to…but I shouldn't. But there's this yearning in his eyes for more than a hug. God, those deep brown eyes. I wish I could have seen his dimpled smile just one last time. He opens his mouth to say something, but then closes it shut. He gives a forceful half smile, as if that took every bit of strength out of him. And with a nod, I look away from him—it still hurts to see him. I turn away, my back towards the rest.

"I'm ready." I say to Arsalan. I'm not ready —I'm not ready to walk away from AJ, but I have to. I can't forgive him just yet. Or ever. I'm not sure. But, as I'm walking away from the K-Pop star who stole and broke my heart, I look over my shoulder one last time and catch a glimpse of him, tears in his eyes.

Goodbye, AJ. Goodbye.

◆ ◆ ◆

"You didn't have to walk me up, Arsalan. I'm a big girl." I say as I fidget my key into the lock.

"Oh, I know. I saw that at the club the other night." He teasingly elbows me gently as I push open the door, shaking my head at my night full of rage.

"Oh, shit! We forgot to pick up the stuff from the store Jace told us to get on the way back." I slam my hand to my forehead as I set my phone and purse on the kitchen counter while Arsalan locks the door behind him.

"Eh, it's fine. Maybe he shouldn't have called us at the last minute. I mean, why would he need peanut butter, ice cream, wine and... god, I can't remember the rest of that list, not so late at night." He laughs at Jace's chronicles as he leans against the counter, crossing one leg over the other.

"Well, that's Jace for ya." I chuckle, grabbing a glass from the drying rack.

"Yeah, he's a strange one." He uncrosses his legs. "Hey, Zara...there's something I actually want to say."

Oh, shit. What could this be about?

"Yeah...go for it." The glass still in my

hand, and suddenly I forgot why I needed it.

He holds onto the counter with one hand, hovering right over me, looking directly into my eyes.

"The other night...at the club, I'm not sure if you noticed me acting differently."

I did, but I shake my head as if I didn't notice.

"Well, there's a reason for it." He clears his throat like there's something stuck, stepping closer to me. "I'm not really good with my words or feelings so, I'm gonna try to be as blunt as I possibly can."

Oh, my god. I gulp loudly, trying to prepare myself for what I think he's about to confess.

"When you held my hand on the dance floor, I didn't like it," he says as he takes the glass out of my hand and sets it on the counter. My eyes following it, I notice my screen lights up, messages from Jace. "I didn't like it because... that's not the way I pictured us holding hands for the first time. And then when you asked me to kiss you, there was nothing more I wanted to do at that moment but...again, not like that. Not while you were drunk with a heartbreak."

Oh god, I think I know where this is going.

He moves closer, forcing my back to meet the roundness of the edge of the counter.

"I like you, Zara. I liked you the moment I met you."

Oh, shit. There it is. He cups my cheek

lightly, gazing into my eyes—the eyes that once hated the sight of his.

"I've never in my life felt so close to someone. I don't know what it is about you but...you make me care. I haven't been able to stop thinking about you."

"Arsalan, I—"

"Zara, please. Just...let me finish." His breath touches my skin as he whispers. "I know you don't feel the same about me...but is there a chance that you might, somehow?"

Do I? I stare at him, looking into his eyes to see if I do.

"Hmm? Is there?" He glances at my lips, making my heart flutter the way it did after I yelled at him before the dinner at my parents. Do I like him?

"I—" I stutter at the sight of him switching his gaze from my eyes to my lips.

"Tell me you don't feel even a little for me...and I'll back off," he whispers, still having his eyes on my lips, brushing the edge of his thumb against my flustered cheek that feels like it's slightly on fire.

"I...I—"

Jesus, is that all I can say right now? Might as well say captain if I'm going to just say that!

"Do you want me to back off?" He moves his lips closer, and his warm breath touches my lips that...are now curious about his. As my eyes move away from his and graze against his lips that are wanting a taste of mine...I feel oxygen is slowly starting to dissipate from my vicinity. Do I want to kiss him? Or is it because I'm heartbroken? I'm not sure—I'm not sure about anything. But what I do know is that...somehow, there is a microscopic part of me that wants him to clear my curiosity.

"Zara..." He says my name so softly, I whimper at his wanting tone. My breathing gets fast, my chest rises and falls like I just sprinted a mile. Gosh, what's happening to me? He places his other hand on the side of my cheek, which is as warm as my beating heart. And with a longing look into my confused eyes, he presses his warm lips against mine. I don't fight back. I let him press his lips against mine. It feels so different, so strange, but no—no, I'm not ready. I shouldn't be ready.

His large hands depart from my face, introducing themselves to the curves of my waist. With a single quick motion, he picks me up and sets me on top of the counter, brushing his hands against my thighs and running them down to my knees, forcing my legs to wrap themselves around his. It's like he wanted to be close to me and couldn't get enough. I should stop. Why can't I though? It doesn't feel the way I did when AJ and I kissed, but...still, as different as this is, it's nice. What am I feeling? Why am I feeling this way? There doesn't seem to be anything that could stop this right now. Nothing at

Creaaaak.

Is that the…door?! I push Arsalan off of me to see what opened the door all by itself, but… that's the thing, it didn't. Someone did.

"AJ?" My heart has officially stopped and fallen into my stomach. How the—what the—what?!

He's frozen in place like he'd just seen someone from the dead come back to life, flowers in his hands, and Jace's keys dangling in the keyhole.

"Oh—I, uh." He stutters over his words, then one foot over the other, backs away.

"AJ!" I call after him, jumping off of the counter, taking a step forward, but I get pulled by the wrist.

"Don't go after him, Zara!" Arsalan commands with begging eyes. Gripping his hand around my wrist, I couldn't even twist my hand.

"Arsalan, please. I just need to talk to him." I wiggle my wrist in hopes of ending this struggle. "We will talk about this later, I promise."

But he doesn't let go. His clenched jaw shows anger, but doesn't match his pleading eyes.

"Please, Arsalan!" I finally let out a cry.

Jaw still clenched, eyes still asking for me to stay, he finally loosening his grip. Without a beat, I grab my phone and run out the door without looking back.

AJ runs down the stairs, moving so fast it looks like there's a chance his legs could split into pieces.

"AJ!" I call out, charging down the stairs. But he doesn't stop. Why am I running after him?! I don't know. All I know is that I need to know why he came.

"AJ, stop!" I cry out as I hop off of the last step of the stairs. Finally, he does, back towards me. I clasp my hand on his shoulder, forcing him to face me. "Why'd you come?!"

There's a tear stuck at the corner of his eye, unable to move as long as he doesn't look at me.

"I—I don't know. I don't know why I came, I just wanted to see you one last time before I left tomorrow."

At last, he gives up and slowly raises his gaze at me, allowing the tear drop to glide down his freckled cheek.

"I shouldn't have come. I shouldn't have been so selfish to see you. I shouldn't—shouldn't have hurt you the way I did. And now..." He scoffs, wiping away his trickling tear, "I've lost you forever and I–I cannot tell you how it kills me to accept that you've moved on. But you should. And...I won't come in between that anymore. It's time for me to let you go. I—" He swallows his cracked voice, only it's making my heart feel as if it's cracking as well, "won't be selfish with you any longer."

I hold back my tears and the words that I

have the utmost urge to say.

"Goodbye, Zara. I'll always love you." His top lip quivers as he lets out a silent cry, saying the words that seem like they killed every part of him. But without another, he turns around with no sliver of hesitation, and walks away...becoming smaller and smaller as he disappears into the dark.

I hate myself for wanting to stop him. But, most of all...I hate myself for still wanting him.

Buzz, buzz, buzz!

My phone vibrates in my hand that's as cold as a lifeless body. It's Jace.

"Hello?" I say, clearing the lump in my throat.

"Hey, I've been messaging you! AJ begged me to give him the keys to surprise you. That's why I asked you to stop by the store to grab stuff to buy him some time to get there before you do. Zara, I swear I said no, but he was so adamant about it...said he just needs to apologize one last time, and I thought you'd want that. So, I—"

"It's...okay, Jace. He left." I say without sounding like I'm broken. I don't want him to feel guilty for giving his keys to him.

"Oh, okay. You have to tell me all about it, I'll be there soon but...I did something CRAZY." His voice lights up with excitement. "Zara, I—I love Ari. I just love her so much. I didn't tell you this yet because...well, it's a bit too crazy, even for me—"

What can that possibly be?

"You might think I'm insane, which I know for a fact I am…but this surpasses all the crazy, spontaneous shit I've done."

"Jace, what is it?"

"Zara…I bought a ring last week. I've been carrying it with me everywhere I go and…I just asked Ari to marry me."

What in the name of Saturn's rings did he just say?

"WHAT?!" Everything that just took place easily zipped out of my head.

"Yeah, I KNOW! I'm crazy, but maybe what's even crazier is that…we're getting married at the end of this year around Christmas time—on the day I met her! We're thinking Australia! I'm so excited—"

And as he continues to talk about the single greatest moment of his life, my head feels like it's losing blood as I wrap my oxygen deprived brain around the fact that this wasn't the last time I saw AJ. Or the fact that I won't be the only friend of his at the wedding, but also Arsalan. AJ…Arsalan…and me, all at a wedding in a different continent. What can possibly go wrong?

BOOKS IN THIS SERIES

Falling In Love In

Falling In Love In Korea

Falling In Love In L.a.

Printed in Great Britain
by Amazon